Weights and Measures

Jane Fraser

Published in UK by Watermark Press 2025

©Jane Fraser 2025

The moral right of Jane Fraser to be identified as the author of this work has been asserted by her in accordance with the Copyright, Designs and Patents Act, 1988

All rights reserved

No part of this publication may be reproduced, stored in a retrieval system or transmitted in any form or by any means, electronic or mechanical, including photocopying, recording or any information storage or retrieval system without the prior permission of the copyright owner.

A CIP catalogue record for this book is available from the British Library

ISBN: 978-1-8380043-6-1

Typeset in Book Antigua

Cover design by nb-design.com

Printed by Imprint Digital

Watermark Press
www.watermarkpress.co.uk

This novel is dedicated to the memory of
Richard Harold Froom (1922-2024),
my dear Uncle Harold, poet, pen pal, proud RAF man,
and first reader of *Weights and Measures*.

PART 1
SEPTEMBER 1939 – DECEMBER 1939

PART 2
JANUARY 1940 – SEPTEMBER 1940

PART 1

SEPTEMBER 1939 – DECEMBER 1939

Mum was
Born in 1916
So
she was
10 in 1926
20 in 1936.
23 in 1939.

Dad was born
in 1918
So he was
10 in 1928
20 in 1938
21 in 1939.

CHAPTER 1
JIM

Jim picked up one of the boots arranged in order of size on the scullery steps and spat at the uppers. It was done as much in response to the words the Prime Minister had just sputtered over the wireless, as merely for a bit of spit and polish.

Old rituals from his army days were hard to let go of. Impossible really. So this Sunday, just as every other Sunday, before lunch, without fail, he polished the family's footwear in readiness for the week ahead. If he didn't, then the world might fall apart or slide into some moral quagmire. But even his compulsive use of the brush and the cloth, the tin of black Cherry Blossom, all the elbow grease he could muster, and all the saliva he could secrete, couldn't prevent it happening all over again.

He picked up the partner to the boot in his hands and held the pair of lace-ups together, staring into the leathers: a distorted reflection in the sheen, forty-eight years of age, old beyond his years, a man just trying his best to hold everything together for the family, to lace up life just like the boots which he brought to his face and sniffed.

They weren't brand new. They were hand-me-downs, re-soled and re-heeled by Mr. Renowden, the cobbler, in his little front-room shop just up the road at 251 Middle Road. At first they were his elder son, William's, and now little Teddy was about to step into them. Lots of people couldn't afford new shoes in the terraces of Swansea East he kept telling himself. That was his excuse, anyway. And then he spat on them again, beginning to buff purposefully in a monotonous back-and-fore rhythm with the large, bristle brush from the shoe-cleaning kit he kept in its place under the sink.

The boots held in his sinewy, butcher's hands still revealed the peculiar traits of William's gait: impressions in the uppers; depressions of his big toes; wear on the outer heel of the right foot. With a small cloth, he rubbed the leather in small, circular movements that matched his thoughts. What now? What would happen to William and all the young men being sucked into this war with Germany again? Though he knew in his heart that this time at least there was a just case. That Hitler was an evil, conniving, little bastard. But thank God, the government wouldn't be coming for Teddy. They wouldn't get their hands on him for war fodder like his big brother and his father before him. Not yet.

Having completed Teddy's boots to his military satisfaction, he turned to the rest: Rhoda's little children's size nines which looked dwarfed besides Dora's adult's size eights, his wife, Mary's, size sevens, and his own size tens. Jim rubbed hard on Rhoda's tiny shoes. At four, she was too young to understand the implications of what had come down the airwaves, but no doubt, she'd learn soon enough. He wanted to rub away all that was about to happen, seeing an ever-increasing circle of ripples spreading from the outside in, and the inside out. The world was a small place now and everything was on the bloody move again. All over the place.

But just before dinner on an unseasonably warm and sunny early September morning, all his family's shoes were good and ready for a pretend parade and an imaginary inspection from army top brass. Job done. Stand down Sergeant Froom.

He started to whistle. It filled the disquiet in his head as much as the small scullery where Mary stood sturdy in her wrap-around pinny and slippers at the gas stove making the gravy. He knew his whistling repertoire bored and irritated her. *Stuck in his head*, she said. But he felt comfort in its familiarity: they were tunes he'd sung in unison with the men when they'd marched up to their bollocks in mud and shells to supply the troops on the Western Front, *It's a Long Way to Tipperary* and *Mademoiselle from Armentieres, Parlez Vous* pounding out in four-four time: left, right, left, right, left, right. He never talked about any of it with Mary. He had no words. And anyway, talking's not what men did, even with their wives. Especially soldiers.

So instead he whistled, saluting her when she called him to the table as she always did, him then pretending to play *Come to the Cook House Door, Boys*, on an invisible bugle to summon the kids for food. He knew that anyone who might observe him would see the old soldier in him, enjoying the drills and sheer predictability of it all. What they wouldn't see was that all the ritual was an invisible crutch, an involuntary tic, that held him together and helped him to just about get through every day.

There was no response to the bugle call. Bloody kids. Dumb insolence they'd have called it in the army. Would have put a man on fatigues. The children – though at twenty, Dora was hardly a child – usually came rushing at the signal for food, and today it was a nice piece of brisket that he'd cut and kept back which had been in the Rayburn in the scullery cooking for hours. He opened the back kitchen door in case his call to mess had not been carried, but they weren't in the top or bottom yard as he'd expected them to be on such a fine day. He walked past the coal house, down the steps to the lower level, across the cobbles to the redundant stables, and peered in through one of the side windows.

They were all inside, surrounded by what Mary called his *paraphernalia* which was essential for the butcher's shop: sacks of sawdust for the wooden floor; stacks of empty liver tins for the customers who always nagged him for free waste-paper baskets; rolls of greaseproof paper; and yesterday's newspapers for wrapping the meat. What headlines would tomorrow's *Daily Sketch* carry, he wondered, imagining himself endlessly cutting and stacking those newspaper pages on the counter-top for years to come, the print screeching WORLD AT WAR AGAIN! and the stories vaunting the heroism of 'our lads' rather than the truth about the carnage that was happening all over again. War to end all wars, they'd said about the last one. My arse. Lies, lies and yet more lies. Bloody government.

He pulled himself up, returned to the scene beyond the window where the stuff he'd assured Mary would be put to good use, still lay untouched: tarnished mirrors; dismantled wooden bedsteads; and an old upright piano against the far wall. The sight of his old garden tools from their little rented cottage back in

Devon saddened him: what call was there here for a spade, hoe and rake in an end of terrace house with a stone yard rather than a veg plot and lawn?

Through the window he could see Teddy sitting on his old, military trunk with the metal rivets, pushing Rhoda back and fore on the rocking-horse – a shabby but well-loved family heirloom. It had seen better days. Sad to think she'd be the last of the four children to sit astride its yellowing, paint-blistered body and tug at its balding mane. It did the job though, Teddy being smart enough to know how to keep Rhoda pacified. Jim counted his blessings for Teddy giving him some respite from the red-headed spitfire. Despite his love for her, she was hard to handle and he didn't know quite where this one came from; or perhaps he did. They weren't all like Mary in temperament and he wondered if it was true what they said about people with red hair. But then Dora, William and Teddy had inherited his red hair too; but not his *ways* as Mary called them.

He didn't quite understand where Dora came from either: she was so different from him – and Mary – for that matter. Not one to share much with them about her life and they didn't see a lot of her. But today, he watched her maintaining her bike with the drop-handlebars and the cross-bar. She'd bought it for practicality and speed. It was upside down on its stand while she pumped up the tyres, kicking them to test the firmness. Rag in hand, she greased the chains and lubricated the cogs to keep everything in good working order. It was satisfying to see her looking after things like this, having respect for possessions. She loved that bike, and Swansea's inclines didn't put her off, not one jot. She was built for them. Chorus girls' legs, he would have called them. But not out loud. Dora didn't seem to care less, anyway. She seemed to care only that her muscles were strong enough to negotiate the toughest of Swansea's hills. As representative of the women's cycling club, she'd even conquered the notorious cobbled Constitution Hill in a bet, had seen off the competition, all men, put out by being defeated by a woman, no less.

Jim worried more about the betting than the fact Dora rode

a bloke's bike. Perhaps gambling was in the blood. Mary knew about this side of him but she didn't know the scale of it or its insatiable pull. For a moment, he felt his guts turning over, remembering the new boots he'd failed to buy for the children again because he'd found himself a bit short. He looked at those lovely children, safe for the time being there in the old stables. But God knows how long the nonsense would go on this time. There was talk it would all be over by Christmas. But his churning innards told him this was unlikely. They'd said that before and look what happened.

Unnoticed at the window, he felt detached from reality: a middle-aged man, now too old for the call up, carrying an invisible load, his feet feeling as though they were still trudging through the sludge of Flanders.

He took another look at Teddy. Earnest little Teddy, sitting there in his knee-length trousers, his hand-knitted socks and hand-knitted pullover oblivious to the fact that everything was in flux. As ever, he was dutifully performing the role he'd fallen into as babysitter to the uninvited girl who'd been born on Mary's early and unexpected change. As much as Mary adored Rhoda, he knew she struggled. Only once had she said that she'd felt *all hollowed out*, but that he wouldn't understand. So they didn't talk about it anymore as she was very touchy and it seemed he always said the wrong thing. As challenging as Rhoda was, she was a cherished gift to them both and he vowed he'd never refer to her as an *afterthought*, the way he'd heard his mother refer to him when he was a child.

Jim feared the unknown. Change was not easy company. Better that pattern remain the order of the day to keep him on track. Left, right, left, right, the tempo that constantly beat out like a metronome inside his skull.

Separated only by a thin pane of glass with a crack in it, he couldn't whistle to distract himself, or sing his army songs out loud as a salve to soothe the unease in earshot of the children. And yet, the words of the song he used to sing to the now absent William, when he'd sit him on his lap as a little lad, still crept in, silently held in his memory. But they didn't ease the ache and somehow made it worse.

> *Climb upon my knee, Sonny Boy*
> *Though you're only three, Sonny Boy*
> *You've no way of knowing*
> *There's no way of showing*
> *What you mean to me, Sonny Boy.*

CHAPTER 2
MARY

As always, Mary opened out the table with the drop-leaves, in readiness for Sunday dinner in the living room. Normally the family ate in the back scullery, but Sundays were different. It was the one day when they were allowed to be a proper family: a private unit, tucked away from public scrutiny in the shop, where the greaseproof paper that hung behind the front window signalled that they were closed to custom.

Mary took her place and prepared herself to watch Jim do the things he did every Sunday. God, he made such a song and dance of everything, standing in front of his captive audience with his blessed *cutty knife* from Devon, a trusty, bone-handled knife held in one hand, and a steel in the other. In theatrical gestures, he sharpened the blade until the sparks flashed, running the edge of the thin blade along his finger to test its bite. Mary noticed the children start to smile as they always did. She was very aware that they knew what was coming next and she worried quietly what they really thought of him and his habitual performances. She knew he worried about this, too. But Jim, being Jim, would never let it be known. What sort of father did they regard him as? One who they tolerated? Mocked? It didn't stop him though. Compulsion drove his repertoire until the predictable end they all knew so well: taking the knife to his face, saying, *Shave anyone?* as he stretched his jaw tight, dragging the blade across his cheek where no stubble would dare to be seen, shop days or Sundays.

Mary was wondering if he could tell by her face that she was thinking, *just how many more times will you do this?* She looked at the kids and feared it wouldn't be too long before they too would all finally say, *Dad, we've had enough of this one*, as each in turn would outgrow his sad-clown's circus tricks: pretending to magic his thumb off one hand only for it to reappear on the other; rubbing a three-penny bit through the surface of the table where it would re-emerge underneath; blowing successive smoke rings from his cigarette that reached all the way to the ceiling. But none of them said anything. Not today.

Mary continued to sit upright in her chair, wondering why she was so hell-bent on assuming this posture. Perhaps it wasn't only down to the corset she wore because of all the babies she'd born, all the babies she'd lost, or the lumbago that gave her gyp, or to stave off indigestion; but she was aware there was no give in her at all. No sign of a slouch. She said grace as she always did; though like Jim, she didn't believe.

"For what we are about to receive may the Lord make us truly thankful. Amen."

"Amen," they all echoed, and then tucked in.

It was when Mary took the rice pudding out of the range in the living room and put it on the table and Rhoda was screaming: *I want the skin. Give me the skin. I always have the skin,* that the fact that they were now at war with Germany came up. She skimmed off the burnt topping speckled with nutmeg and gave Rhoda what she wanted, as she always did, shouting, *give me strength.* She couldn't take any more today. The other two had what they were given and she and Jim had what was left.

"Make the most of it, kids," said Jim. "Bloody Ministry soon will put a stop to all this."

"We'll be making do for a good while to come, if you ask me," said Mary.

Jim could make of that what he wanted. Mary didn't raise her head as she said it, but continued to spoon up every last drop of the milky pudding, best china dish and dessert spoon poised away from her and not towards her, just as she'd been taught to do when she was in service. Perhaps she too thought her world might fall apart if she didn't hang on to what was the 'right' thing to do. Or perhaps she thought she could place her family, or even herself, on the road to God knows where with the right social graces, set them free from the butcher's shop at 141.

Sometimes she felt as if she was still in service; but she kept quiet for fear of upsetting Jim. She knew he carried a lot. And she knew he vexed about what she might think in private. God forbid, she have her own thoughts. He was aware he wasn't much of a breadwinner: a hard worker, yes; a good provider, no. She remembered his sister, Kit, had upset him, criticising his capacity to look after a wife as Kit felt a husband should. For one of the only times in his life, despite his prickly ego, he'd shared what Kit had told him: *You couldn't keep pussy, Jim*. It had bit hard and she knew it was festering still.

CHAPTER 3
JIM

Up until now, Jim had found it impossible, for many reasons – and excuses – to make things happen at Middle Road. As perverse as it sounded, he wondered if this time at least, war with the Hun would present opportunities for him and he'd prove Kit wrong. Make her eat her words. But God knows how.

As he looked at Mary, her rimless glasses sitting on the end of her nose, her fine, fair hair turning prematurely grey with its streak of yellow-stained nicotine from the Woodbines at the front, he knew he'd failed her. He couldn't keep a bloody cat. Kit had told him so to his face. Try as he might with the betting, it never came off. Though he never stopped hoping. Deep down, he didn't believe he was a bad man, he was just a man who desperately wanted to do good by his wife and his family and give them the things he'd never had in life. Christ, he never wanted anyone to endure the grind of poverty he'd suffered back on the farm as a kid and in the years that followed. But he knew he was a fool.

"It's not going to be easy, this," he said, opening his arms out, palms up to heaven like some corny preacher in an American film, dramatising the sweep of the challenges they all had ahead.

No-one said a word, though he knew they well understood what he was alluding to. He looked at the empty chair at the side of the room where they stacked all the dining chairs Monday to Saturday. Mary looked up at him and wiped a tear away with the hem of her pinny, thinking of William. He watched her get to her feet to begin clearing away the table and make a start on the washing-up. The sooner she'd be done with him and all this, the sooner she could get back to her knitting. He guessed it was the equivalent of his whistling.

The air raid warning siren sounded soon after Jim had rearranged the living room and readied it for the week ahead, when the dining room had to function as a thoroughfare between shop and scullery, rather than a place of fleeting family comfort. As he was re-stacking the dining chairs, Teddy looked at him for reassurance.

"It's only them practising today, Son," he said.

"It's horrible," said Teddy, placing his hands over his ears.

"Be alright, Son. Now be a good lad, and take Rhoda up the park for a couple of hours. Put her in the push chair if you like. With a bit of luck, she'll drop off after all that rice pudding. Let your mother and me have a bit of a chat. There's a lot to be thinking about."

With the younger two out of the way, and Dora back at work on her bike, Jim sat down in one of the two easy chairs at the side of the range. He took a Woodbine out of the pack and lit up. Apart from these two shabby chairs and a tiny side table, there was just a small sofa tucked up against the wall. One of the legs had gone and it was propped up with a couple of the pile of moss-covered bricks that he'd stacked at the bottom of the yard for when the time came. As he studied the sofa, he dragged on the cigarette. Another bloody chore that he hadn't got round to.

The bricks supporting the sofa had fallen down from the separating wall with 139 which was his responsibility to maintain. He'd get round to the sofa and the wall soon, he'd promised Mary. Then again, perhaps the wall wouldn't need rebuilding now as Louisa next door had a garden rather than a yard and it would make sense they'd want quick and easy access to the Anderson shelter she'd be installing as per ruddy government directives. He blew the smoke out, realising that with a bit of luck, the job might not need doing at all.

Mary sat opposite him in an identical chair. The sun was September low and she was almost in shadow. She looked like a faded version of the girl he'd married. Was it life or him that had done this to her, made her age before her time? Not much sun ever got into the living room with its one window facing onto the top yard with its high stone wall. Nor her life, if he was honest. He was glad of the warmth of the range to take the chill off things.

She was knitting again, fag in mouth, which she could keep in place, clenched expertly between her lips. He didn't know how she did it: drag on it so intently, take it down, and then exhale, all no-hands. She just sat there clicketty-clacketting as the ash grew longer until it could hold out no more, falling onto the small mat on top of the lino at their feet. With the heel of her slipper, she ground it in hard. He wondered if she'd like to grind him down too, squash him into the mat, suck the debris up with the Ewebank she'd be getting out later and setting to with vigour. She did the heel-grinding without looking up from her knitting. The surely-to-God monotonous pattern of her life was revealed in her actions, the way she said his past was stuck inside his head. He knew he was stuck in the present too, immovable in his attitudes the way he'd been stuck up to his balls in slime as a young man.

"He's asked for a pullover," she said. "A roll neck."

Mary's words broke Jim's thoughts and he looked up at the mantelpiece where she tucked the letters in a rack. He could see the envelope, William's handwriting on the front, forward sloping, full of flourishes and loops. School-learned.

"Must be the fashion with Air Force lads, nowadays," she said, smiling. "He said he didn't mind a shop-bought one. But it's not the same, is it?"

"No. You're a good knitter, Mary. You could knit for Britain!"

And he looked down at the Fair Isle tank top he was wearing, smoothed it over his thickening waistline. The whole family was knitted from head to toe by Mary.

"He says he's going to need one with winter coming up. And when he gets to the other side. He can't say when, but it's in the air."

"I don't like to imagine him going over there," said Jim, thinking back to a younger version of himself.

"He's quite happy at the moment, he says. Whether that's just for our benefit, I don't know. But he wants to get going now. All the waiting is killing him. Be nice if you read his letters, Jim. Dropped him a line now and then. Everyone else seems to be writing to him. Even your *favourite* sister Kit. And Sybil. He says that he's happy that she hasn't forgotten him. Yet."

"I can't bring myself to read them, Mary. I'll leave it to you to keep me posted. You're good like that. But I hope things don't fizzle out with him and Sybil, though. She's a nice girl, isn't she? Hard to thinks she's the Bowen's stock."

"Yes, she's a lovely girl. No wonder both William and Dora took a shine to her. I know Dora and William have been back and fore to London what with one thing and another, but they've always seemed to pick up where they left off," she said, pausing and admiring her handiwork, the even rows, just the right amount of tension, before turning over the growing jumper and starting on a row of purl. "It's beyond sad, that William and her are apart. But she's very close to Dora. So that's good."

Jim well knew the sadness of separation. Yet the camaraderie of the Forces was something he'd never been able to forget. It was just over twenty years, but what was twenty years? Less than a generation. But he had forgotten how to enjoy himself and wondered why he couldn't settle on anything. Now he couldn't even fix the bloody sofa. No wonder Mary knitted. The noise of bone needle against bone needle set his teeth on edge but he put up with it the way she surely put up with him. He sat in the chair and continued smoking in silence, listening hard as the all-clear sounded outside.

CHAPTER 4

MARY

As Mary got into the rhythm of her knitting, she mulled over the pickle the country was in again. Things had been a long time brewing and perhaps that had given the government chance to prepare for the inevitable. So, perhaps Chamberlain was not so daft after all. And neither was she.

People would be surprised, shocked even, that a girl who'd left school at fourteen, had four children, was middle-aged, and married to a butcher, would dare engage her mind in matters that were perceived to be the prerogative of so-called 'learned' gentlemen. She hated the way people put you in a box to fit what they wanted to think. And keep you there. Stop you from daring to be different from them. Though as yet she hadn't had the nerve to holler over the shop counter that she relished delving into *Hansard* every week, eager for it to drop through the letterbox by Willy James' paperboy. Jim knew. But he didn't get involved in the discussion of the nitty-gritty. He told her not to get herself so wound up about things that she couldn't change.

She had to believe that she had it in her to make change or otherwise what was the point of it all? She thought herself a bright woman, literate and interested in people's lives. That was politics to her. When she was a young girl, despite being poor, politics was a subject that was never off limits around the dining table where current affairs had been argued (amicably most of the time) with her eight brothers and sisters. Some of them she'd thought were Communists, but she thought of herself as Liberal. Perhaps increasingly Socialist. She missed all that debate rather than the tittle-tattle she had to endure in the shop, and when she was dealing with little Rhoda, bless her heart.

So now when she'd read *Hansard* every week, she could keep

an eye on proceedings in Parliament, who said what and when. No-one could get one over on her. Not any of the ridiculously hopeful Conservative parliamentary candidates that would come canvassing at the door, nor the Labour MPs that always got in around this Ward. She'd tell the party's representatives straight, whatever their political persuasion, who'd been vociferous or mute at Westminster proceedings for God knows how long, and who hadn't stood up one bit for those they professed to represent.

She liked the people who lived in their Cwmbwrla area of Swansea: she thought them honest and hardworking and a darn sight more sociable than where she'd been brought up in Hampshire. In these rows of terraces, there were no Lord of the Manor types or Country Squires, and cap-doffing wasn't a custom. She'd settled quickly when Jim and her took over the corner shop and she became *the butcher's wife*, Mrs Jim Froom. She remembered how she'd found it harder to adapt to a new name than a new place, and wondered why she was not Mrs Mary Froom. It was then she realised that her old self had been erased and a new one created at the moment she'd written her maiden name for the last time on that marriage certificate in the church. Indelible. Mary Read, Spinster of the Parish of Fordingbridge, was no more.

What she did gain, she supposed, was a standing in the community because she and Jim were 'in business', if such a thing mattered; but she wondered where Mary Read had gone, and often questioned – to herself at least – why she was expected to live in Jim's shadow. If there was some respect afforded to her because she now lived in a corner shop, she hadn't earned it herself. It wasn't Jim's fault, either. He was as much a victim of expectation as she was.

Mary often felt restless because she didn't have a role that was as important as Jim's, or William's. It wasn't fair really that she'd been forced to go into service because her father had said she was just a girl and that's what girls did. How else would someone of her plain looks get on in the world unless she was given a leg up by a man of means? Jim was no man of means; her mother had said as much. Yet she'd loved him. She could, and would, look after him as he was expected to look after her. That wasn't fair either, the way he struggled to do his bit as a good man. She didn't want to be a man. She just didn't want to be restricted by being a woman. At least things were changing now and Dora had a choice. She was in control of her own destiny, it seemed, switching professions like that. But what about herself? What could she have been? Had anyone ever asked her about her dreams? No. Not even Jim. She was just middle-aged Mary. Mrs Jim Froom. Butcher's wife.

She longed for Rhoda to be in school. She was a bright and forceful child but Mary was just too old to have a four-year-old shadowing her all day when she had so much to be getting on with, helping Jim in the shop and trying to keep on top of all the things that needed doing around the house. Rhoda was a child who would not submit to being enclosed in the playpen, not even for a quick half hour, nor was she one to sleep. Mary would have another year to wait until she'd start school. A year was a long time especially with a war going on.

She felt the living room closing in on her, especially now they had to stack the wooden black-out frames there ready for when darkness fell. They didn't bother about the shop or the room behind as no-one went in either after dark. She felt angry when she thought of the space in that room – the middle room – as it was called. Just wasted. Jim hadn't got around deciding what to do with it, whether to expand the shop backwards for more storage, or to do it up and use it for additional living room. The war would be over and they'd all be bloody dead by the time he ever got round to anything.

CHAPTER 5
JIM

Slaughterhouse day was a Monday. Apart from the same old customers trudging in daily, their tongues well-oiled for a natter, Jim didn't see many people. Being a butcher was a lonely old business. The slaughterhouse was as good as it got.

He felt especially empty this morning. He hadn't seen Dora at breakfast as she'd cycled off early in readiness for her shift on the ward at Mount Pleasant Hospital. On her return from London, where she'd been for almost four years, she'd been adamant it was time for a change. It was futile to argue with that one. She knew her mind. Being a cashier had paid the bills, but it wasn't for her. She wanted a profession, to have some intelligent conversation with women of her own kind. Some *camaraderie*, she'd called it, with a kind of wistful longing. He wondered if she'd picked up the word from him and who she was in cahoots with. She seemed never to be at home. Perhaps he wasn't the only one carrying secrets.

He'd said a quick goodbye to Teddy as the boy had run to catch the 83 bus. He hadn't wanted to be late so early in the term at Dynevor. It was hard for Jim to acknowledge that he was now in form three, but he had to remember that just because Teddy was physically small, it didn't mean he wasn't growing up. Perhaps growing away. But he had brains, too, like all his children. He'd passed the 11+. Not many of the kids in Cwmbwrla passed the scholarship and he'd overheard some women in the shop, almost whispering to each other, that it was only because Teddy came from a shop, insinuating that he'd offered someone on the adjudication board some bribe to get him a coveted place. As if, he, Jim Froom, had the resources to give Teddy a leg up in the world.

He was glad though they all had brains and were school-learned rather than book-learned as he'd had to be after leaving school at nine years of age to go and be some toff's 'boy' on a local farm working for his keep and less than a shilling a week. He could remember standing all day in the fields, protecting the crops, flapping his arms every so often to fend of marauding crows. Penny a day he'd got for that.

This was the time when he'd looked after, and slaughtered, animals as part of his 'boy' role. Of course, he wasn't to know then that butchery was what he'd ultimately end up doing, in a shop of his own. Well, it wasn't owned outright. Even though it had his name on the front, it was rented. But then, nobody but he and Mary knew that so it didn't matter really, did it?

Even though he felt more alone than usual, he decided not to take Rhoda with him to the slaughterhouse that Monday. In the past, on occasions when Mary had got to steaming point stating in no uncertain terms that she wanted everybody out from under her feet, he hadn't flinched from taking all the other kids. But that Monday, he didn't want her to be part of all the things that went on there. He couldn't understand how the men that worked there could endure the things they did, and then he realised that he did a sanitised version of the same job; he was just a little further down the line: a carver-upper and chopper and slicer of things that he felt had never been living, breathing animals. Just carcasses. Meat for human consumption. He liked the diagrams he had on the wall behind the block: a breakdown of the particular beast into its cuts so that customers could see at a glance what they were buying. He liked the names: shin, hindquarter, forequarter, flank, belly, loin, rib, rump...they were devoid of the life of the whole and it made him feel a bit better about things. He wondered if surgeons thought about bodies and corpses like that. There couldn't be that much difference between being a butcher and a surgeon, surely?

Distracted, he took off his slippers and stepped into his polished boots, setting off as though he was going on a military exercise. It was only about a fifteen-minute walk between 141 and Ellis Davies' abattoir and butcher shop, and he kept his back straight and his arms gently swinging by his sides just as he'd been taught.

He raised his cap to old Granny Weidenbach who was coming out of her front door at the top of the steps opposite at 142, thinking it a quirky, old gesture to do here in Cwmbwrla. It was something better suited to when he'd been nothing but a farm boy.

"Morning Mrs. Weidenbach," he said. "Lovely day."

He pronounced her name Whydenbar as did all the people in the row, but his way of saying it came with a long rolling 'r' at the end of bar. He still sounded like that poor little Devon 'boy'; he couldn't rid himself of that.

"Yes. Awful news though, Mr Froom."

She had always called him Mr Froom. Never Jim. Most of his customers did, come to think of it. Showed him respect. He didn't even know her Christian name and he always referred to her as old Granny Weidenbach though he had no idea of how old she actually was. He'd never known a Mr Weidenbach in the seven years since they'd been in Middle Road. Until now, he'd never thought about her name: she was just who she was; but today he wondered how the hell she had wound up with a German surname? She probably thought the same about him. What brought a man with a funny accent to Swansea where he ended up a butcher? The money, of course; to escape poverty; to put food in our bellies. As to why she was here, he had no answers, and if it hadn't been for what he'd heard on the radio yesterday, he probably wouldn't have been thinking about it at all. That's what war did to you: changed the way you thought. He ticked himself off for having such thoughts and carried on along Weavers Avenue. He didn't like to think of himself as a bigot. He was many things, but he hoped he wasn't that.

He reached the bottom of the hill where the avenue joined Pentregethin Road, one of the parallel roads – Carmarthen Road was the other – that ran either side of his road which was logical to call Middle Road now, he thought. He turned left, walking past the row of crumbling terraced houses that backed onto Cae Bricks. It was pretty rough there, so rough he'd always warned the kids to stay clear of it. Though he'd never seen it, he'd heard talk of women, stripped to the waist, boxing blotto on Saturday nights. It was said they drew a fair crowd, money changed hands, and there was often blood and bruising.

He'd never stoop to be part of such a spectacle, not these days. Though he knew all about rough, all about shame. He didn't like to think of those days, without Mary by his side, working to keep him together. He'd come alone to Swansea on the paddle steamer from Ilfracombe in the mid-1920s to check out whether Swansea would be a good place to move with the family. It was a strange sort of reconnaissance exercise, an expedition into the industrial unknown. He'd have done anything back then to earn a shilling. It wasn't that he wanted to be a rich man. But he didn't want to be poor again. There was a difference.

He remembered when he was put in the ring with a black man on a Saturday night. It was when he'd turned up like a stray cat, penniless, at his sister Kit's and her husband Bill's place. They'd had a butcher's shop back in Tredegar then. The Welsh Valleys was where it was all happening; where the work and the booze and the money were in good supply.

It was bloody Kit who suggested he step into the ring and see if the crowd would throw some coppers in his upturned cap for him. He'd never forgotten the disdain in her voice. But he didn't have much choice seeing as he'd exhausted all his chances in Swansea. He'd drunk too much, getting into trouble in nearly every temporary job he'd been lucky to get in one or other of the many pubs down by the docks where he'd save the beer slops in a bucket and water them down and try to make a bit of money on the side.

That night, in the ring in Tredegar, he'd been knocked clean out and ended up on the floor of a local pub. When he came round, he could see that the cap was full: coppers, three-penny-bits, even some tanners and florins. Pity money, no doubt. Bill had come for him and taken him in, black-eye and all, much to Kit's disgust. He'd never forgotten her face: that sneer, those pursed lips. He'd wanted to ask her who the hell she thought she was all high and mighty. She'd come from the same pitiful stock as him but now she was the Lady of Commercial Street in Tredegar, married to a Master Butcher. But he shouldn't be so hard. Bill had offered him the apprenticeship. He'd become Bill's boy, like he'd been a farmer's boy, learning the meat trade and obtaining certificates.

He'd never had a certificate in his life so he'd taken the offer gladly and it had set him up for the life he had now, such as it was.

Later, Kit and Bill had moved back to Swansea, to buy a fancy shop in Dyfatty near both the Hide and Skin and the town centre. It was a good spot. Plenty of buses and trams passing, and people on the hoof. And it had an illuminated sign outside with the HARRIS family name shining out across the neighbourhood in burning gas. Bill could keep more than a cat and wanted all the world to see. Or perhaps it was Kit who wanted the recognition. He doubted he'd ever have a shop with an illuminated sign but he couldn't get the burning image out of his mind: that bloody gas shining out just so everyone knew how high up they'd come.

He was nearing Ellis's slaughter house, tucked behind a terrace of identical grey houses, out of sight, approached by a long alley. The cries and squeals from the animals were no different this morning from any other Monday. Strange how they sensed what was ahead of them. He'd heard men – well, boys really – cry like this, strange sort of primitive sobs before they went over the top. The men who worked here were used to it, anaesthetised like the livestock. Jim touched his cap and the men raised their bloody hands to say good morning in response. Poor buggers. Their rubber aprons, with the deep pockets to hold knives, were streaked red, and they sloshed across the yard in rubber boots, past the sides of the deep gullies that ran full with fresh blood diluted by the water flushing through.

Jim was used to the smell. It was stronger here than in his own shop, heavy with the stench of death and the warm, almost sweet odour of freshly dead flesh. It got everywhere, up through your nostrils, in through the pores of your skin. You could never be free of it. It lingered on your hands and in your clothes long after the scrubbing of them. Mary always told him that their house stank of blood and guts, but after all the years he'd got used to it.

Pigs were being hefted into a large, circular tank of boiling water. He didn't flinch. At least, they weren't put in live. This scalding had to be done to de-hair them before they were brought, with skin as smooth as a baby's bottom, to hang snout down from a ceiling hook and later grace the shop at 141.

He didn't see any live lambs or young beasts. It was just the hearing of them, before they were stunned unconscious with a metal bolt in the brain. Most were already slaughtered. Silent now.

He walked through the opening into a stone annexe off the yard, which housed the newly-sticked cows and lambs suspended from the hooks, heads down, their gashed necks leaking blood into the channels in the stone below so as to drain away. Men with hoses helped the process. The animals were already de-bowelled, skinned and drying in the hanging room, to be delivered later by Ellis's new-fangled lorry to be unloaded at his shop.

He liked to be thought of as a discerning buyer at the abattoir, to assess the stock and instruct the slaughter-men as to which beast he wanted for delivery, viewing them like a Sergeant Major inspecting his troops on parade. He walked down the line, looking for imperfections and noting those in prime form for cutting and selling and making the small profit he slaved for. He could spot a good carcass. He felt powerful when he instructed the yard men which beast he wanted and they told him they'd be sure to tell Mr Davies, and that they could tell he had a good eye and knew what to look for. He was a Master Butcher after all. JC Froom. Family Butcher. Bugger Kit and Bill Harris.

After he'd done this, he walked back across the yard, and tapped on the glass of the back door of the house. He knew Maud would recognise his characteristic knock and she was at the door in a flash.

"Dewch mewn, Jim," she said, ushering him inside. "Eistedd lawr and have a cup of tea. I'll give Ellis a call."

Jim knew that Ellis wouldn't need much coaxing away from the grind of the usual Monday cutting and chopping.

In the man stepped, grinning madly as he rushed to shake Jim's outstretched hand. Ellis' felt cold, fridge cold, from the blessed fancy fridge he could afford to invest in.

"Croeso, Jim, Good to see you, boy. And what a day it is! What a bloody business we're all in now, eh?" he said, releasing his grip and rubbing those hands together in glee as if he expected Jim to be sympathetic to his greedy joy. Jim could feel a strange excitement coming off Ellis. Why he was acting so smug and self-assured, Jim didn't know.

What Jim did know was that Ellis was, what Mary called, a *clever bugger*. The way she said it wasn't as a compliment and he had to give it to Mary, she was a very knowing woman. Ellis had a nose for things. To Jim's knowledge he had always stayed within the law, but he reckoned it was just by a whisker. He was doing alright by the look of him: the fridge, the men he employed, the fact that he was into processing and 'manufacturing' meat as the Ministry called it. He knew all the tight-arsed Gower farmers at the mart and so far, it seemed he was making a good profit through it all. Ellis and Maud. Bill and Kit. There were butchers who were carving out a damn good living. What was wrong with him?

Jim sat in the kitchen, all ears, letting Ellis have the floor as he spouted his views on what was likely to happen in the meat trade now that war was finally here. Jim sat there and bled Ellis like the animals in the drying house, draining every answer that might be useful to him in the months to come. As he slurped his tea, and the steam perhaps clouded his vision, Jim decided that he would do something himself to profit out of the black market possibilities that *clever bugger* Ellis guaranteed were looming large on the horizon.

Jim was a betting man after all and as he listened to Ellis spouting, all full of himself, he thought that he, Jim Froom, might be on to a winner, if only he could get away with it. Meat was surely going to become a commodity that would be difficult to get hold of. There was always a price to pay in war. And there was always a price that someone would be prepared to pay in war. He tried not to let the workings of his mind make themselves visible to Ellis. He'd keep this close to his chest. For now, Jim was more than happy to sit in the kitchen and plot. To think Mary belittled his man-to-man discussions with Ellis about the meat trade. She said if it were two women sitting over a cup of tea it would be called, gossiping, or chin-wagging. But he'd show her that all this chat would pay-off one day, seeing the pound, shillings and pence before his eyes. But he wouldn't tell her. Not yet.

CHAPTER 6

TEDDY

By mid-September Teddy, like every member of his family, had been issued with a gas mask. As he set off each morning for school, he thought he would crumple under the weight of the mask encased in a cardboard box hanging over one shoulder and his battered satchel slung over the other. Though he was just thirteen, he already felt he was struggling to carry the weight of the world. Rhoda was a point in question. He felt like an unpaid babysitter as most of his so-called free time he'd have the spoiled madam constantly in tow. *Just do as you're told, Teddy*, he thought. And it wasn't just about Rhoda. His mother and his father both put on him too. But he never said anything.

He found it easy to pretend the war wasn't happening. At least not in Cwmbwrla. Even though he duly carried his gas mask daily to school, the blackout frames went over the windows at dusk, a bucket of sand and a bucket of water and a stirrup pump stood on every street corner, it still felt like make-believe. By the end of September, and his first month back at school, not even a single bomb had dropped. He felt let down if he was honest. All a damp squib. So he and his best friend Raymond from number 89 continued to play in the local park. There, they'd have a kick-about with other local lads and the young, whizz-kid footballer, John Charles, who lived nearby and who would come and weave magic with his togs. Teddy could tell that even though the Charles boy was only eight, his boots were touched with stardust. He'd probably play for the Swans one day. He was jealous in a way he couldn't put into words, not about the football, but the fact that 'Charlo' knew what he was going to do when he grew up and it seemed like nothing or no-one, would ever get in his way.

Sometimes Teddy would play at war, down on his belly,

slithering through the grass, camouflaged by the twigs and browning leaves. He'd close his index finger tight to his middle finger and make stuttering noises to mimic the imitation rifle he held in his hand to kill his friend, now turned foe, who pretended to play dead. This felt more exciting than just talk of what was going on in Europe: that was boring.

But it wasn't boring when he went to the woods with Raymond. They always headed off on foot – they called it a route march – all the way to the Penllergare Estate. It was another world there. Another time. You could smell the past in the old trees. The derelict mansion had eyes which bored into you. The deep lake held secrets and the waterfalls gushed with danger. They'd climb trees and fix the rope they'd carried with them and swing wildly out to the lake, let go of the rope and bomb into the lake, thrilled by the cold, still water.

Since he'd started another year at Dynevor, Teddy's mother had felt obliged to knit him a new pair of woollen bathing trunks. He'd tried to say *no thank you* politely but she'd insisted on creating a new version of the normal, grey-ribbed style by inserting a chevron with the Dynevor school colours of amber and black down each side from waist to thigh. Didn't she realise he was thirteen now? In form three? She tried to knit her way into all their hearts.

On that last Saturday of September, Teddy felt Raymond's eyes boring into him as he emerged from the water. Raymond couldn't contain his laughter and was bent double at the shore of the lake. He knew then it was the trunks that were heavy with the water they had absorbed. They were sagging and baggy, the crotch somewhere between hip and knee.

"I can see your John Thomas," laughed Raymond.

Teddy put one hand over his privates and tugged at the elastic to yank up the trunks.

"I will if you will," said Raymond.

"You're on," said Teddy

After that they stripped naked and dived like baby seals, their hair flat to their heads as they bobbed to the surface, the young skin of their hands crinkling with the time they'd spend putting the world to right as they frolicked in the water. They swam to the side of the lake where the waterfall roared and let the spray pound their bodies.

Teddy imagined that there might be spies camped out among the thick foliage or holed up in the decaying mansion. They decided to talk in whispers. They wondered whether they needed to develop a code. Trees had ears. Houses had eyes. How would they cope if they were taken prisoner? Name. Rank. Serial number. No more than that. They considered how long they could survive submerged without being spotted. If they breathed under water with the aid of a straw, they could last days, weeks even.

Later, when they were chilled through, they towelled themselves roughly so that their skin felt chaffed. Then they dressed again in their outdoor clothes and prepared a makeshift camp with fallen branches and the mildew tarpaulin they'd brought in the knapsack with them as they did every time they went wild. Finally, they lit a fire and poked it with sticks until it roared, sitting by the crackle of the tinder and twigs, each full of his own thoughts while they cooked spuds in an old saucepan and dined on them like princes. And when they were full, and tired with the swimming and the eating, they absorbed the heat of the flames until their blood warmed and their feral selves became tamed again. They sat and watched the burning, until the embers turned white, cooled, and finally became ash, which signalled it was time to make the trek home.

When he was with Raymond, the world felt good. But when he got back home, his stomach was fluttering and he felt frightened of something that he was unable to put into words.

He went to bed early, racing along the long, dark passage, past the closed, glass door to the shop through which he could see the iron hooks suspended from the ceiling, silhouetted by the light of the moon. For a moment, he thought he saw dead beasts hanging there. Ridiculous. It was a Saturday. Nevertheless, his heart was knocking against his ribs when he'd pounded up the first flight of steep stairs, crossed the small landing next to the bathroom, and up the final three that led him to the refuge of his bedroom.

Teddy loved his bedroom. There was a fireplace – though no fire was ever lit – a chest of drawers, and two single beds: one for him, and one for William. But for now he had the room all to himself.

In normal times, Teddy would sometimes climb onto the chest of drawers in front of the back window, and sit cross-legged gazing out at the lights twinkling in the ascending parallel rows of houses in the distance at Mayhill and Townhill. Usually, it was like fairyland. But tonight it felt as if all the brightness in the world had been switched off.

Later, as he lay in his bed, he heard the comforting, slow, rhythmic chug of the pistons of the steam train loaded with its waggons of coal, as they battled the steep gradient through the Gorse embankment. It was like a lullaby, this pattern of ordinary life.

Ordinary too, was the hooter which sounded at the tinplate works at Cwmfelin at ten, to tell the world that the afternoon shift was over and the night shift would begin. And at six o' clock it would repeat to inform the world that that shift too was over and the morning shift would start. And the day after that, because it was another Monday, he knew he would wake to the thud of his father chopping on the block below, which was a sign that life was going on as it always had. At times, he felt the sound might wrap its arms around him and prevent him from ever leaving. At other times, he feared that everything might suddenly come to an end.

CHAPTER 7
MARY

Mary had found it hard to sleep since she was on the Change. The hot flashes soaked her nightgown and she thrashed around in the bed, trying to ease the restlessness in her legs. It felt as though insects had taken up residence under the skin. Why she continued to try and stick it out and not get up and move around, she didn't know. It would feel like defeat if she gave in. She already felt she'd lost too much.

She worried that by getting up, she'd disturb Jim, though she needn't have vexed as he seemed oblivious to her torment; he slept through it all. But his wasn't a peaceful sleep either. Most nights she was aware of him moving his legs constantly, though his moved in a regular tempo, marching to a drum that was unseen and silent, to her, at least. The counterpane rose and fell as he swung his legs, and she noticed he'd worn away a patch in the flannelette in the base sheet with the force of his heels coming down hard. Sometimes he told her his feet ached in the mornings, after he'd held them rigid all night long. Sometimes he saluted in his sleep. Other times he whimpered.

Most nights she just lay there and endured this time of life, waiting for a crack of light to appear before she got up. Then she went straight downstairs to get on with her chores before Jim rose.

One by one, she crumpled yesterday's pages of the *Daily Sketch* into balls, not too tight, allowing some air to remain. There was nothing in that paper that was worth reading anyway. She poked last night's ash through the grid of the grate and brushed it into a layer of newspaper ready for the bin. She placed the remaining cinders in the hearth. With the grate cleared, she placed a layer of her rolled paper balls on the grate, shifting from knee to knee on the mat. She wasn't getting any younger. She'd be forty-four next birthday, and it was hard being a woman of this age. She reached for the sticks that she'd stacked in the hearth overnight, two vertically, two horizontally, two vertically, two horizontally, and so on. She repeated this pattern with the sticks on top of the paper and then replaced the cinders. She wondered why she'd taken on this role of fire-maker. Christ, how she'd like to come down to her clothes being warmed in front of the range once in a while.

She struck a match and lit the newspaper, watched the paper, char and blacken, disappearing before her eyes and turning to flame. She hoped the sticks would catch. They seemed dry enough, starting to spit and give off a pale, yellow flame. She gazed into them and then added the house coal from the brass hod, lump by lump, so as not to starve the fire of oxygen by suffocating it with too much coal. She felt starved of oxygen sometimes, too.

Just to make sure her efforts lighting the fire weren't going to come to nothing, she took a double page of the newspaper and held it up against the fireplace. There was something very satisfying about seeing the *Daily Sketch* being sucked in, listening to the roar, the way the energy of the flames took hold of the paper and drew it into itself. As it charred and burned, she poked the conflagration into the body of the fireplace, watching it rage and being dragged up the chimney. Then she put the guard up and went into the scullery.

It was still quite dark there. This morning she wanted to see, and feel the sun. She wanted an outlook. Some perspective, the way she had when she looked out of the kitchen back in Devon. Space for her thoughts and dreams to expand. But her mother was right. You couldn't live with just a view. It didn't pay the bills.

She took a cup of tea and walked softly in her slippers along the passage. It was just after six-thirty and still there was no sign of movement from upstairs. She walked past the door to the shop and on along the passage that led to the front door, opening it on to the row.

Standing on the threshold, she breathed in. It wasn't in any sense beautiful, but proof there was indeed space beyond the terraced houses. She felt less stifled, her body temperature coming back down. Kilvey Hill loomed in the distance to the far left of the frame, denuded and burned yellow by chemicals and copper of the industry in the Lower Swansea Valley.

She remembered how she'd laughed until she'd peed herself when someone had painted a very excited stallion on the face of Kilvey Hill. She thought back to Jim's face and how he hadn't known whether to join her laughing or chastise her for laughing so lewdly. Did he think it was unwomanly? In the end, he'd laughed but she promised him she wouldn't belly laugh about penises in public. Or whistle with her fingers between her lips to call the kids as she was more than capable of doing. She didn't understand why Jim had told her that it was vulgar for women to whistle. As always, Jim had a saying for this: *a whistling woman and a crowing hen are neither fit for God nor men*. She didn't find it funny and worried Jim did; pretending to show authority like other men did. He whistled: why shouldn't she? It gave her a feeling of freedom, the way that sound came out of her lips, making her feel powerful and carefree.

Between Kilvey and Townhill lay the valley, and at its mouth, the docks. This morning the sea was not yet blue, but in the autumn dawn, somewhere between purple and navy-black. The port was busier than usual, scores of stationary ships as far out as the horizon. That didn't bode well. Sitting ducks for German bombers if they ever came. They'd be in trouble for supplies then, alright.

She sipped her tea. The street was still sleeping. Not a soul stirring. The milk-float had come and gone and the bottles were lined up outside the front doors opposite. It would be a while until the postman did his round. Even Dennis Haywood, the local lineman from 131, who kept his motorbike and side-car stuffed with copper wire in the top shed in their yard at 141, wasn't up and about yet. Arthur must have been having a lie in, too: dear Arthur, the taxi man, with the gammy leg he'd brought home from the war. He lived on the corner of Weavers Avenue and kept his Morris 10 in their yard, too. Mary recognised that she and Jim were lucky to have a side and back entrance that the others in the row didn't.

But then she saw it. How she didn't see it immediately she didn't know. Her mind had been on the faraway. But at 142, someone had obviously been up before the rest of the world rose, and left their mark in white paint on the dark-green front door. NAZI WHORE. LOOK OUT.

Mary felt sick. It suddenly all felt very real, this war. Already it had come to Cwmbwrla: not with bombs, or gas, or burnt or bloodied bodies, but with a paint brush. Ridiculous. This was just old Granny Weidenbach's house. She wasn't even German, for God's sake. She simply happened to have a German name.

"Jim. Wake up. Quick," shouted Mary, as she shook him roughly out of his sleep.

"Is it the warning siren?" he asked, coming to in a tremor. "I went back heavy."

"No. Get up. It's old Granny Weidenbach. Some hoodlums have been up to no good. They've daubed her front door."

"Bastards," he mouthed, getting out of bed. "Any excuse and they're off."

"I'll get Teddy to fill a bucket of hot water and get a scrubbing brush. You make a start by finding some white spirit. Wherever it is!"

With Teddy and Jim still in their pyjamas underneath their overcoats, the three of them mounted the steps of 142. The curtains were still drawn in the two windows that overlooked the road. So far so good.

"Go easy with that," whispered Jim to Teddy as he instructed him to get going at the already dry paint with the rag doused in white spirit.

As Teddy rubbed, the white paint began to smear and the words slowly became indistinguishable until they were finally obliterated.

"It's disgusting," said Teddy.

Mary smiled sadly at Teddy as he carried on rubbing.

"There. That'll do. I'll scrub it now and she'll never know," said Jim.

He picked up the brush and loaded it with carbolic soap and went at the door. He was working as quietly as he could but it obviously wasn't quietly enough as they heard the porch door open, and the latch turn and then old Granny Weidenbach stood on the threshold, her face as white as the long Winceyette nightgown she was wearing, a hair net covering her curlers.

"It's alright Mrs Weidenbach," said Mary.

"What's happening?" she asked, her voice shaking, her hand going to her chest to calm herself.

Mary looked at her and saw a very old woman, yet she guessed that logically she couldn't have been more than fifteen years older than she was herself.

"You had some visitors in the night," said Mary, softly. "All gone now."

Old Granny Weidenbach looked at the bucket, the foul water inside.

"I can only guess," said Old Granny Weidenbach. "But thank you anyway for trying to clean up. It's not the first time. But you can't scrub away the filthy thoughts however many times you get your brush out."

"Don't say such things," said Mary. "I'm not going to give up on trying to make it all a bit better, even if I don't get beyond Middle Road. It's not right; and I can't stand back and do nothing. So I'll do what I can."

Old Granny Weidenbach looked a tragic figure to Mary, standing there in the early light, her head to toe whiteness framed by the architrave.

"Come across with us," said Mary. "The range is lit and I'll get the kettle on and make a nice cup of tea."

Mary took Old Granny Weidenbach by the arm and helped her down the steps, across the road, and into the living room at 141. She sat her down in one of the chairs in front of the range and got a blanket for her. She signalled with her eyes for Teddy and Jim to hop it and get themselves ready for the day while she saw to the old woman. Seven years in Middle Road and she knew nothing about this woman really. Nothing at all.

Old Granny Weidenbach told Mary that she'd left Swansea as a young girl. Just fourteen, she'd been, when she'd gone into service for a family in the East End of London. She'd only been eighteen when she'd met her husband – Berndt – a German.

It wasn't unusual back then as there were so many German immigrants in London at the turn of the century. He'd been a hard worker. A sugar boiler. Slowly, he'd earned some money, saved hard, and bought a shop – a confectionery – in Shoreditch. They'd married and then they'd had their daughter, Doreen, above that little shop. Life was good and Berndt had loved London. It was more relaxed and liberal than Germany in those days. Then it all changed; almost overnight.

"1914 it was when they came for us. Louts. Just like those that came here last night," she said to Mary. "People we thought we knew. From our own community."

"What happened?"

"They smashed our windows and threatened us," she said. "It wasn't just us. It was all the Germans in the area. Aliens they called us. Told us to get back to where we came from. I suppose they thought I was German too. But perhaps they meant the Welsh too," she said, with a smile.

Old Granny Weidenbach said that after that things got worse and after War – the first one – was declared, they seized assets – the shop – and interned Berndt along with all his other compatriots.

"He was a sweet maker, a sugar man, not a spy," she said. "I never saw him again."

Mary listened and thought of Berndt, and also of her own two brothers lost in the same conflict. She listened as the old woman told her that Berndt had taken his own life; and without any money and with a small child, she'd come back to her parents' house in Middle Road.

"Funny how we all ended up here," said Mary.

"Mmm. We've all got our own stories to tell. We never know by looking at someone what's been going on in their lives. Anyway, I've got my faith. It's kept me going all these years."

"That's good," said Mary.

"Have you got faith, Mrs Froom?" she asked.

Inside, Mary was stirred and angry. She had always thought that practical help was more effective than faith, and preferred the man Jesus to the notion of a God. Jesus got out there and tried to do something about the injustices he saw: turned over tables in the temple; jumped to the defence of Mary Magdalene and the poor.

"No. I don't believe in God," she said. "I wish I did. It must help a lot. But I do believe in fighting wrong when I see it. And maybe that's sort of the same thing."

CHAPTER 8
JIM

Even after all that occurred earlier that morning, Jim prepared himself with a wet shave before opening up. It was as much of a ritual as the boot-cleaning, and had to be executed to the letter before he could present himself to the outside world. Being clean-shaven equated with clean-living. He'd never forgotten what the army had taught him.

But this morning he was unsettled – and not just by Old Granny Weidenbach. Last night, Mary had taken down a letter from the rack and read the news. His chest had tightened to hear that William was, as he feared, really *on the other side*. He hated seeing his son's handwriting. Seeing it in print made it true.

The text was heavily censored, but Mary could read between and beyond the lines and tied together everything William had told them was likely to happen. 59th Squadron had now been moved to an airfield and camp at Poix, near Dieppe in Northern France. The Squadron couldn't understand why Hitler hadn't already marched into Belgium, as he'd been braying about, when to be honest, Britain and the Allies were ill-prepared. William was on reconnaissance missions in the Blenheims with another two crew members. They knew the mad man would invade, they just didn't know when. They had to be ready. And no, he wasn't as afraid as he thought he'd be, and not to worry, for it wasn't as cold as he feared. Jim felt sick to his stomach but knew he couldn't show, now he had to try and pretend to be the man he thought he should be for Mary.

So he stood in front of the bathroom mirror and with his bristle brush lathered his face with the foam from his shaving mug, like a soldier. He soaped-up his sideburns, his upper lip, his jaw, chin and neck. Then he took his cut-throat and felt the edge of the thin steel blade. He'd been careful to give it a good stropping as he didn't want it tugging at his skin. Stretching his jaw, and holding it in position with his left hand, he began to work the blade methodically across his skin, just as he'd done in his army days. Nowhere was the hint of overnight growth allowed to remain and cast a shadow on his face. He didn't rush. When he was done, he rinsed the blade under the cold water tap and dried it carefully. He couldn't afford for it to rust.

With his morning ablutions complete, he looked in the mirror and approved of this version of himself that he'd present to his customers. The looking glass didn't reflect what was going on inside his brain, the pounds, shillings and pence leaping about all over the place. The mask he had created hid the prospect that he might be working on the wrong side of the law soon. But sod, the rules. What did the Ministry care about him?

Jim padded downstairs in his slippers. Rhoda was still sleeping and he knew Mary liked it like that so she could get on top of things in the morning. He went into the living room and was met with the warmth of the range, his starched white coat and blue and white apron laid out on the back of the chair close to it. Sometimes he couldn't believe that Mary still loved him enough to do these little touches that meant so much, getting the fire alight in the range before he came down, putting the kettle on, making him his toast and dripping.

He went down the two steps into the scullery where Mary stood at the sink. Then he lifted the lid of the settle and took out his polished boots, sat down, and laced them up. He didn't say anything to Mary. They didn't chat much in the mornings anymore as he found it difficult to come around and didn't like to do small talk. God knows he had enough of that to do in the shop. He knew Mary understood this by now. She turned her face away and presented her cheek to accept his kiss. It was a quarter to nine and he was fully prepared to face the world.

He strode along the passage, his leather soles echoing on the tiles and off the green, distempered walls, bare apart from the phone that hung on the wall on his left, opposite the cupboard under the stairs. The phone was his life-line. He and Mary had readily agreed to having it put in. Not many people who lived in their patch could even think of having one.

He'd put the idea to Mary that it would be a good thing for the neighbourhood. People could come in to use it when they had an urgent need. Jim assumed Mary liked the idea of the phone singling them out, the fact that they were special. He presumed she'd welcome the fact that they could make a bit of money out of it too by charging every time it was used. He presumed a lot of things about Mary.

Jim had managed to get the motivation to mount a small shelf next to the black Bakelite phone on which was placed a little notebook with a pencil and a glass jam pot for the coins. He'd thought 6d a call was a bargain. If Mary knew the real reason he'd had the phone installed was to place his bets on the horses with the local bookie or his runner, she didn't say. His betting cost his family dearly at times. And Mary didn't know the half. Aye, he thought. Best keep it that way, and all.

He belched as he entered the shop, walking across the wooden floor boards sprinkling them with sawdust. Then he stood next to the white marble slabs inside the shop window, reaching above him and beginning his daily task of unpicking the individual sheets of greaseproof paper hanging from the hooks. One by one, he took each sheet down, placing the papers in a pile and the hooks in a tin, ready to be used again later, when it was time to lock-up.

As each paper was unhooked, it revealed more and more of the queue that was already forming outside. All women. They all seemed to look the same: drab coloured, tightly-belted coats; headscarves tied around their hair, knotted under the chin; familiar shopping bags at the ready. Jim tried not to make contact with those eyes of theirs, imploring him to open up. Putting him under the pressure of a performance he didn't want.

He looked at the walnut clock that hung over the doorway to the passage. Five to nine. He wouldn't be rushed. He placed the ashtray on a stand next to the shop door, adjusted his tie, turned the sign that hung on a piece of string from CLOSED to OPEN and then finally, unbolted the door, top and bottom.

He cleared his throat ready to get into role. He was conscious he did this. Mary had told him he had a shop voice that he could switch on and off, telling him there was no need for *affectation*. He hadn't known what affectation meant, but he assumed it was something like pretending. He didn't want to ask: it would only drive home how different she was from him in so many ways.

"Morning, Ladies. How are we today?" he said, as, in an orderly fashion, the women filled the space on the other side of the counter with the smell of stale cigarette smoke, and dampness. With them came the bite of the October morning. This weather was better for trade.

"No need to close the door, Mrs Squires," he instructed. "Nice and fresh this morning. Now, who's head of the queue here?... Mrs. Brooks, usual, is it?"

Every Tuesday was neck of lamb day for Mrs. Brooks. He'd never make a fortune out of her from 140. She could make a stew that would last all week for her and Mr Brooks out of this cheap cut. Mean buggers.

"I heard you sorted Mrs Weidenbach out earlier, Mr Froom? You know she's German, don't you?" she said.

"I did indeed. Was more than happy to. And she's not German by the way – as if that makes any difference."

"Well, she was married to one. And it will make a difference, Mr Froom. Make a difference to us all."

He tried not to rise to the goad. Of course, it would make a bloody difference. But Mrs Brooks was a bigoted bitch.

"This alright for you, Mrs Brooks?" he said, holding up the meat, wishing it were Mrs Brooks who he'd taken the cleaver to, and was now hanging limp in his hand.

"Lovely, Mr Froom."

He walked to the Avery scales and placed the neck on a sheet of greaseproof paper to weigh.

"Sixpence halfpenny? Is that too much for you?"

"It'll do fine," she said. "Don't want to go spoiling anyone."

Mrs Brooks handed over the exact amount and he placed the sixpenny-bit in the sixpenny-bit compartment and the halfpenny in the halfpenny compartment, and tried to regain his composure as she went out of the shop. He knew if he told everyone who came into his shop what he really thought about the world – and them – he'd have less of a business than he did now. Everything was such a ruddy compromise and he hated himself for it.

He looked deep into the till, to the wooden compartments at the back which didn't hold money, just tucked-up memories: a curl from Dora's red, childhood hair, the first milk tooth he'd pulled out from Teddy with a cotton thread, one of Rhoda's early attempts at writing her name on a scrap of paper, a fading sepia image of William on the rocking horse, a signed photograph of Mary which she'd sent to him when he was at camp in Bulford, and even a picture of himself in uniform soon after he'd been made a sergeant. He closed the drawer of the till quickly when he looked at the image of himself in uniform with the three stripes, stifling another burp, and quickly returned to the next customer.

There was a steady flow of trade throughout the morning. He stood at his block listening and looking up from his chopping and his cutting from time to time to see the women's faces, so animated, in the mirror behind him. There were snippets of gossip that seeped into him: who was under the doctor; who was having a hard time with their husband; who'd joined up; who wasn't long for this earth judging by the colour of them; how so and so managed to put up with the in-laws now they were living in rooms in the same house; how they felt a change in the weather; how they didn't think this War would come to anything.

How could women talk like this? They seemed to talk about everything and nothing, and they did it so easily. He believed they found relief and some measure of comfort in the talking for talking's sake and wondered why men didn't talk like this. As if they'd had their tongues cut out by some invisible force or just passed facts back and fore to each other, filling the awkward space where their feelings were meant to be.

CHAPTER 9

MARY

Saturday mornings were always busy in the shop and Jim didn't even have time to come through to the scullery for a cup of tea mid-morning, so Mary carried the tea to him on a small tray. She paused at the ever-open door separating the shop from the passage, held open by a large, iron meat hook hanging from the ceiling bar. She could see the back of Jim as he stood at the block, stooped, his face reflected in the mirror behind. He looked old. Tense. She wondered where the young soldier had gone, the one she'd seen marching past her garden gate when he was training on a route march at Bulford. Those four years before they married at the end of 1918 had made him go in on himself in ways he wouldn't talk about. The man she saw in the mirror was a shrunken version of the one she'd loved, and he seemed to be getting smaller every day. But this side of him wouldn't be apparent to his customers.

She placed the cup of tea down on the smaller block at his side and touched the crook of his arm, feeling the stiff fabric of the white coat he put on every day. His uniform. His eyes smiled at her from the reflection, crinkling and showing the lines, but he didn't look around to face her. There was a customer in the shop.

It was at that moment she felt more invisible that ever. She had an almost spiteful urge to make herself seen. She'd make him take notice of her. She'd bloody make him move the decrepit piano out of the old stables and have him put it in the middle room. She'd instruct Mr Eynon, the blind man with the tuning fork from Ravenhill, to come and check if the keys were all working and advise as to whether it would need to be restrung. Once the tuned piano was in place, they could light the fire in the cast-iron grate and hunker down together, breathing new life into 141.

Who knows, perhaps they might even sing as they used to.

Mary decided that Guy Fawkes' night was just the impetus needed to get Jim to shift both himself and the piano. There were no outdoor fireworks this year because of restrictions, so she planned a little brightness indoors, instead of the small bonfire they'd usually have in Louisa's garden next door.

They'd never made an extravagance of November 5th – it was a practical way of disposing with the garden debris made more exciting with a couple of shillings spent on sparklers, Catherine Wheels, and no more than a couple of rockets, and potatoes cooked in their skins in the fire. They'd stopped having the Jumping Jacks even though the children loved them. Jim said he couldn't stand them after the War. So that was the end of that.

Mary was already mourning the loss of the event before it had even happened. She'd taken it quite for granted until it wasn't allowed. It made her want it more somehow, and in her imagination she made it out to be better than it actually ever was. She didn't think Jim would miss it, as he was always afraid of the fire getting out of hand, or one of the fireworks burning the children, or one of the squibs not lighting first time and then going off in someone's hand, or face. He was afraid of a lot of things, Jim, and so he took complete charge of everything, running it like a military operation.

Guy Fawkes fell on a Sunday so she decided on a get-together in the middle room. She commanded Jim to get a team together to move the piano from the old stables. The timings couldn't have been more perfect, and as soon as Jim had shut the door to the last customer, and she'd cleaned up the shop, they were ready for her to direct operations.

Standing at the old stables' door, she shouted at Jim and the assembled team to be careful: it wasn't worth a lot, but it was precious, the old upright Townly that used to belong to her mother who'd taught her to play when she was a little girl. It was mahogany, with a golden, twirling flower of walnut veneer placed above middle C, and a pair of swivelling, brass candlestick holders. She could see that the keys had yellowed during the time it had been idle, and a couple of them were chipped, too.

Never mind. She was no Beethoven; but she could read music and play by ear. Jim had told her she could hold a tune well, too, and she was pleased that she'd passed on some innate, but unused talent, to William.

"Assume positions," she bellowed. "Now, on the count of three, lift. One. Two. Three. Lift."

"Christ Almighty," shouted Jim as they lifted the weight. "Worse than a bloody coffin."

They took it easy in short stages, pausing, and resting every couple of feet, faces red, backs stooped. It was indeed worse than a corpse-filled coffin. You could put that on your shoulders and share the load.

"This is the worst bit. Take it easy up the step," said Mary.

She watched the piano assume an angle of forty-five degrees as the men manoeuvred it up the step, then turned to guide it in through the scullery door. When they placed it down for a moment, Mary noticed that Jim was sweating. She worried about him. He wasn't getting any younger.

They sped up as they undertook the last leg, along the passage and into the middle room, Mary watching intently as the piano was carefully positioned against the far wall, feeling that the room had been needing this instrument for a long time to make it come alive. It looked as if it had always been there, perfectly at home.

"You boys can bring the piano stool and then you're dismissed. A good job jobbed!"

Once the men and boys had done her bidding and left the room, Mary walked up to the piano stool and touched the worn, leather seat. She caressed the impression in the centre where her mother's behind had sat for all those years. Now it would accommodate her almost identical rear. Opening the lid of the stool, she was met with the smell of musty sheet music. So many memories were held in those notes: her mother playing to accompany her father back in Fordingbridge; herself at her mother's side trying to master scales and fingering.

The piano *was* her old self back when she was Mary Read. Something of her that belonged to no-one else. She felt protective of it as if it were her own body. She didn't want anyone else to touch it, to treat it with anything besides the respect it deserved.

She would make a sign: *AT YOUR PERIL*, for everyone to know they had to keep their mitts off it. After all, Jim had one for the phone.

All of a sudden, she felt better. She delved through the sheets until she found what she was looking for. Opening the music, she placed it on the music desk and then sat on the stool ready to play *O for the Wings of a Dove* as she'd done in the past to accompany William. As her fingers touched the keys, she felt him standing beside her as he used to, his young soprano voice clear and true, intent on making as perfect a rendition as possible. Abruptly, she was overcome with melancholy, and closed the lid over the keys. She quickly nestled the music back inside the stool. Yes, it was a good idea that she'd planned a little get-together later. She could do with something to lift her spirits. She would strive to look forward rather than backward as much as she was able. After all, what other choice did she have?

As Mary came out of the middle room and made her way along the passage, Jim was on the phone. He made no attempt to put the handset back in the cradle or lower his voice anymore. She knew all about it. He was standing there with a pencil and his little, black book making a note of his bets. And no doubt his debts. But at least he was open about it and not out and about doing things behind her back. She'd learned by now that it was no good trying to stop him by constant nagging. It was a hard habit to break even though it was hurting them as a family. No wonder the kids went without new boots most of the time. Still, married him was all she had done, not beatified him. She wondered if he'd ever be able to move – or she could make him move – a few inches from what he'd been made to understand a man to be made of: what had been beaten into him as a child, and drummed into him as a soldier.

"I won't be long," he said, as he placed his hand over the mouthpiece as she passed.

She just shook her head at him and made her way to the range and sat down in her chair, picked up her knitting, and waited. It was like waiting for a naughty child who expected to be punished.

"Well?" she said. "Is this *the* sure bet?"

"Don't be like that, Mary. It's got good form and the odds are great. It's the 3.30 at Newmarket. *War Admiral*."

"How much have you put on?"

"Half-a-crown. It's 100/1."

"And the form?"

"Triple Crown winner."

"There'll only ever be one winner, Jim. And it's not you. How much longer are you going to go on lining other people's pockets? Wasting your – and my – hard-earned cash."

"I've got a good feeling in my waters about this one, Mary. Trust me. Dead cert."

"I do trust you, Jim. But with horses you're a fool. Which little bleeder were you on the phone to this time?"

"Frank. He's down the Gate House."

"I might have guessed. Propping up the bar. Touting for more trade from all those boozers. Idiots the lot of you, men. And to think you believed I didn't know this was the real reason you had that phone put in in the first place. You just can't help yourself, can you, Jim?"

"No. You're right, Mary. I can't."

"Well at least you're honest about that. I'd skin you alive if I ever learned that you were down the Gate House, wasting any more of our meagre wages on a whim. And you can forget about your dreams for Teddy. Over my dead body will I have him going to a stables. Jockey, my foot. He'll never be a Tim Hyde, or some other Irish winner. With a bit of luck, he'll be too big soon. He wants to follow his dreams, Jim, not yours. Have you ever bothered to ask him about his?"

"Good God, Mary, not yet. Haven't had time."

"Time? You know nothing about a lack of time. Try putting yourself in my shoes for a while. And you should know, he wants to be a surgeon, Jim. And he's got the brains to be whatever he likes, so help him realise his dreams not have your second-hand ones fill his head."

"I never had the chance, Mary."

"You're like a stuck gramophone needle. It's not about you now, Jim. It's about the kids. Their futures. So don't bugger up their chances. They're up against enough without you."

CHAPTER 10
JIM

Following his ticking off, Jim thought he'd better pull his socks up. He didn't want to incur Mary's wrath again. God knows she was up and down enough with women's troubles.

He whistled as he helped Mary get ready for their little Guy Fawkes 'do'. He took the Teacher's whiskey from the cupboard under the stairs, along with a bottle of peppermint and glass tumblers, and set them out on top of the table in the middle room. He made a promise to himself that he wouldn't hit the bottle later. But he still had a taste for it and knew he was more than partial and couldn't drink in moderation. He could either have none or too much. Nothing soothed him like being drunk. It took away the things that he couldn't get out of his mind from his days as a sergeant. But it was short lived and the guilt was always worse with the hangover. His life was really a constant hangover from those dark days.

His spirits were raised when he saw that he was pleasing Mary by playing a willing part in the occasion. She never stopped, poor woman. He watched her as she brought some of his homemade sausages out of the oven of the Rayburn and cut them into small pieces and speared them with little sticks. He didn't know where she'd got that idea from. She'd also got some new-fangled sliced bread in, and had made sandwiches filled with shrimp paste, cut into triangles with the crusts off and arranged them on a doyley-covered plate. She didn't want a big fuss, she said. It wasn't a fancy spread; more of a just-take-us-as-they-find-us evening. For someone who said this, she was certainly pulling out all the stops. How long they would have these little luxuries Jim didn't know. They'd no doubt have to pull their belts in after Christmas. But for now, they'd enjoy.

"Have you asked Raymond up?" Jim asked Teddy.

"Yes, Dad. He's bringing some sparklers."

"That'll be good. And for you to have some young company with all us old fogies," said Jim, ruffling Teddy's red hair. "And you can keep an eye on Rhoda. Let your mother have a bit of a rest and enjoy herself."

"Don't worry. Me and Raymond will look after her. As usual…"

Jim's response was stopped in its tracks when Dora came into the middle room. Her hair was freshly washed and had a lustrous, red sheen. She wore a green dress and court shoes. He couldn't remember the last time he'd seen her dressed up.

"You look very smart, Dora," he said. "Expecting anyone special, are we?"

"No, *we're* not, Dad. I've just made a bit of an effort that's all. For myself. It's a relief to get out of uniform now and again, all that starch and cuffs and caps and tight belts."

"I thought for a moment, there was someone you'd met at the hospital you'd like Mum and me to meet? A handsome young doctor that you're sweet on, perhaps?"

"No. there's no young man joining me," said Dora. "Only lovely Sybil. I've asked her over for company."

"Marvellous. I'm glad you and her are such good friends. She must be missing William so much, poor girl. Good that she's got you to stand in for him."

"I'm not a stand-in Dad. I've been friends with her for years as well, remember," she said tersely. "And don't worry about me finding a special someone. I'm only twenty. I'll make sure I find the right one, when it's time."

"Well, that told me good and proper, didn't it, Son" said Jim to Teddy, feeling unsettled as he watched Dora stalk off out of the room. "Hope Mein Fuhrer comes back from the scullery in a better mood. Don't want her spoiling the evening."

The guests came via the front door. Arthur was the first to arrive with Muriel, his wife. Jim played host, took their coats, hanging them on the hooks in the passage and ushering them into the middle room where Mary and the rest of the family were waiting. Jim was relieved to see that Dora had put a smile on her face as she poured the drinks. He watched Arthur limp towards the fireplace, turn, and warm his backside. Jim knew the War hadn't been kind to himself, but it didn't show like Arthur's physical disability. Mr and Mrs Haywood – Dennis and Irene – were next, followed by Old Granny Weidenbach, Graham and his wife Doreen, and their little girl, Joan, who was around the same age as Rhoda. Sybil was last to arrive and seemed a little shy in the room, until Dora went up to her, put her arm around her, and settled her down with a drink. They were so close, those two.

Jim felt proud to see the room full, the fire roaring in the grate, smiles on everyone's faces. The shop-come-house had always drawn people to a party. He liked that. If it hadn't been for the wooden frame tacked with blackout fabric that he'd put in place just before dark, and the sparklers that were now being lit indoors, and the fact that his elder son was on reconnaissance missions *on the other side*, you wouldn't have known there was anything amiss with the world.

Mary suggested a singsong and took to the piano.

"Any requests?" she asked, swivelling her backside on the stool, looking over her shoulder.

Jim was in his element singing, *It's a Long way to Tipperary* and *Pack Up Your Troubles* with this band of men. All, apart from Graham, had seen active service on the Western Front, and now they were marching and swinging their arms with their drinks held in one hand, while Mary kept them in time at the piano in a little room with a concrete floor in Cwmbwrla.

"How about some modern ones?" sighed Dora.

"How about, *Somewhere Over the Rainbow?*" suggested Teddy.

"Good choice, Teddy," said Dora. "It's from the film, Mum, with Judy Garland."

"I haven't seen the film, but I've heard it on the radio. I'll give it a go, by ear."

She practised a few chords while everyone chatted.

"I didn't know you two had already seen *The Wizard of Oz?*" said Jim to Teddy and Dora.

"I went back in the summer," said Teddy. "With Raymond. Don't you remember me telling you about it? How the film changed from black and white to technicolour?"

"The summer seems another age now."

"You should take Mum," said Teddy. "She'd love it. And you might."

"Yes, that would be good. I'll get tickets for the double seats at the back. Get the usherette to shine the torch at us and tell us to stop cuddling or else she'll have to throw us out," said Jim, winking. "So what about you, Dora? Where did you see it?"

"At the Plaza. Same as Teddy."

"With anyone special?"

"Sybil," she said, smiling gently at her friend.

Mary said she was about as good and ready as she'd ever be. Teddy said he'd give it a go. He was no William, but he'd try. He took a sip of lemonade, and went to stand near his mother.

Jim watched and listened. It could have been William standing there: the tone of his voice, the look on his face. William, who had been given a chance in life with the singing lessons at Carmarthen Road with Stanley Owen. He'd got the scholarship to London. He'd done what he wanted to do so far in life, chosen his own path. Little Teddy had just come behind, the third child, plodding along, demanding nothing, almost bringing himself up. Jim didn't even know he had it in him and wondered what chances he'd take in life. There was a lot about Teddy he didn't know. It would appear there was a lot about all his children he didn't know. Maybe about Mary, too.

CHAPTER 11
MARY

It had seemed like a good idea to have a party on a Sunday night, but the next morning, Mary could see that Jim's head was telling him a different story. Gone were the days when he could drink like a navvy. In the fug of the scullery, she watched him as he tried as best he could to monitor the pot on the Rayburn, trying to shield his forearm from the boiling fat that spat as the beef trimmings rendered. All week, he'd stored the offcuts in a large meat tray under the block in readiness for the dripping he was now making.

She could tell he was on the cusp of being sick. Even her stomach was curdling at the stench.

"You alright, Jim?" she asked, not without a degree of perverse pleasure. "Struggling a bit this morning, are we? Wish we hadn't had *just* that last one?"

"I'll be alright in a bit," he said. "It's worth the effort. And the smell."

She knew he was right. When he'd open the shop the next morning, he would have cut the dripping into blocks by weight for his customers who relished JC Froom's homemade dripping. For most in the neighbourhood it was the staple for breakfast or supper, spread on a chunk of bread or toast. She was happy that he was happy when he saw his name on the front of the waxed paper that contained the dripping.

As the fat broke down, Mary kept an eye on him as he ladled the hot liquid through a sieve into a deep bowl to cool and set solid white. His hands shook continuously. He returned the bits from the sieve to the pot and repeated the process. Every last drop counted. He then lifted the pot with the boiling liquid and placed it safely out of the reach of Rhoda who sat on the scullery steps drawing, out of harm's way. Mary was on the sausage-making. Like the dripping, JC Froom had a reputation for beef sausages. No muck. Not all rusk as some used in what they had the nerve to pass off as sausages. She felt good knowing small things like these.

Mary didn't know how she did it. She'd had almost as much Scotch as Jim. Perhaps women were built to withstand pain: menstruation, pregnancy, miscarriage, childbirth, sleepless nights, menopause, this list was never ending. Life was surely an endurance test and she didn't want to be found wanting. So now she stood at the side of an old bench where the red sausage-making machine was set up. She and Jim called it the canon. She was bent over a china bowl, mixing the beef she had minced and seasoned and added just a little bit of cereal and preservative. Where she got the energy from she didn't know. No hint of a hangover. Stamina as well as strength.

"I'll stuff the canon and turn the handle," she laughed. "You look fit for nothing."

Mary picked up a dollop of the mixture and pressed it into the body of the canon while he took his position at the other end, where there was a steel aperture through which the sausage-meat mixture was forced to come out the other side magically as a sausage. Jim placed the lace-like sheep's intestine onto the tube and rolled it along its length so it could contain the meat as it emerged. He looked at Mary as he was performing this action, very deftly, with his thumb and index finger as he would when he used to put on a rubber.

"What d'you think of my skills, Mary?" he laughed.

"You're a naughty old man, Jim Froom. Keep your mind on the job or you might go blind! You know what they say. I'll crank the handle."

It was hard work, but she didn't complain as she put her back into her task while he kept his fingers on the nozzle, guiding the continuous tube of sausage meat into the casing, and on into a waiting bowl.

"I'll let you loop today, Mary, if that's alright."

"Good grief. Allowed to loop? You must be poorly. Sit on the step with Rhoda and keep her amused while I finish off."

She watched him walk to the sink to swill his hands under the tap, drying them on a lamb's loin cloth before walking to the step. He then sat down and picked up Rhoda and put her on his lap. She beamed at him and it made Mary's stomach flutter with the love he had for their last child. She choked back the tears as Jim bounced Rhoda up and down on his knee and they chanted the words that she loved to listen to on the Billy Cotton show on the wireless. Funny how they both had a love of horses: her love so innocent; his, a costly pleasure.

> *Horsey, horsey don't you stop*
> *Just let your feet go clipetty clop.*

"Again, again," squealed Rhoda.

Nothing was ever enough for Rhoda, Mary realised as she twisted and pinched the sausages, forming a string of perfect loops. She'd go on and on demanding until she'd worn Mary out. She just didn't have the knack with this one. More skills with the sausages. But she and Jim were a good team. Not many couples could work together for so long without coming to blows. They were an established, if not always profitable, production line: dripping, sausage, as well as all the children. Sometimes it felt to her that she had melted into Jim and become a single person. This was both good and bad. She heard Jim starting up the action rhyme with Rhoda again and she knew she was a lucky woman most of the time, when she saw how tender he could be. Definitely no saint, but patient. How she wished she could be more like that with Rhoda and just pour this moment into a bowl and watch it set solid like dripping.

CHAPTER 12
JIM

During the autumn Jim had found the weather to be much like the war: apart from a cold spell in early October and the first week of November, it had been milder than he had expected. So much so that he felt he was going to be caught suddenly off guard.

About the weather he was right. The second week of November bit hard and it seemed not to get light at all. A single, naked bulb hung over the counter, and Jim nevertheless marvelled at the electricity that had been put in enabling the two, shabby gas lamps that previously lit the space behind the window to be taken away and dumped. The white wall tiles behind the block gave off a sickly glare. Jim was glad when the street light directly outside flicked on in the early afternoon with its gentle glow that it wore like an orange halo. He would have preferred it if it had snowed or been frosty, but what fell from the Swansea skies was freezing rain that cut to the bone. Old Dennis Heywood was up to his eyes in it, repairing the lines that had sagged and finally collapsed under the weight. Black ice formed unseen on the pavements that caught some of Jim's customers out, many of them coming a cropper. He made a point of getting up earlier in the mornings and shovelling the cinders from the grate in the range into a bucket and scattering them on the ice outside the front. He didn't want to be responsible for anyone getting hurt. Not on his watch. Not again.

This included the birds, too. From the kitchen window he looked out at the scores of sparrows in the yard: on the lids of the bins, and on the wooden bird table, desperate for a crumb. They looked sadder this year. Greyer. He made a point of making sure there was fresh water left outside and that there was left-over bacon rind to hang from the bird table.

A single robin appeared and would perch on top of the stone wall and Jim singled it out for special attention, taking it a saucer of milk when it was safe from Whiskey, the cat. It sang a cheerful song to break the dullness of the cold mornings. Jim felt that perhaps the little bird had singled him out too, and taken up winter residence in 141. It became a daily visitor and it warmed his heart.

The house was cold. The water froze in the lead pipes and you didn't want to hang around in the bathroom. He and Mary sat close to the range in the evenings, so close that Mary's legs, above where she'd rolled her stockings down to her ankles, became red and mottled, reminding him of the bully beef he used to supply the front lines with. He knew it wasn't a pretty thought, but he couldn't get the comparison out of his head. Hell, he couldn't get those times out of his mind, full stop.

It was hard to leave the dying embers at night and rush to the bedroom where the flimsy peach curtains stuck fast with ice to the inside of the window panes. He undressed at speed, sitting on the edge of the bed, not daring to touch the lino with his bare feet. It was so cold that he sometimes wore his dressing gown in bed and piled overcoats on top of the sheets, and the blankets, and the eiderdown. He wore a nightcap that Mary had knitted him and the bedsocks. He found a warmth of sorts nestled into Mary's body, though Mary insisted that these days their contact was purely for practical purposes and they'd be safer from now on sleeping back to back. He missed Mary in that sense. He ached for her. He didn't like endings. Yet he realised that their family couldn't withstand another baby.

CHAPTER 13
MARY

Mary licked her finger and turned down the top corner of the page in the Radio Times for Saturday, 11th November. The Queen was addressing the women of the nation on the Home Service: 9 o'clock. She wouldn't forget.

The powers that be had pushed the actual service of Remembrance forward to Sunday the 12th as they didn't want to halt any production in the war effort. It was change like this that brought it home to Mary how serious things were getting. The next day, she and Jim would listen in to the service as they always did, and Jim would well up and be on the verge of crying as the bugler played *The Last Post*, but Saturday night was the night for the Queen.

Mary put Rhoda to bed early, and for once, the little madam didn't make a fuss. Be grateful for small, mercies, Mary told herself, hoping that Rhoda wouldn't wake up later and interrupt proceedings. So she found herself with an hour to spare to get herself ready for the broadcast. She and Jack always took anything to do with Armistice very seriously. It was a serious business, war.

Every year at this time she and Jack would remember all the family and friends who never got to get to middle age like they had. She could only recall her two brothers, as twenty and twenty-two-year-olds. She knew Jack remembered the men he'd fought with, as well as the men who made it home in some form or other, like Arthur with the limp from across the road; Bill Burman with a steel plate in his head; and Mervyn Demery with the shakes, all neighbours, living in Beattie Street. And now there was William to worry about, too.

Mary ran a bath and the pipes juddered with the force of the water. She knew Jim wasn't serious when he told the family that they shouldn't waste water and that if they filled the bath too full – above the invisible mark – a man would knock at the door and come upstairs with a ruler to measure it. Nevertheless, she turned off the taps pretty sharpish. It would be a dip rather than a wallow. She'd leave the water for Teddy, and he'd leave it for Jim. She didn't need to think about Dora as she'd seen to herself earlier and had gone out to the pictures with Sybil. Again. They were so close.

She got out of the bath, dried, put on her brassiere and corset, and then her housecoat. She rubbed the mirror with the damp towel to clear the condensation and looked at her reflection. She saw herself as being on the road to fifty rather than being almost forty-four. The smoking was etching fine lines above her mouth. She'd give it up, she vowed. When this war was over. She counted the crows' feet at the corner of her eyes. It was true. There was one for every decade. She rubbed Nivea into her face with vigour. But she couldn't undo what the years had done to skin that was too fair and dry for smoking. She hoped the measuring man was a figment of Jim's imagination, rather than a real live male who'd come across her naked.

She went into her and Jim's bedroom and sat in front of the dressing table, brushing her hair, examining the amount that came out in the brush. In her palm, it resembled a grey mouse. *A grey mouse*, she said to herself. Was that what she was too? What mark had she managed to make on the world so far? She put down her brush and dabbed some scent behind her ears. She'd had it for years. Lily of the Valley. What was the point of wearing scent when she never went anywhere? Shop. Scullery. Out the washing line. Into town. Off to bed. She took out her best frock from the wardrobe. She couldn't remember the last time she'd worn it. Probably before Rhoda was born. She put it over her head and adjusted it down over her waist, her hips, smoothed out the slightly flared skirt. She checked herself in the mirror. The blue suited her. The colour matched her eyes though she had no idea if spots were still in vogue. She wasn't one for fashion. The puff sleeves came down to her elbows which she liked; what she didn't like so much was how the buttons of the dress pulled, the fabric gaping across her breasts, how she had to do the thin belt up on the last notch. Never mind. It would have to do. She hitched up her stockings to the suspenders of her corset and then stepped into her lace-ups. She couldn't bear the idea of a heel, not with the fluid she was recently retaining around her ankles; but at least she'd got out of her slippers. She couldn't listen to the Queen in her slippers.

When she entered the living room, she sat down at the side of what she called her knick-knack table in readiness. She liked her things to be always at hand, where she could find them. *Her* possessions on *her* table: knitting pattern from *Woman's Own*; tape measure; pin cushion in the shape of a lady with a dirndl skirt; blue and white china pot containing a crochet hook, small scissors, nail file, magnifying glass, and a letter opener, and next to it, a dish of Mint Imperials. She swore by them, for her indigestion and her breath.

Until Jim and Teddy came back downstairs, she would knit. She was still underway with a pullover for William. Even though he'd asked for only one, she was doing him a few in the same style so he'd have a change. Knitting was about all she could do from an armchair at the side of a range to offer practical help in this war effort. To keep her son warm.

The process not only kept her hands busy; but her head engaged, focusing on things other than children and worry. She glanced at the mantel over the range where William's latest letter was in the front of the rack. She'd have to get cracking on the jumpers if they were all to be done by Christmas when he'd said he'd be home on leave – if Hitler didn't march into France and Belgium and the rest of the Low Countries in the next six weeks, of course. They hadn't been all together for years what with him being away, and Dora in London.

She took a look at the clock. Ten to. Not long now. She switched on the wireless and turned the dial to tune in to the Home Service. It crackled through the airwaves until she found the station and perfected the indicator line over the exact wavelength until the sound was clear. Almost ready.

Jim came in with a clean shirt and a dark tie with one of Mary's sleeveless plain pullovers on top. He stepped into his shoes, polished for the occasion, then reached up to the mantel shelf and took down the two red poppies that Mary had bought from the British Legion when they'd come around collecting door-to-door at the beginning of the month. She took hers from Jim and threaded the stem through the top button hole of her dress. Then she reached over and attached Jim's to his pullover with a safety pin, stroking his hair off his forehead and kissing him gently.

Just as the pips sounded on the hour, they took to their chairs, and waited for what her Majesty had to say.

"She's a lot better than him on the wireless," said Jim. "Poor sod, that he is, to have all this thrust upon him and his family."

"Shh," said Mary, leaning across and turning up the volume. "You're right, but I'm listening to what the Queen has to say for a few minutes."

Whether it was the heat from the range, or the emotion she felt listening to the Queen, Mary felt a flush rise from between her breasts, spread across her chest, her neck and face. She must have looked a sight but she didn't care about that at the moment. She shuffled her bottom in the chair and strained her ears to try and take in more of what was being said. She felt that the Queen was almost in the room with her, such was the intimacy of the wireless, drawing her in, Elizabeth almost chatting to her, woman to woman. She imagined that all the women in Great Britain might feel the same, desperate to hear someone who seemed to understand what they were feeling at the moment, eager to raise their spirits and press home that just like the men, women were doing a wartime job that was valuable too. She needed to hear that. And her heart went out to the plight of the women of Poland and France that the Queen was talking about, and how they were already suffering so much. Hitler was a monster.

Up until this broadcast she had thought of herself as redundant in the war effort – that little grey mouse – but as the Queen spoke about the sacrifice of the men and the boys who had joined up and the danger they were facing, she also spoke about the role of the women they had left behind who had to keep the family going and keep up the spirit of the community. The women would need to be strong when these men and boys came home. It would be a new world then. A fresh beginning for men and women.

Mary could tell Jim was intent on what the Queen was saying too. He didn't interrupt again for the course of the broadcast, without her even have to tell him off. When the Queen had finished her speech, the national anthem played and Mary and Jim got up from their chairs as they always did when they heard *God Save the King*, standing quietly, backs straight, until it had come to an end.

"Well, what did you think of that?" asked Mary, not without an air of confrontation, as she switched off the wireless.

"I think she's right," said Jim, taking the wind out of her sails. "I've always thought it's the women who need medals pinned to their chests in war for their bravery and their suffering."

"Do you mean that?"

"I do. They're made of strong stuff to take all that they do," he said.

"I've felt a bit useless on occasion, if I'm honest, Jim. As if I'm not important. I mean, not that I want William to be in the Forces and facing danger, but he has a role. And you, Jim, you're in the Fire Watch now and even though you don't wear a uniform, you have tasks to do, if, and when, needed. And you meet with other men – it gets you out. Being useful."

"You're useful too, Mary. Important, I'd say. Look how people around here always turn to you."

"Don't overdo it, Jim. I don't feel strong – inside – yet people think I'm strong, I know. When someone dies, they come knocking. Ask me to help with the laying out. If someone goes into labour, I know I'm the first they come to. I suppose what I'm saying is that what I do isn't noticed. Sometimes, I feel worthless."

"You're not worthless, Mary. I couldn't get by without you. Or any of us."

"I expect even Dora will be off as soon as she can to do something with the nursing. Or joining up. I can sense that she wants to be an active part of what's going on. That it's not enough for her being here with us at home. I suppose I've felt like that sometimes."

"Oh Mary. You'll get through this. And you've got to be *here* good and ready for when things get back to normal. Because they will one day, and people will need you then because they'll bring a lot back with them from the war," said Jim. "Things will be going in a different direction then."

"I'll carry on with what I'm doing as best I can for the time being and I'll knit. I'll knit for William. I'll knit for Sybil to try and keep her happy. And I'll knit for Dora and Teddy and Rhoda and of course, you, Jim Froom. I'm going to knit for victory, stitch by stitch, row by row. And when it's all over and we're through the mincer, I'm going to emerge in a different form. I don't know exactly how, as yet. But I know I'll be changed. We'll all be changed. Just you wait and see."

CHAPTER 14

TEDDY

Teddy hated the weeks approaching Christmas: it was the busiest time of the year in the shop. The second Sunday of Advent was the day for the Christmas order board to go up. Winter had set in now and Teddy deliberately slid and swerved across the ice on his way to the old stables to get the blackboard which came out every year. On the way back with the order board, he noticed the little robin in the garden. He knew his father would be glad to think it was keeping an eye on them all at 141.

"Give us a hand, Son," his father said as Teddy carried the board through the scullery and on towards the shop. "Get a chair."

As usual, Teddy did as he was told, carrying the wooden chair from the scullery into the shop where his mother was carrying Rhoda, whining in her arms. The hook was still in position on the wall next to the door to the passage, so Teddy steadied the chair while his father climbed up and hung the string on the back of the board and put it in position.

"It's not level, Jim," said his mother. "Up a bit. Right... ... That's it. Perfect."

"I hate bloody Christmas," said his father.

"You don't mean that, Jim. You like it when it comes. There's an extra day this year as it's on a Monday, so don't moan. And William will be here. It's for the kids, remember," said his mother.

Teddy listened to his father huffing and puffing at his audience as he hoiked himself up onto the marble slab in the window. He wasn't getting any younger and Teddy had a fleeting image of himself putting on his father's white coat and butcher's apron when he was too old to want to anymore. He didn't like the look of his future self. Why wouldn't Dora consider it? She was good with figures and accounts. But he knew that with William in the Forces, his father would be thinking he'd automatically be the heir. He pushed the picture out of his mind and watched his father attach a poster to the meat hooks in the window for the Christmas Carol Service at Babell Chapel.

Teddy turned away from the window and looked at the board and the smudged remnants of a sprig of holly and a Christmas pudding drawn with coloured chalks by his father last year in an attempt to get some Christmas spirit into the shop.

"I'll sort the board out, Dad. Leave it to me," he said.

He climbed onto the chair and stretched to refresh the pudding and the holly. He didn't want to erase them completely, just make them come alive again. He chalked on the green leaves and the red berries, added a few more currants to the Christmas pudding, and created an assortment of crackers and a red Santa at the very top. In block capitals he wrote CHRISTMAS ORDERS in white chalk in the top centre under the illustrations and underneath, ruled three vertical lines from top to bottom. One column for CHICKENS; one for GEESE; and one for DUCKS. There was no call for Turkeys, as yet, in Middle Road.

He got down from the chair and stood back and admired his handiwork.

"You're a proper artist, Son. They're teaching you something at that school of yours," said Jim, winking at him.

"I'll never make an artist, Dad. It's Dora who's the artist in the family. Or haven't you noticed? She's always sketching in that little pad of hers. Though she won't let me see what she draws. A surgeon, I'm going to be, remember?" said Teddy.

"I know you want to be a surgeon. Your mother told me."

"So why have you never asked me yourself, Dad?" asked Teddy, knowing full well the reason he hadn't asked was because he feared the answer he would get, which was both sad and infuriating. His father couldn't bear the thought of change, or him leaving and this was worse since William had joined up.

CHAPTER 15
JIM

There was no let-up in the cold spell, which was good for business. When Jim unbolted the door and took down the greaseproof paper from the window on the Tuesday that week, he saw faces on the other side of the counter that he hadn't seen all year, and knew he wouldn't see again after the so-called Festive Season. What was it about Christmas that made these women behave like this? As though they were preparing for a siege? They'd have a shock sometime in the New Year when the rations would probably come into place. He couldn't wait for that, he thought, rubbing his hands together.

"There's no need for you to be in here, Mary. It's cold and you've got enough to do," he said.

"I'll give you a hand. I can see you're rushed off your feet. Anyway, Louisa's come in to help me a bit in the house and keep an eye on Rhoda. Rhoda's *helping* her clean the brass. You know how much Rhoda likes listening to her stories. This is a rest for me."

"I didn't see her come through the shop…"

"She came over the wall. She didn't want anyone to see she might be doing things around the house for us."

"Good. Don't want the neighbours to think we're made of money," he laughed.

"She's getting us a bit of lunch. She'll eat with us too. It's company she wants more than the wage, Jim."

"Poor Louisa. Awful to be on your own like that for so long and lose a husband so young. And a child. I can only imagine."

"Right. What's to do?" asked Mary.

"Keep me from strangling these bloody women and write up their Christmas orders. You write better than I do."

"Yes, Sir," said Mary, saluting, knowing full well that what he said was true.

One after the other, each customer asked where the birds were coming from this year and whether they'd be plucked and feathered. Jim said they'd be coming from Morgan Beynon, Pitton Farm, Rhossili, in Gower, same as they always did. And yes, they'd be plucked and feathered by old Mrs Beynon in the outhouse there just as she always did. And yes, they'd be fresh as they weren't due into the shop until the Thursday before Christmas. They'd still have the heads and feet on but he could chop those off if so wished. And yes, the giblets would be left inside so they could make a good gravy or have them roasted up on Christmas Eve. And yes, he'd know the total before they came into pick it up and all they'd have to pay was the balance after he'd taken the Christmas Club money they'd been putting by, week by week, all year, so it wouldn't be so hard when the time came. All this he said, through gritted teeth.

He called out the orders to Mary who chalked them up in the appropriate column: Duck, Mrs West 133 Middle Road, 5lbs+; Goose, Mrs Squires 119 Middle Road, 7lbs+; Chicken, Mrs Hill 125, not too big! Typical, he thought, as he watched Mary from behind, knowing that she was trying to hide her laughter. There was a lot of work for no profit with poultry and some of the money that had been put-by in the Christmas Club he had already used as it came in. At this time of year, he felt that he was working for almost nothing. But it wasn't nothing. He'd known what nothing was at one time in his life and this wasn't anything like nothing.

Trade tailed off towards lunchtime and they had a quiet spell. They leaned against the counter to get their breath back, and looked out to the road.

"Bloody hell, said Jim. "I can't believe it in this weather."

From the shop, Jim could see only the back of Old Granny Weidenbach: her broad rear seated on the upstairs' window sill opposite, wedged in position by the edge of the bottom of the lower sash which she'd brought down tight across her lap to stop her falling out. She had a chamois in her right hand and was cleaning the outside panes, in the way that was employed by most of the women in the row. But most of them didn't bother in this bitter weather.

"You'd never get me doing that," said Mary.

"But why is she doing it now? She must be freezing."

"Christmas," said Mary. "Women go a bit mad at Christmas."

Jim was fascinated as he watched Old Granny Weidenbach shuffle along the sill on her bottom, stretching her arms to reach the top panes. She swivelled her backside and looked across her shoulder, waving her chamois to say hello.

"Good God," said Jim. "She's fearless. I can't look."

"It's never the accidents that you think you see coming, Jim, it's the other stuff that creeps up and catches you out. Because there's a war going on, I tend to think that the stuff of ordinary life is on hold. That's dangerous. Life goes on: people die, babies are born, people fall in and out of love, some have accidents doing the ordinary little things, not hanging out the window of a terraced house."

"I don't like you talking like this, Mary. I'm shutting up shop now. I suggest we go and have some dinner with Louisa and Rhoda. It smells like bubble and squeak."

Jim followed the aroma of cooking to the back scullery. Louisa must have had the cabbage and spuds frying all morning on the back ring of the gas stove. She couldn't get the hang of the Rayburn, she said. Couldn't come to terms with cooking being done inside an oven, where she couldn't keep an eye on things. She used the gas stove at the side. Jim preferred the Rayburn for all things to do with the shop and he knew Mary liked the gas stove for domestic use. She also had the range in the living room. Louisa called her *Thee-Stoves-Mary* sometimes and Jim didn't know how Louisa kept her sense of humour after all she'd been through. She still talked about *her Stanley* who'd been lost in the War and *her Julia* who'd been lost to the Flu epidemic soon after.

It was probably why she was fussing over little Rhoda, tying an apron around her to keep her clothes clean before Rhoda sat still enough to eat. She was plating up the bubble and squeak and scraping the burnt and crispy bits off and immediately taking them off her plate. For someone who demanded the skin of rice pudding, Jim couldn't understand this. But Louisa could handle

Rhoda, whereas his poor, worn-out Mary maintained she couldn't do a thing with her. And Rhoda loved Louisa. Her Auntie Louie, who snuggled her in her big bosom and told her stories from a cloth book and the depths of her imagination for hours on end while sitting on the scullery step. *Tell us another one, Auntie Louie*, she'd say. And Auntie Louie would always oblige.

"You've sat there so long, Louisa," said Jim "that you've worn down the stone step and left the impression of your arse for posterity."

As they all sat down to dinner, Jim told Louisa that he and Mary had been entertained by Old Granny Weidenbach hanging out of the window in mid-air in the freezing cold.

"You won't laugh when I tell you what's happened again," said Louisa.

"Go on." said Jim,

"She had *visitors* again in the night," said Louisa.

"What? Like before?" asked Jim. "Filthy bastards."

"Close your ears, Rhoda," said Mary. "But your father's right to be cross. What has that woman done to deserve that?"

"Well, she married a German and that's the only justification to some," said Jim. "Animals, they are."

"It makes my stomach turn over. I'd like to take the law into my own hands and sort it all out. I'll pop over when we finish up, Jim. See how she's doing," said Mary.

After dinner, Jim said he didn't have time to hang around chatting. Work to be done back in the shop. He walked through the living room, the smell of Brasso strong in the air. He looked up at the mantelpiece where the brass letter rack was now gleaming and brimming over with letters from William. He glanced at the hearth wondering why they felt the need to put on display so many remnants of conflict. It was like the bloody Imperial War Museum. The last war, the war before, the one now, were with them still. There was a large, brass shell case, golden now, and used to house the poker. It had been fashioned by Jim's cousin, Romney, who was a dab hand with metal. He'd made a smaller shell case into a cigarette lighter, too, which Jim and Mary used to ignite their Woodbines. On either side of the range was a matching pair of sizeable and very heavy brass stirrups, which Jim would often use for weightlifting, grunting as he raised them up to his shoulders. Originally, they'd been attached to leathers and hung either side of a horse in the Boer War. They'd been given to him and Mary as a wedding present. You couldn't account for people's taste.

Jim felt compelled to pick up the small brass tin, engraved with a picture of the Princess Mary in profile, with her initial M ornately etched on either side, and a list of countries; *Belgium, France, Japan, Russia, Monte Negro,* and *Servia* with the Latin, *Imperium Britannicum,* taking centre stage along with *Christmas 1914*. With a heaving stomach, he recalled how he'd been placated with it, as had every one of the millions of other poor souls stuck away in Flanders that Christmas. It was the Christmas Day he'd been made a sergeant. He'd never forgotten the surprise and pride Mary, his Mary, had shown when he'd told her of his promotion.

Inside the tin, which he now held in his hands, was a black and white photograph of a very clean-looking princess in profile, robed in a fancy white dress and pearls, seated on a padded stool. It was signed, *Mary,* and underlined. There was a printed card with a sprig of holly with red berries – just like the one that Teddy had done on their order board this year – though this one sent 'Best Wishes for a Happy Christmas and a Victorious New Year from The Princess Mary and friends at home.' What a load of shit! thought Jim, as he stomped out of the room. Bloody Princess Mary! Victorious? So much for that! Just a ploy to keep up the spirits of the masses. Wonder what they'd come up with this year and in the years to come, for he didn't think this war would be done by Christmas. His own Mary had more idea what was going on in the world than bloody Princess Mary…

CHAPTER 16
MARY

The street light at the corner outside the shop window flicked on just before half-past three. Mary was glad to see its yellow glow seep into the shop and go some way to lift the afternoon gloom that lay thick above the pavements. This freezing fog and ice showed no sign of easing. She was relieved to see that the light had come on in time for the little ones to come out of school when the bell would soon go for home time.

There was a lull in the shop. Most of the women were already on their way to the school gates to collect their kids. Next year she'd be doing that and it couldn't come soon enough. She chastised herself, physically slapping herself on her wrist for wishing little Rhoda's life away. And her own. Life was precious. Especially in wartime. She pulled her packet of Woodbines out of the pocket of her pinny and handed one to Jim.

"Have one while it's quiet," she said, striking a match and lighting hers first and then stooping to use the tip of her lit cigarette to light his, as she held it tightly between her lips.

"Marvellous," he said, filling his lungs with his first drag.

They stood together near the ashtray, just inside the shop door, and looked out. Mary noticed Granny Weidenbach coming out of 142, slamming the door after her, and then turning to make sure that she had closed it properly. She pushed against it with her hands and turned as if to leave as though she was finally satisfied that it was secure, and repeating the action over and over again.

"She's cutting it fine," said Jim. "She needs to get her skates on if she's going to be there in time to get little Joan."

"She could do with skates with these pavements," said Mary.

Mary and Jim were about a third of the way into their first Woodbine when they saw Granny Weidenbach pick her way down the seven steps opposite. She reminded Mary of Jim's new little robin friend: a body that seemed too round and big for spindly, twig-like legs.

As Old Granny Weidenbach reached the pavement and went to turn right towards the school, those little legs went from under her, and she slid along the pavers and landed hard on her bottom. She didn't move. She lay immobile in her coat and hat, splayed and silent outside her own home.

"Jesus Christ," said Mary stubbing out her cigarette in the ash tray, and rushing out across the road.

Jim belted after Mary and they both knelt at Granny Weidenbach's side and assessed the damage.

"Don't move her, Jim. Just in case," said Mary. "I'll phone Dr O'Kane at the surgery for a house call in a minute. Once we've settled her. It's going to be alright," she continued, holding Granny Weidenbach's hand.

Mary could see that she'd lost her colour: her skin a sickly pale colour with the fright under the diffused winter light. She must have really come down hard on her arse. Doreen would have a fit. She wasn't the calmest of women.

Mary could see Jim's face drain, too.

"You alright, Jim?" she asked.

But Mary knew he wasn't. Knowing Jim, she guessed he would feel like retching. Things always affected him physically as if it was somehow his fault. He was always like this when anything out of the ordinary happened, even if it turned out to be nothing serious in the end. He was always on high alert.

"I wish I'd scattered ashes on the pavement outside 142 and not just outside the shop. I could have stopped this happening," he said.

"Not now, Jim," Mary said.

And turning to the old woman she told her that everything was going to be alright. But she somehow didn't think it would be. Her mother had always said that old age began with a fall.

Mary made sure she popped across to 142 a couple of times a day in the week that followed to take and collect Joan from school. Mary also delivered gallons of clear, chicken soup. She had always believed it a cure for all ailments and believed that the Jews were right when they said it was food for the soul. But despite the soups, she was going downhill rapidly.

Dr O'Kane came daily but couldn't prevent the pneumonia that had set in. Despite the warmth and the love of her family, and the honey and the lemon, and the poultices on her chest, and the goose grease rubbed on the soles of her feet, and the soup that she must be drowning in, Mary knew Old Granny Weidenbach was fading away and seemed past caring.

"C'mon Mrs Weidenbach. There's so much to look forward to," said Mary. "We've even got William coming home for Christmas. You know how he has a soft spot for you."

"I'm tired, Mrs Froom," she said. "Ready to go."

"D'you know, Mrs Weidenbach, in all these years, we've never called each other by our Christian names. Daft that, don't you think?"

"It was the way I was brought up, I suppose. And you being in business and all that."

"Well, I think it's about time you called me Mary."

"Mary. Lovely name. Like our Blessed Lady. And the old Queen."

"And the Princess. Common as muck," said Mary, smiling.

"Gertrude, I am, though Berndt used to call me Trudy, and Therese is my second name. My saint's name."

"Mine's Ann, but I'm neither a saint nor named after one," said Mary, laughing.

"You are to me," said Gertrude. "Isn't that right, Doreen? She's been good to us all here at 142 hasn't she?"

Doreen nodded and blew her nose into her handkerchief.

"I'm not having a good death, Mary," said Gertrude, softly. "Even though I've been praying and using my rosary."

"You're not dying, Gertrude," said Mary. "You've just had a nasty pull. We'll get you back on your feet. Isn't that right, Doreen?"

Doreen was weeping now, her face puffy and swollen. Mary feared she'd have two patients on her hands soon.

"Sometimes death is the only cure, Mary," said Gertrude. "My mother used to always say that."

"Mothers aren't always right, Gertrude."

"I feel it's my time but the Lord won't let me leave. Help me, Mary. Please. Look. My mother and Berndt are waiting for me. Can't you see them?"

Mary watched as Gertrude stretched out her arm and grasped at the empty air as she might to remove a delicate cobweb or lace veil. She'd seen this often enough with all the people she'd witnessed on their journey to death, just before the end.

Gertrude's lips were dry, but she was refusing to eat and drink anything. No point, she said. And Mary knew enough to know she was right.

"I'll moisten your lips. Make you a little more comfortable. There," said Mary, dipping the flannel in the cold water, squeezing out the excess water and gently dabbing the face cloth on Gertrude's parched lips. "That'll make it easier. Suck on it, if you like."

"You could make it easier still and help me to let go if you prayed with me. That should do the trick," said Gertrude, a smile beginning to furl at the corner of her moistened lips. "You and Doreen help me on my way. Give me permission to go."

Even though Gertrude was deadly serious, Mary still saw the sense of humour on her face, heard it in the tone of her weak voice.

"But I'm a heathen, Gertrude. A non-believer. Don't know if my words carry any clout."

"You're a good woman, Mary Froom. A real Christian. Look. *The Lord's Prayer* might do it," said Gertrude. "Get down on your knees at the side of me, you two, and we'll give it a go."

Mary gave Doreen an eye-roll and Doreen got up from the chair again and walked slowly towards her mother. Mary got down on her knees one side of Gertrude and took her left hand, and Doreen took to her knees on the other side, taking her mother's right hand. Together, they started to pray, Gertrude praying along in a barely audible voice but as hard as she could:

> *Our Father which art in Heaven*
> *Hallowed be thy name*

Before all three of them came to the AMEN, Gertrude's voice

had trailed off, her eyes shut. Doreen started to sob, when suddenly Gertrude lifted her lids again and said in a loud voice from who knows where:

"Well, that didn't work, did it? Try something else. *Psalm 23*. That should do it," said Gertrude, and she took the other women's hands again as Mary and Doreen started to chant:

> *The Lord is my shepherd I shall not want*
> *He maketh me lie down in green pastures...*

Mary heard Gertrude's breathing become looser and it rattled as though she was drowning from the inside out. Mary looked at Doreen and Doreen understood. And by the time they had got to the *Yea though I walk through the valley of the shadow of death*, Gertrude had passed.

"She's gone, hasn't she?" said Doreen

"Yes. She had her way in the end. We did as we were told and made it a little easier for her."

"If I'd have known it was going to be this quick, I'd have called the priest to give her the last rites," said Doreen.

"Well, you weren't to know, Love," said Mary. And I think we did a good job ourselves. She seemed happy. Content."

"I'll have to call the priest now. She'd have wanted that."

"You do what you think is right. I'll go over and call him if you like. And Dr O'Kane."

"We'll have to get her upstairs and changed into a clean nightie and put into bed with fresh sheets before he comes."

"Who? The doctor or the priest?"

"The priest."

"I'm sure he won't mind her here, will he?"

"I want to do what's right. So he can pray for her soul when she's cleaned up – you know what I mean – and arranged in her bed. I'm going to fill her a hot-water bottle. It'll stop her from feeling the cold."

Mary sighed. Poor Doreen. Of course Mary would deal with the practicalities of the laying out. She always did in the neighbourhood. It was all the religious palaver she didn't understand. Nor the hot-water bottle. It was too late for the doctor and the priest as far as she was concerned. There was no possibility of that lovely woman's soul hovering around and being stuck in purgatory or going to eternal damnation. She was glad the priest wasn't there before she died, the old woman had nothing to ask his pardon for. It was others who should be asking for pardon. The vandals who'd daubed her door and no doubt contributed to her anxiety. The living left in this house had more need of both doctor and priest. But if it made Doreen happy, she'd get the doctor to come first and call Jim over so that between them all they'd carry Old Granny Weidenbach and get her into her clean bed with the laundered sheets and pull them up to her chin where she'd lie with the painting of the Blessed Mary hanging on the wall behind her, as required, before the priest came with all his pontifications, incantations and holy oils. As for Mary, she'd had her fill of piety and genuflection for one day.

CHAPTER 17
MARY

Mary kept one eye on the clock, one eye on the roast pork in the bottom oven of the Rayburn, one eye on the pudding steaming on the gas ring, and one eye on Rhoda as she clambered on the chair to open a window of the Advent calendar that Mary had pinned to the side of the scullery cabinet. She knew the arithmetic didn't make sense, but she needed to be everywhere this morning, needed eyes in the back of her head.

Doreen had made the calendar for Rhoda, it being a tradition they had carried on at 142 throughout the years since Berndt had been gone – he had introduced Old Granny Weidenbach to this German way of marking and counting down the days to Christmas Day when they'd lived back in London. It was a naive attempt: three wise men, a Christmas tree, a crib, Mary and Joseph, and a star and a donkey here and there, but beautiful in its own way, and did the job of keeping Rhoda occupied for five minutes and giving herself some brief breathing space. Today was the 21st. A Thursday.

Mary bent down with the customary groan that was now an ingrained habit that little Rhoda imitated. She basted the pork. The crackling was coming on a treat. The scullery smelled like a normal Christmas when it was anything but, the air thick with the aroma of slow-cooking meat and simmering dried fruits, orange candy peel and glacé cherries. She thought about Advent with a capital A and the imminent arrival of Jesus Christ. But she was more concerned with advent with a small a, and the arrival of William, who was due home by Saturday if all went according to plan, and more urgently, the poultry which was due to arrive on Morgan Beynon's lorry, as promised, by half-eight at the latest. And of course, Louisa, who was coming surreptitiously over the wall soon, she hoped. She was coming to keep another pair of eyes on Rhoda so Mary could go into the shop where Jim and Teddy had been at the ready since just after 7 o'clock.

Jim had skipped his breakfast. She knew how much of a state he always got himself into about matching the correct type and weight of poultry to the customer. No doubt he'd be giving Teddy instructions about cleaning down the marble slab in the window in readiness. Once a sergeant, always a sergeant. It had never been what you'd call an exciting run up to the Festive Season for any of them at 141.

She took two glasses down from the cupboard and filled each with a good glug of Harvey's Bristol Cream. Every year around this time the sherry came out of the cupboard under the stairs. She took an egg, separating the yolk and beating it into the sherry with a fork and then added a heap of sugar.

"Mum and Dad's little tonic," she said to Rhoda, winking, and putting her finger to her lips. "Our little secret."

She believed what she was saying. It was part of the annual ritual that would get Jim and her through the next couple of days with the onslaught of customers and the heavy work-load. Jim always told her it did him the power of good and that it fed his nerves. If it did that, she'd keep up the tradition.

Good as her word, Louisa announced her arrival with her characteristic tap on the glass of the back scullery door, and then opened it and let herself in. She was carrying a few packets of red and green crepe paper. Mary felt her indigestion come on. It always did with stress. Or guilt. Yes, she'd made a cake which she was feeding daily by pricking the underside of it with one of her bone knitting needles and pouring in more than a little rum. Yes, the puddings were steaming away and she'd placed a tanner in each of them, and wished as hard as she could that this war would end soon and her children would be safe. And yes, she'd washed and aired the bedding ready to make-up William's single bed in the back bedroom. She'd done all the functional things. But the house was still comfortless. Jim didn't see the point of what he called *wasting money* on frivolities like trees and decorations. He could be such a killjoy on occasions as though he continually wore a hair shirt of his own choosing.

But Louisa was overflowing with joy as she entered the scullery.

"Don't worry about us this morning, Mary. We've got things to do. Isn't that right, Rhoda?" she said. "Santa's little helper is going to make some decorations ready for William's homecoming."

Mary realised how bare the living room looked. The sofa had still not been fixed. It looked nothing more than a route between shop and kitchen. She was a bad mother. A guilty mother.

"That's lovely, Louisa. You think of everything. Sometimes I don't feel I have time to think at all. I'll leave you two to work your magic, then."

"All we'll need is a few of your bits and bobs from the knick-knack table if that's okay? Scissors. Some thread. A couple of darning needles…"

"Be my guest," said Mary, as she took the tonics and went through to the shop.

"Dinner at one? It'll be boiled ham and parsley sauce. You need something put in front of you, what with all the work you've got on," she shouted after Mary who was almost at the end of the passage.

"D'you know, Louisa. I should have married you," she laughed, wondering for a moment whether it would indeed have been a better choice.

"Bugger off," said Louisa, putting her hands over Rhoda's ears. "I'll give you a shout when we're ready."

The shop was cold. December cold. Mary shivered as she entered. It was an unforgiving bitter spell and the ice on the pavements hadn't melted since the beginning of the month. Just as she had predicted, Jim had Teddy on duty in the window, wiping down the marble slabs with lambs' loin cloths. Thirteen years old and the poor sod was flat out, a woollen bobble hat on his little red head in an attempt to keep in what little heat there was, and fingerless woollen gloves. At least she could knit. She wasn't that bad a mother, surely.

Mary could see that Jim had left the shop door open as it didn't seem as if it made any difference to the temperature. He was facing the pavement. He looked bulkier this morning. Must have been the thermals and the layers of pullovers he had under his white coat. She could see the smoke rings he was blowing rising up into the grey, listless air. How long he'd been standing there waiting for the lorry, she could only guess. Every year she told him that the poultry wouldn't arrive any quicker by watching. *It's like a pot*, Jim, she'd say. But it didn't change anything. He was set in his ways like the marble slabs in the window.

Mary walked up to him and put her arm around his girth. He took her hand and smiled.

"Here," she said handing him the glass. "This will do the trick."

"Thank you, Mary. Shouldn't be much longer now. Sorry to have you doing all this. Again."

"It's alright, Jim," she said gently. "I knew what I was getting myself into when I married you. We're in this together."

Mary heard Jim clear his throat and gob onto the pavement. She worried about his chest. And her own. They should give up the Woodbines, but Jim maintained that the fags were good for loosening the phlegm and that he'd get progressively better as the day wore on and the more he smoked. It seemed there was some stupid sense in this.

Mary heard Morgan Beynon's lorry before she saw it. The road was quiet, people not yet up and about, just the grinding of the gears as the lorry changed down from top into third as it started to negotiate the incline below, and then from third into second as it passed Babell Chapel, and then into first as it came into view at the bottom of the row, finally pulling up outside the shop with a yank of the handbrake.

Mary, Jim and Teddy stood together ready to receive the poultry. Mary could see inside the cab: Morgan Beynon at the wheel, his wife nearest the pavement, and wedged in between the two of them, was old Mrs Beynon, who'd obviously finished with her plucking and feathering in the outhouse on the farm and come along for the ride. Mary wondered how many times she'd ever been off the Gower peninsula as she looked so out of place, a little woman all dolled up for the occasion, wearing a black hat with a pin in it, what looked like her best Sunday coat with a brooch on the lapel, and a shawl draped around her shoulders. Yet when she raised her hand to wave and smile, Mary saw that she didn't have her teeth in. In a strange way, she reminded Mary of the poultry that was now being unloaded off the lorry in cardboard boxes: plump bodies but scrawny necks with sagging heads, pointy beaks, and scraggy, colourless, flecked skin.

"Just put them on the floor, Morgan. I'll settle with you now. How much do I owe you?" asked Jim.

Inside, Mary and Teddy started on their allocated jobs, laying out the poultry in the window, which, to be fair, Morgan had separated into ducks, geese, and chicken, for Jim to weigh and tag when he'd finished with him.

Jim remained outside on the pavement, deep in conversation with Morgan and she wondered what it was that was so important to keep him there in the freezing cold, yakking to that farmer. She wasn't that keen on him. Never had been. But the poultry was good.

The two men then ended their conversation and came into the shop. Mary heard Jim mutter, *Bloody Christmas*, as he shut the till drawer after paying Morgan.

"Nice and fresh. Killed yesterday. The old woman didn't finish until midnight, up to her bloody neck in quills and plumes," said Morgan. "Heads and feet still on as you asked, mind. Giblets inside. Oh, and I've got a net of swedes on the lorry. A little thank-you off the farm for you, Mary," said Morgan turning, to talk to her directly.

"Well, you certainly know how to woo a woman, Morgan. Thank you very much." she said, as Morgan returned with the net. "Will you have a cup of tea or something stronger. One for the road, perhaps?"

"That's very kind of you, Mrs Froom. But I'll not be stopping. Going to be a long day. And I've got the women with me…"

And with that, Morgan was off, thanking them all for their custom and wishing them compliments of the season, before he turned the engine over and the lorry chugged away leaving behind a cloud of filthy diesel.

CHAPTER 18
TEDDY

Teddy stood at his father's side like the butcher's boy he felt he was being moulded into. One at a time, he handed his father the poultry, as his father took his cleaver and hacked through each bird's neck and legs just above the feet, before chucking the remains in the waiting tray at the base of the block. Teddy was then instructed to stand at the order board while his father weighed the bird. Teddy tried as best he could to bird-match the customer's request according to weight and fear of an earful. He watched his father trussing the feet of each bird together with string, then tagging and labelling them, putting those that he was going to have to deliver around the neighbourhood into a sheet of greaseproof paper and then swaddling them in newspaper.

Teddy lugged the poultry to the basket of his bike, leaned up against the outside window, and methodically arranged them according to the route he'd take: firstly the bottom of Middle Road, to Mrs Pember, Mrs Boyle, and Mrs Grinter; then through the square at Cwmbwrla – Willie James the newsagent and the Italian cafés at De Marco's and Zanetti's, then hell for leather along the flat of Approach Road to Mrs Williams with the disabled son in the wheelchair, and onto Pentregethin Road to Mrs James at 339 with the adenoid problem who talked through her nose but always gave a good tip; all the way up, thighs burning, high in the saddle, to Maes Glas Road, to Mr and Mrs Rundle; onto Torrington Crescent, Upper Gendros Crescent to the O'Rileys, O'Connors and the O'Shaes and then back to the familiar territory of Middle Road, to the old bakery at 328 and the post office at Price's at 251, where Norman, the son with polio, shuffled along on his backside across a splintered, wooden floor, his legs spread and encased in iron callipers, while his mother worked behind the counter grill.

He hollered into the shop before he set out, telling his father to not, under any circumstances, dispose of the poultry's dismembered parts while he was out on deliveries. As other children would be writing letters to Father Christmas and stuffing them with hope up the chimney, he had something far more malicious up his sleeve planned for the discarded poultry feet. This is what a traditional Christmas was all about at 141 Middle Road. He'd make sure to keep a few back for when William arrived home, too. Get him in the Christmas spirit. He surely wouldn't have forgotten, or outgrown, this ritual. They'd sort Rhoda out a treat. Frighten the living daylights out of her.

CHAPTER 19
JIM

Everything was going according to plan, including the little ruse he had discussed with Morgan about the possibilities they could work on in the New Year when rationing would finally come in.

The timings of the morning couldn't have been better and by Saturday lunchtime most of the regulars had picked up their birds from the shop. A few stragglers who hadn't ordered in advance, came in after two o'clock hoping that Jim had something left. Mrs Hill was one of them, hoping he had a neck end of lamb that she could turn into a feast as she wasn't partial to poultry. She also took some fillet steak for the bloody canine. It would appear that Mr Hill wouldn't be having much of a Christmas again this year, thought Jim, as he cussed silently and then said *Merry Christmas* perfectly politely to her as she took her leave.

Even though he was exhausted with the physical and mental strain of this time of year, not to mention the man to man chat he'd had with Morgan, Jim felt the weight start to lift from him as he wiped down the block and re-arranged his knives. He could finally allow himself to think about the short Christmas break and the fact that his boy was coming home. A couple of days was better than nothing. He and Mary had never taken a holiday. Being in business was a bit like being in prison. He felt his ribcage relax as he took the meat hooks and put up the sheets of greaseproof paper inside the shop window and turned the sign that hung on string behind the door from OPEN to CLOSED.

He looked at Mary as she soaked and wiped out the trays, swept up the sawdust, and got down on her hands and knees to scrub up. He kept believing that he'd finally pick a winner on the horses. One day. He kidded himself that he was not out of pocket. Like the booze, he knew he shouldn't; but it seemed the habit was all consuming. He felt shaky knowing that he couldn't even have his usual Christmas season flutter this year as the race grounds were frozen all across the country, from Newmarket to Aintree. All the races cancelled. He looked again at Mary, cleaning up after the mess, and feared that one day she'd be cleaning up a lot more if she ever got wind of what else he was doing in his other life. He was a fraud of a man. A pretend everything. A had-been sergeant and a liar who feigned to be part of the Community Fire Service, going to its meetings in earnest, only to throw dice and play cards, and chuck more money he didn't have down the drain at the Old Bakery in Phyllis Street.

But this was the time of year to keep believing. His son would be home by three. The last letter Mary had read out, necessarily lacking in other specifics, stated that he should be into High Street Station on the dot. He'd make his own way home from there in case there were any hiccups. He hadn't forgotten how much needed to be done in the shop. And he warned them not to fuss. There was just one thing he'd like though if it didn't put them both to too much trouble – and to not read too much into it as he wasn't *exactly* sure about how she felt about him – but he'd like to invite Sybil to come for tea on Christmas Day. A week hadn't gone by when William hadn't written to her and it would mean so much.

CHAPTER 20

MARY

Mary lit the fire in the back bedroom and turned back the bed she'd made up for William, stroking the pillow where he'd soon lay his head. She imagined him on a crowded French train with other servicemen rattling through the vast, flat, Normandy countryside until they got to Calais or was it Dieppe? She couldn't be sure. She saw him board the ship, perhaps standing for the whole time it took to cross the Channel. She hoped he'd get his connection into London and cross the city until he reached Paddington and find the right platform quickly for the GWR train to Swansea. With a bit of luck, he might find a place to sit, even if it was a corridor, the guard's van or a goods' truck. He would be beyond tired. But he was on his way to her.

She then made sure that everyone was scrubbed up in honour of his return. She got in the bath with Rhoda, then Teddy took his turn, and then Jim. Dora was still on a shift at the hospital. Or so she said. At times, she seemed as absent as William.

Mary watched Jim put a tie on and even though it was a Saturday, took out his shoe-cleaning kit and stood brushing his shoes as though he was going on parade, whistling as he brushed, and spitting and rubbing like a demon, trying to work off the crippling feeling of anticipation. She felt her stomach turn over at the sadness of it all: him never failing to believe that nourishing and protecting the shoe leather with polish would be enough to protect his family from the unpredictability of life.

Just as she'd done when the Queen addressed the nation on the wireless, Mary got out of her slippers, put on a frock, brushed out her hair and let it hang loose. She took out her compact and powdered her face, realising how old and tired she looked in the little circular mirror. She closed it down sharpish. Time was passing too quickly. She now had a twenty-year-old daughter who was a working woman; an eighteen, almost nineteen-year-old man, as a son who was serving his country; a thirteen-year-old son who was turning into a man too early because he had to; and a four-year-old baby who was sucking the very life out of her. What was it about Christmas that brought all these things home so starkly?

Yet on the surface, everything was seemingly under control: clean shoes, beef stew simmering in the Rayburn, table set, dining chairs arranged around the table in the living room. It was good to see half-a-dozen of them waiting to be sat on again.

Until they sat down to supper, there'd be mince pies and home-made scones that Louisa had made and arranged on the best china plates with doyleys. There'd be jam sandwiches and bread pudding. Anything he fancied. There were even decorations that Teddy was now pinning to the walls: drapes of red and green crepe paper that had been threaded and pulled tight to form beautiful ruffles by Rhoda, all by herself, so she said. No one argued. No one dared. This was not to be a Christmas for conflict. No politics. No religion. Everything except the here and now was off limits.

By the warmth of the range, Mary's family waited and listened to the time tick by. The chimes of the walnut mantel clock signalled that it was four and William was still not home. By then it was dark and Jim had put the blackouts in place at the windows. Mary wondered what William would make of seeing his home turned into a mini-fortress. There was she trying to imagine what life was like on the front line for William when no doubt William, like all the Armed Forces lads, would be imagining how life had been transformed in their own particular neighbourhoods.

Everyone was restless. Teddy kicked his heels over and over again against the back of the chair, Rhoda whined that she was starving until Mary gave in and stuffed her with some Custard Creams and Jim accused her of spoiling their daughter to which Mary retorted that she was worn out and anxious and needed some peace and quiet, so she'd feed her as she pleased, so there!

From time to time she stood up and went in to the scullery and sighed as she opened the oven door, took the lid of the stew, gave it a stir and repeated that she was glad that she'd done something in a pot as it wouldn't spoil, so it didn't really matter that William was late.

CHAPTER 21
JIM

At six o'clock the still-waiting family was startled out of anticipation by the sound of brass instruments, a drum, the rattle of a tambourine and the occasional clash of a cymbal. The racket broke the tedium and drew Mary, Jim, and the children from in front of the range, towards the shop.

They trooped up the passage, and took down their overcoats from the pegs in the passage behind the front door, and Jim climbed the stairs and brought down a couple of blankets off his and Mary's bed. It would be worth the chill for a ringside view. Teddy walked back and fore carrying a chair each time and set up the four near the shop window. Jim unhooked a couple of sheets of greaseproof paper – just enough so they could all look out without too many unwanted eyes peering in.

But he needn't have worried about prying eyes. Tonight the streets were deserted except for the small band of the Salvation Army which had congregated directly under the streetlight outside the shop. There they stood, men mostly in their caps, and one woman with a bonnet tied with a bow under her chin, as they did at this time of year every year. In the freezing fog, the pavements already glistening with frost, they looked spectral under the glow of the lamp: faces pale with cold, and breath pluming as they took a small rest between each carol.

Jim noticed Mary dabbing her eyes with the corner of her cotton handkerchief – though she insisted she wasn't crying; it was just the cold – as the trombones and euphoniums started up on *While Shepherds Watched their Flocks by Night*. This one always got to her despite her disbelief in the Virgin birth. Jim glanced at her and knew she knew what was coming next. Just as the Salvation Army came every year to stand outside 141, so Jim would give his own rendition:

> *While shepherds washed their socks at night*
> *All boiling in the pot*
> *A lump of soot came tumbling down*
> *And spoiled the blooming lot.*

Teddy turned and put his hand over his mouth and did a pretend yawn. Even Rhoda seemed to have a vague recollection of this version, though she still thought her father was funny. Mary wondered when Rhoda would stop finding her father funny. Probably a long time before she'd stop believing in Father Christmas.

Jim got up and drew back the bolts on the door, top and bottom, so that Rhoda could run out and put some coins from the till into the bucket for the Salvation collection. Tonight she looked suitably angelic as she dropped in the pennies and halfpennies, turning and looking for acknowledgement with wide eyes and a wide grin. That was what Christmas did to you. Transformed you.

As the band began to play *Silent Night*, the music competed with the sound of the 83 bus struggling up the road. Jim turned his head and could see the headlights piercing the thick fog. Perhaps he'd be on this one. He couldn't stand the waiting much longer.

The double-decker drew nearer and as it did, he was there: William, with the clippie behind him, standing on the open platform at the rear holding on to the silver aluminium pole, ready to hop off. It was as if the Salvation Army had been summoned by some unknowable force to welcome him home.

For all the excitement, the Frooms stood rooted to the spot in the shop doorway as they watched William, his kit back slung over his left shoulder, tread towards them. They listened to the firm, leather-treaded, rubber-heeled steps of his RAF-issue shoes, getting louder and louder as he drew closer.

Jim held back his tears as Mary stretched and kissed William on the cheek and nuzzled into his great coat, the brass buttons indenting her cheek. Jim could smell the coat: it was damp cold and smelled of cigarette smoke and that distinctive sootiness of a long journey by steam train. He felt he could breathe out for the first time in months. It was only frozen points on the line at Bristol that had made him late.

The band played on with *Away in a Manger* as Jim stood almost to attention to receive his son. He embraced him, not tightly, more of a pat on the back and then a handshake, man to man, and then watched as William roughed-up Teddy's red hair, swept Rhoda up into his arms, and embraced Dora.

"Let's get you in," said Jim to William. "You're freezing. And you must be starving. Your mother's got something on the go so we won't be long."

Stepping into the shop, William unbuttoned his dark blue great coat and Jim helped him out of it, standing behind him to receive it as he slipped his arms from the sleeves. It weighed a ton. He'd forgotten how his used to feel on his then young shoulders. He hung the outer garment on one of the empty meat hooks high on the steel rail. William took off his cocked hat, and Jim took that too and used another hook as a temporary wardrobe. The canvas kit bag was next, which William instructed everyone not to look inside as Father Christmas wouldn't be bringing any presents if they did. There were no presents in it anyway, so no point in looking, he said. All that was in there was his flying jacket, his flying boots, his helmet, and his leather gloves with the white silk linings which he'd show to Teddy and Rhoda in the morning, when he felt less tired.

Jim took the load of the dirtied kit bag and suspended that on another hook. He took note of the name: William Peter Froom; the rank: Wireless Operator; the squadron number: 59; and the serial number: 619761. The choirboy with his thick, red hair who used to wear a cassock and a white surplice with a ruff and sing as free as a bird in high soprano now stood in the shop with a regulation short back and sides and a stiff air-force-blue serge uniform. War was a brutalising business. He looked at the face. He had finally grown into that face. Was it less than a year ago that William's Froom teeth seemed over-big for his fine features and scooped out cheeks? In that short time, they'd become the perfect fit. In front of him in the ordinariness of his own shop, was the grown-up man he'd been himself once upon a time. And he was sick to his stomach to see his younger self confront him.

CHAPTER 22
MARY

Mary couldn't quite believe that this year they had Christmas Eve off. A whole day to get over the pestering customers and to be just the six of them. Family. Some good was coming out of 1939 after all, and it seemed more likely that Mary would kill her family with an over-indulgence of love and food than would a bomb or a bullet.

She looked on at an almost picture-perfect domestic scene, glad of a breather from the demands as Rhoda, who was fixated with her eldest brother, tugged on William's shirt as a signal for him to plonk her on his knee and read to her. She wanted *The Tale of Peter Rabbit*, because, she said, it had William's middle name 'Peter' in it. Mary was delighted that William was the star attraction.

"An old mouse was running in and out over the stone doorstep...." Mary listened as William started the tale. He was a natural storyteller: the pace, the music of his voice which now had traces of accents from all over the country including a little of her and Jim's rural lilts along with a good dollop of Swansea, and traces of London where he'd had some of the edges knocked off him in those years at the Choir School.

Rhoda knew this story so well that she mouthed along with the words as William read. Mary thought he'd make a lovely father, and wondered if Sybil was indeed the one. At the end of the story, Mary heard Rhoda tell William that she loved that tale because it was about her family; as Peter Rabbit had Flopsy, Mopsy and Cotton Tail as brothers and sisters, and there were four children in her family too. William told Rhoda that he was delighted she could count and that she would do well to carry out the moral of the story which as to always listen to your parents. Mary didn't know how much truth there was in that.

It was a day for indoors. Jim said that it would freeze his balls off if he ventured outside for which he was chastised by Mary who said to him, what is the point of Rhoda being read books which they hoped would improve her behaviour when he used the language of the trenches? Rhoda laughed and said, Dad, you need to go and wash your mouth out with soap and water.

As Mary pottered back and forth between the scullery and the range, peeling spuds and swede ready for the morning, and criss-crossing the heads of the sprouts, checking every now and then on the giblets and the sausages she was roasting, her family sat and chatted, Jim and William nodding off from time to time. For once she didn't begrudge their forty winks even though she wanted to squeeze every waking minute out of them.

The ambiance was abruptly interrupted by Teddy. Just as he had threatened, he was making use of the discarded poultry' feet which had been stored in a tray under the block. Into the living room he bounded, chicken foot in his left hand stretched out at arm's length, its long white tendons in his right. He raced towards Rhoda. Mary saw her little face freeze as Teddy stood close to her, pulling on the tendons in time: open, close, open, close, and as he did, the white claws stiffened, stretched and spread, as he held them within sniffing distance of his sister's face. If this wasn't enough, he pulled a spare out of his trouser pocket and thrust into William's hand who couldn't resist joining in either, and within seconds, both boys, the child-boy and the man-boy, were tormenting the life out of Rhoda.

"Stop it. Stop it" she squealed. "Tell them, Mum."

Mary looked on powerless as the boys she'd created laughed, and Jim, the man she'd chosen, started out of his sleep to join in the assault. How naturally cruel men could be sometimes. Especially when they got together. No wonder there were wars.

"Cut it out, now, the lot of you," she shouted. "Why do you boys always have to spoil things? It's Christmas Eve, for God's sake. This will all end in tears if you don't, just mark my words."

The episode had ended as Mary had predicted, Rhoda flouncing out of the room in floods of tears, dramatic shrieking and breath-holding. Mary had clipped the three *juveniles* – as she called them – around the ears and they all apologised to Rhoda who eventually let out her breath as Mary had firmly told her that if she didn't, she'd *burst her bola*. It was a phrase she'd picked up since she'd been at 141, and thought it a much better description for an exploding stomach.

As she got up early on Christmas Morning to make everything ready for the family before they came down, she wondered if there'd be any more tears. Christmas did that to families. Why was it that Christmas always made you look back with a longing for a time when everything seemed to have been perfect? It wasn't real. Any of it. It was just a feeling. Nostalgia for times or a place that never were. *Hiraeth*, they called it in Cwmbwrla. But all there was really was what was happening now.

As she took a match to the paper in the range, she wondered if Jim had got her a little present or whether he'd give her a few quid *to get herself something nice* as he didn't know what she'd like. He wasn't a mean man. He just didn't think. It wasn't about the money. *It's the thought that counts*, her mother had always told her. She'd like him to prove her wrong; just this once.

She switched on the radio and tuned into the Home Service as the fire caught light. The King would be speaking to the nation at three o'clock so she'd make sure they'd be done with dinner by then so they could listen in to hear what he had to say, and how he said it, poor bugger. But for now, with the flames in the hearth, and the carols coming down the airwaves, all was well at 141.

In the calm before the family descended, she thought about the day before and why, when they'd been sitting waiting for William from three onwards, Jim hadn't wanted to listen to Carols from King's. *I can't bear it this year, Mary*, he'd said. So they'd left it at that. As she tried to make sense of it she realised it was the War. This one. The last one. All bloody wars as far as he – and she – were concerned.

In the firelight, all time melded. Jim and his war. William and his. Despite all the hope and the season of joy and peace the world was raging again. She thought of Old Granny Weidenbach and Berndt and lives gone to waste. She thought of Louisa next door, who, despite the invite to join them for Christmas dinner, wanted to have her own company and spend her day with the ghosts and memories of Stanley and Julia who she'd loved and lost to war and its aftermath. Mary needed to shake herself out of this maudlin mood, needed to keep strong.

A little later Rhoda came charging into the living room, shouting, *he's been, he's been*, holding one of Mary's hand-knitted Christmas stockings. It wasn't exactly bulging, but there was a flashlight, some monkey nuts, a tangerine, and another book by Beatrix Potter from William that had been extracted from the depths of his kitbag. Mary smiled. It was good to see Rhoda happy. And appreciative.

One by one they came into the living room and sat together around the range. Mary looked in hope to see if there was anything for her.

She watched Teddy, happy as ever, with what he was given. William had given him two bullets that had been welded together at their bases and to which he had attached some of his old boxing and swimming badges. Mary thought it an odd gift. But that was boys. Yet, the badges made her stomach tighten and her indigestion start to play up. It was as though he was relinquishing all the things he'd achieved when he was younger, passing them on down the line.

She watched Dora as she unwrapped what Mary had bought in Ben Evans' department store: the bicycle clips elicited more of a positive reaction than the bath cubes; and the diary with the brass lock and key was a huge success, as was the sketch pad.

Mary reached in the corner and got out her large shopping bags which contained all her 'extra' gifts. She could tell by everyone's faces that they knew what was coming. *Oh, some socks,* said Jim. *Just what I needed.* Dora said the same and Teddy and Rhoda. She delved into the bag and pulled out not one, but three, plain, roll-neck pullovers for William, identical in style, but not colour. There was one in pale blue, one in fawn, and one in dark brown.

"To keep you warm, over there on the other side," she said.

He held the pale blue one up against his chest.

Mary knew then that she'd done the right thing. She could be close to him all the time. That wasn't possible with those shop-bought ones.

"Well that's it," said Mary. "I'll be getting on with things," she said, looking around one last time just in case.

Rhoda had drawn her a picture: a man in a striped apron, a small woman with glasses, and four children of various sizes, holding hands.

"It's beautiful," said Mary. "I'll pin it up in the scullery."

Teddy handed her over the sheet music for 'Bless This House', Mary realising that he must have saved up all his coins over the year for it. She loved this song, and Jim, when he was in the mood, often used to sing it. Now she could accompany him on the piano.

"What a lovely thought, Teddy," she said. "Perfect."

"I went in Snell's in the Arcade in Alexandra Road. I go past nearly every day on the way to school. You ought to go in there, Mum. It's a beautiful shop and old Mr Snell was very helpful."

"Time, I need, Teddy. But you're right. I ought to make time and have a nose around there. Mr Music, they call him around Swansea. Did you know that?"

"No, I didn't. But I can see why."

Mary turned to accept William's gift.

"You know my weakness," she said, kissing him on the cheek. "I'm going to keep these chocolates and the tea. These French ones are too nice to be eaten."

"You're going to gorge on them after dinner, Mum. You won't be getting any more of these for a while." said Dora.

"If you insist, then… we'll share later. Bit of a treat," she said as she rose from her chair and started to make her way to the scullery.

"Mary. Now don't drop down dead, but I've got you a little something," said Jim. "All off my own back, I might add. No prompting."

"You shouldn't have, Jim" she said. "What is it? Dust pan and broom? New T-towels?"

"Oh ye of little faith," he said. "Open it and see. You might be surprised."

Mary took her scissors from the knick-knack table and cut through the string. She wound the remaining length up and put it in a tin for when it would come in handy as she did with the brown paper which she folded neatly. Inside, there were two heavy-ish items swathed in white tissue paper, which she gently opened to reveal the gifts. She couldn't quite believe the thought – or the expense – that had gone into the purchase of a matching tortoiseshell hand mirror and pure bristle hair brush. She felt like crying and also interrogating him as to where he'd got the money to splash out on these luxuries which she knew they could ill afford. Betting, no doubt. Or the Christmas Club.

"They're beautiful," she said, fondling the gifts. "Not that I needed them, mind. Have you gone into debt for these, Jim Froom? Tell me the truth."

"No. I had a little win when a horse came up earlier in the year and I put it by. I didn't *re-invest* it as you might have thought."

"You deserve a medal for this," she said, leaning forward and kissing his forehead.

"Now you can get on with the dinner," he laughed, as she skipped down the scullery steps like a young girl.

CHAPTER 23
JIM

After dinner, Jim stood at the side of the sink with Dora while she washed and he wiped. He was glad to get out of the living room as Mary was making such a fuss getting the table ready again for Sybil's arrival.

"You'd think she was expecting the arrival of the Queen of Sheba," said Jim.

"Well, she is a very special girl, Dad. William's lucky to have her," said Dora, rubbing at the dishes with an almost crazed zeal.

"There'll be no pattern left on those plates if you keep going at them like that," said Jim. "You're not a little bit jealous, are you? That they're sweethearts?"

"No. Why should I be?" retorted Dora, clattering the plate into the draining rack. "I love them both, Dad. I want them to be happy."

"Your time will come soon. Plenty of eligible gentleman on the wards, I'm sure."

"I'm sure there are, Dad. And yes, my time will come," she mused, gazing out through the window.

Jim followed her gaze into the yard. There was still a little natural light remaining. He wondered why birds always went into a frenzy in this blue-black between dusk and dark. His mood was going down with the sun. He felt it was to do with the tetchiness combined with sadness that was coming off his daughter and he couldn't put his finger on why she was so uppity. He tried to shift the conversation and get himself together. He didn't want to spoil things.

"Look," he said. "Sparrows. On the top of the wall. And the dustbin lids."

Jim noticed that Dora wasn't exactly enthused: she said nothing but she looked out to see what he was talking about. He put down his T-towel and reached in the basin for some leftover breadcrumbs from the bread sauce and then opened the back door and cast them into the air.

"No sign of my friend the robin," he said as he came back to pick up where he'd left off.

"You're almost as miserable as me, Dad. Why so gloomy? I haven't upset you, have I?"

"No. It's just Christmas. All over so quickly. He'll be off before it gets light again. Home in the dark. Leave in the dark."

Jim felt Dora's soapy hand as she took it out of the bowl and squeezed his arm.

"It'll be alright, Dad," she said. "Everything works out in the end."

"Have you seen the robin, today?" he asked quickly, uncomfortable with Dora's rare show of affection and his awkward reaction to it.

"No. Not today. Nor yesterday, for that matter. But that's not surprising, is it?"

"No? Why?"

"Well, William's here, isn't he?"

"You talk in riddles, sometimes. Dora."

"Robins come as a sign that a loved one is near, despite that person being a million miles away."

"There's lots I don't know in life, Dora. I thought that as I got older, I'd know more – and understand everything. But it seems the older I get, the less I know. Funny that."

"I understand, alright, Dad. But the robin will be back. You wait and see."

"That makes me feel a bit better," said Jim, as he carried on wiping and stacking the dishes. "Thank you, Dora. I don't see as much of you as I'd like. But when you are around, you talk a lot of sense."

Everything was winding down. The King had made his sombre speech almost without a single hesitation and then Jim leaped into action as instructed by Mary for Sybil's arrival at five-o'clock. He turned off the wireless and commanded Teddy to fit the blackouts up at the windows and light some candles. Mary said she wanted to make it romantic. Jim surmised it was to hide the shabbiness. Especially the settee.

At the allotted hour, when the family had been instructed not to let the side down, Jim watched William's face light up as he walked Sybil down the passage and into the living room as though he was accompanying her down a church aisle towards the altar. Jim had to admit that they were an attractive couple. Both slight, bright-eyed. He, with his short back and sides, and her, with that wavy dark hair that tumbled past her shoulders.

Jim was proud William was behaving as gentlemen were schooled to, pulling out a chair at the dining table for Sybil to take her seat. Jim watched Sybil closely as she kept fiddling with the single string of pearls around her neck guessing that they must have been a Christmas present from William. Things were serious, then. He'd chosen well in Sybil and the pearls which were a perfect accompaniment for the royal blue twinset she wore. There was nothing flashy about her. She was a level-headed girl, Mary had always said: easy company and a good listener as well as a good talker.

She was a good eater too, by the looks of things. Not faddy. Jim liked the fact that she tucked into the trifle and wasn't worried about her figure enough to refuse a second helping. He could see that Mary was thrilled about this too, as she was about how relaxed she was with Rhoda. If she could get on with Rhoda, she had grit. It would stand her in good stead whatever happened in the future.

Jim was touched when Sybil said that despite her having a lovely time, the talking needed to stop. She didn't want to outstay her welcome as she realised that William had to be up early. In fact, she said, if she didn't leave soon, there would be no point in him going to bed at all.

Jim rose from the table to say goodnight to her, watching as William helped her on with her coat which he'd been warming by the range, holding it out for her while she slipped her arms into the sleeves. He couldn't help but catch a look on Dora's face that he'd never seen before, as William placed his palm in the small of Sybil's back in readiness to usher her along the passage.

Dora sat transfixed at the scene, a single tear running down her cheek which she didn't attempt to wipe away. Or couldn't. Jim was unsettled at the intensity of the emotion and he looked at Mary, and with the deep understanding that years together brings about, could tell that she'd noticed too. Dora rose quickly from the table and made herself scarce.

"Leave her be, Jim," said Mary, stroking his hand. "Christmas, most probably," though she wasn't so sure that was the only reason. "Anyway, let's hope that the lovebirds make the most of their goodnight kiss on the doorstep."

Cold air sliced under the gap in the door between the living room and the passage as William returned. He looked pale and frozen and Jim told him to come and have a sit down with him for half an hour, have a slice of Christmas cake. His mother could help Dora in the scullery. It was her turn after all and she'd been indulged enough for one day so he didn't want her getting used to it.

Jim knew Mary realised he was joking as she made a quick exit down the steps into the scullery so that he could chat to William, father to son. He brushed the crumbs off the table cloth into his palm and stroked them into a saucer. They'd be ready for the robin when it came back. He trusted Dora's wisdom. He took a knife and cut into the cake, through the white icing, the smell of rum that Mary had been feeding it, seeping into his nostrils, making his gut heave. He tried to contain himself. He hadn't touched a drop of rum since the end of the last war.

"They looking after you over there, as they should, Son?" asked Jim.

William replied saying that their sergeant was a fine chap and had the men's best interests at heart. They hadn't lost a man as yet.

"That's good," said Jim. "Every man deserves to be looked after by a good sergeant when they're away from home."

William told his father that he didn't need to be so emotional. He was being well looked after considering the circumstances. And that his father should look after himself for a change, after the run up to Christmas.

"Never mind about me, Son. I'll be alright. And you'll be, too. You're a good son, William. The gods will be looking down on you. And you've got Sybil now. She's a lovely girl. Made for you."

"I know, Dad. You can't help but love her, can you? Nobody can."

"And I want you to know that I love you, Son," said Jim in an unusual gush of emotion. "But I can't see you off in the morning. I just can't. I'll leave that to your mother. I'll say good night now."

And with that he got up from the table and ruffled the top of William's hair, and walked out the door along the cold passage, taking one last look at William's kit bag hanging off the hook in the shop. Not once did he turn his head and look over his shoulder at his son, but instead whistled as he mounted the stairs, his cygnet ring tapping monotonously against the banister.

CHAPTER 24

MARY

Mary hadn't had to set the alarm. It was just after three o'clock. She hadn't slept a wink until then and neither had Jim who she knew had pretended to, and was pretending still, his knees tucked tightly into his chest, trying to feign the breathing of deep sleep. She didn't break the pretence.

She dressed in the cold of the bedroom and then padded along the landing. All the children were still asleep – or feigning sleep – except for William who was in the bathroom, preparing himself to get back in role. She went downstairs and put the kettle on to boil. She'd sort the fire in the range when she got back unless, by some divine intervention, someone other would magic it alight by the time she arrived home from the station.

The toast was under the grill when William came down the steps into the kitchen and put his arms around her. She told him not to be so silly and to sit down and have a cup of tea. She didn't want the toast incinerating. She had to keep an eye on it. They didn't have long.

Whiskey rubbed against the bottom of William's trouser legs, and weaved in and out of his ankles, purring loudly. He stooped and stroked her and went to the cabinet to get a saucer and filled it with milk and put it down at the side of the table. Cats know, thought Mary.

Mary sat down with William at the table, spreading the toast with butter, his first, then hers. The scraping of the knife against the bread sounded over-loud and the words weren't coming easily to either of them. Mary was glad when she heard Arthur's taxi eventually start up in the yard. Good as his word, that man. Up in the dead of night to take her and William to the station. Though she wanted to keep him as long as she could in her little back scullery, she needed the pain of the parting to come and go as quickly as she could.

She left the unfinished toast and the undrunk cups of tea on the table and took a T-towel and dabbed at the remnants of butter on William's mouth.

"There," she said, thinking of all the times, she'd spat on her handkerchief and dabbed his face free of food or dirt when he was a child, though he was nothing but a child now all dressed up in a man's uniform; like fancy dress.

She put her arm around his waist as they walked slowly along the passage and into the shop. She could see Arthur's taxi had been brought round to the front, through the gaps between the greaseproof paper, the exhaust fumes thick and filthy in the frosty air. He must have had the choke out to start in these temperatures.

She watched William stretch, taking down his cap from the meat hook and placing it on his head. Mary helped position it at the right angle. *There*, she said again, when she was satisfied. He took down his great coat and muffled himself up inside its weight. Mary did the buttons up for him, even though he insisted he could do them up himself. *That's not the point*, she said. Lastly, he took down his sausage bag and slung it across his shoulder. Only two days ago he'd carried it like Father Christmas would his sack, weighted down with kit and presents. Now, though it only contained his kit, it looked heavier on his shoulder. Mary took down her coat from the peg in the hall, put it on along with her gloves and hat. She slammed the front door shut after them and placed the house key in her pocket. Arthur was standing on the pavement ready and took William's kit bag and placed it in the boot. Mary got in the back and told William to ride up front with Arthur as he could wipe the inside of the windscreen as it was misting up with condensation. They pulled away and drove slowly down the road. Mary noticed William glance to the left, hoping in vain to see a glimpse of light behind the blackouts at Sybil's at 122.

There wasn't a car on Middle Road as Arthur negotiated the slithery surface as they descended into Cwmbwrla Square. They took it easy along Carmarthen Road, just the occasional skid, and

William doing his bit to enable Arthur to maintain his view ahead. Down through Waun Wen they drove and then through Dyfatty. Mary glanced at the Harris' butcher shop on the corner; but there was no gas sign burning bright tonight. And then they were there, turning into the station at High Street.

It was busier than Mary had thought. Well, she hadn't thought at all. Even though it was Boxing Day there were hundreds of Williams intent on getting the milk train out of Swansea to be back at their bases before their leave passes ran out.

She told Arthur to leave the engine running. She wouldn't be long but she had to make sure William was aboard the train despite his insistence that he didn't want her to catch cold.

She linked arms with William as they negotiated the sea of uniforms in the concourse. The Station Master let them through to the platform where the train was already fired up and steam hissing out from the engine upfront.

She kept her glove over her mouth and her head down as she advanced along the platform towards the front of the train, past the milk tanks and the goods carriages which were already filling fast with men and kit. The doors of the carriages were open from then on and she hoped William might find a space if not in a compartment, perhaps in the corridor where he could sit on his kitbag.

This was as far as she could take him. She'd taken him to the school gate when he'd started school and no further, and this was just the same. There was so much she wanted to say to him about coming home safe and how much she loved him but just like when he was in Infants School, nothing but a set of instructions came out of her lips. *Make sure you get enough to eat. Keep warm. Don't catch cold.* As if these motherly orders would protect him. She watched him board the train and then disappear for a while. She stood immobile on the platform until she saw him reappearing, his capped head and arm poking out between the gap in the corridor widow that he had slid open. She watched his breath in the air and she kept on watching until the guard slammed all the doors shut, blew his whistle, raised his flag and the train steamed out of the station. She waved her gloved hand to mirror his wave and she kept waving until the last of the wagons had left the platform and disappeared around the long, dark, right-hand curve out of High Street towards the viaduct and beyond. Until the last strain of the piston turned to silence.

And Mary & Jim are the ages of Gwallter + Jim.

PART 2

JANUARY 1940 – SEPTEMBER 1940

(June 1940 when Mum & Dad married)

And I had enlisted Orkneys

In 1940

My mother was

My father was

Born 1916
10 = 26
20 = 36
So 24

Born 1918
10 = 28
20 = 38
So 22
4 years older than William.

CHAPTER 25
JIM

The new year started just as the old one had ended: the temperature failing to budge from below freezing for weeks on end. Inside 141, ice formed on the window panes and the thin curtains stuck fast to the glass. Outside, in the back yard, Jim's white work coats hung stiff as corpses on the washing line and snow was packed solid on the roofs of the adjacent houses.

What was different about January however was that the robin was back. Each morning, before he opened up, Jim would make a point of going outside to make sure that his little friend was looked after with stale breadcrumbs and fresh, warm milk. The water he would leave daily was continually frozen solid in the saucer. As the days passed, he reckoned the robin was getting to know him more intimately, edging ever closer, as if one day he might feed out of his hands. The sight of his red breast and the sound of his early morning chirps calmed Jim, while at the same time making him melancholic. Though he couldn't look after William physically, there, on the freezing plains of Normandy, he could attend to this little fellow. It enabled him to face the day ahead.

What else was different was that Sybil, like the robin, became a more frequent visitor to 141. When she'd come home from work and had shared teatime with her parents, she'd pop across to see them all. The shop would be closed by then, but the front door would be left wide open into the porch until Jim locked up at bedtime. She didn't wait to be let in anymore, but tapped on the glass between the porch and the passage with what was now her characteristic 'rat ta ta tat tat' and cheerful voice shouting, *Yoohoo. Only me. Just popping in.*

"She's part of the furniture now," said Jim to Mary as they were sitting in their familiar chairs in front of the range one evening at the end of the month.

"I hope she's not going to see our furniture like *that* for much longer," said Mary, glancing over the top of her glasses toward the settee that still remained propped up with bricks.

"Don't nag, Mary. I'll get around to it as soon as I can."

"Mmm," said Mary. "Pigs might fly."

And Mary returned to her knitting.

"She probably feels closer to William when she's across here with us," she continued.

"Or that she can't wait to get out of the house and away from those bloody Bowens and their holier-than-thou attitudes."

"Don't start Jim. But you are right. It's good that she gets along with us. I mean, we might be her in-laws in the not too distant future."

"That would be lovely, don't you think? And Dora's so enamoured with her, too... What do they find to talk about in the middle room? Think they'd have used up all their words by now."

"It's called being young, Jim. Remember that?"

"I remember, alright. Being young isn't all it's cracked up to be for some, Mary. I wouldn't be young again in a million years."

Jim stared into the fire after that, and all was silent between him and Mary, except for the click-clacking of the needles, intent on finishing yet another pullover. The quiet was interrupted by Dora who came back into the living room, asking anyone if they'd like a cup of tea as she was putting the kettle on. Jim said he'd like one if she was making, to which Dora huffed and said she wouldn't be asking if she wasn't making. She was making for Sybil who wasn't feeling very well and was sitting down quietly in the other room until she felt a little better.

"Worn out with gassing probably," said Jim. What have you got going on in there that's so hush hush?"

"Never you mind," said Dora, pointing at the end of her nose.

"Walls have ears, remember," joked Jim.

Mary looked up from her knitting, noticing Dora's exasperated expression.

"She's alright in there, is she? I thought she looked a pit peaky when she came in, as though she's losing weight?" asked Mary.

"She's just tired, Mum. On her feet all day in the store. She'll settle down again soon. Early days."

"Look after her, Dora. Take her that tea now. And don't hang about in that room much longer. It's cold in there."

"Like pulling teeth, getting anything out of that one," said Jim to Mary after Dora had left the room again.

"They've got things to talk about that don't concern us, Jim."

"Sweethearts and men in uniform most likely."

"Perhaps," said Mary, lowering her head to check her tension.

CHAPTER 26
TEDDY

There was something different about the day, Teddy felt on waking. As he came to, everything slowly came into place. No, it wasn't a Saturday, it was a Tuesday, his mother's birthday, February 20th. How could he have dared forget? She'd kept on at everyone for weeks that she was going to be forty-four and that time was passing and she was coming up to half a century. There was fear in her voice as she said it, as though it was a very significant age. Teddy didn't see why she was making such a song and dance as she was already old, and another six years wouldn't make that much difference.

As he lay in his bed, he couldn't imagine ever being that ancient, although recently he felt he was getting older. Even though he was still obliged to wear short trousers, he sometimes felt loaded down with responsibilities. *Take Rhoda for a walk will you, Son? Take the left-over meat down to the cold stores, there's a good boy; take the deliveries round on your bike.* And even Saturdays weren't that special anymore as Saturdays with Raymond were becoming fewer, and the time wasted on errands for his father, more and more. Getting up on Saturday was like getting up on a school day, only earlier.

His father seemed to be leaning on him more heavily. Teddy didn't even think his father knew he was doing it. It had become an expectation now that he was the only boy in the house. Everything felt it was falling on him in the worst possible way; he was being treated like a man when he hadn't finished with being a boy. He didn't say anything but inside his head a little voice kept saying: *it's not fair, Dad. I've got my homework to do. My studies.* There was no point in saying anything as he knew what the answer would be: *Life's not fair, Son. You'll learn that one day.*

JANE FRASER

He pulled back the layers of sheet, blankets and eiderdown and got out of bed. There was something else that was different. It felt warmer. He drew back the curtains and looked into Beattie Street. A light drizzle was falling, soft and noiseless. Swansea seemed to be back to normal. The milder weather had come at last and was melting the frozen ice off the roofs, the white turning to a slush and dripping down on to the pavements. He hoped this thaw would last, and with the lighter evenings, there'd be a chance to get out to play after school. It had been a long, dark winter.

He went into the bathroom in his pyjamas and had a quick swill, washing his hands and wiping away the sleep in his eyes and the thoughts from his head with a cold flannel. He brushed his teeth with bicarbonate of soda. Back in his bedroom, he dressed quickly, putting his school shirt on over the vest he'd worn under his pyjamas, doing his tie in a Windsor knot as his father had shown him – without a mirror – and then his grey school short trousers, grey hand-knitted socks and grey hand-knitted pullover. He knew he was small for his age and worried about if, and when, he'd start growing and *spurt* as his mother had promised him he would; and then he wondered how his mother and father would be able to afford a new uniform when he did. Not many of the boys in his class – the A stream – would be worrying about things like these. No doubt it would be only boys like himself and the other two who had passed the 11+ at Cwmbwrla School and were travelling much further in their minds every day than the actual one-mile journey on the 83 bus that took them to a different kind of world.

In the little back bedroom, it was the first time he'd felt a little ashamed that his father was a butcher, that they were quite poor, that he wasn't from a family of lawyers or surgeons. He was still going to be a surgeon. He'd made up his mind. His teacher had told him that he could go anywhere in this world if he put his mind to it. He stood on tiptoe to look in the mirror on the wall that had been positioned for William and said, *I'm going to be a surgeon*, before bounding downstairs to the scullery.

His parents and Dora were sitting around the table, his mother automatically rising to her feet as he came down the steps. Dora put her hand on her mother's arm to restrain her.

"Not this morning, Mum," she said, before getting up to put a slice of bread under the grill of the gas stove and instructing Teddy to sit down and be quiet and not cause any trouble as everyone had enough on their plates.

"Happy Birthday, Mum," said Teddy, kissing his mother on the cheek she offered him. It felt wet.

He sat down as Rhoda plonked the toast in front of him. He took his knife and dug out a chunk of white dripping from the earthenware pot and spread it thickly on his toast. It smelled beefy and salty and he could taste it already.

"What's the matter, Mum?" he asked. "C'mon, it's your birthday and the weather's turned. Spring's on its way. Tell her, Dad."

"I've tried, Son, said Jim. "But she's got 'em today."

"And you'd have 'em too, Jim, if you had to go what I have to go through," said Mary. "Who'd be a woman? Coming back as a man, next time, isn't that right, Dora?"

"She hasn't had a letter from William," said Dora, explaining the uncharacteristic mood to Teddy. "She thinks he's forgotten her birthday."

"He'd never forget your birthday, Mum. You know that. It's so close to his. Perhaps something will come second post," said Teddy.

"Ever the little diplomat, Teddy," said Mary. "Come here and give your old mother a hug," she said, as Teddy got up from the table and allowed himself to be drawn into her pillowy bosoms by her strong arms.

In the comfort of the warm smell of her, he thought of William. His stomach knotted. He missed his big brother. William would be nineteen in two days so wasn't that much older than him and look what he was being asked to do. He prayed that the letter would come later with the GPO boy.

Teddy's embrace with his mother was brought to a sudden conclusion by his father, who looked on from his chair. Teddy knew his father couldn't bear this public show of affection.

"Enough of that now, Mary. You'll make a sissy of the boy," he said.

"It would do you good, too, Jim Froom. Perhaps you wouldn't

be the way you are if you did. All buttoned up."

Jim cleared his throat; but didn't retort.

"You'll need to be getting on your way, or you'll miss the bus," Jim said to Teddy "But don't forget, we've got Arthur coming over this evening. I know you've got *plans* - again - Dora, but Teddy, we'll need you to make up a four for a game of Solo."

Teddy unpicked himself from his mother and stepped into his polished shoes and laced them up. Sometimes he felt like the substitute. The replacement off the bench. He took down his gas mask and felt the weight of it as he slung it across his shoulders. It was almost as heavy as the weight of yet another task he would be enlisted for when he got home.

When he arrived home from school Teddy could tell by his mother's face that there'd been a letter from William delivered second post. She looked lighter somehow, and younger than the forty-four she now insisted on telling everyone she was. He felt his tummy loosen. Life was up and down since the war had started, nothing much happening to show there was a war on, but people were on edge. You could never be certain of what mood they'd be in. Either up in the air or down in the doldrums, like his mother who maintained it wasn't just the war but also her time of life.

She stood in front of the range in the living room and took down the letter she'd placed at the front of the letter rack. It was getting full now. Teddy wondered what would happen when there were too many to go in the rack. Or if they'd stop coming. But for the moment he listened as his mother summarised the contents of the letter from his brother: son number one. *It's still cold*, she read, *but the pullovers are coming in handy and I'm the envy of all the boys in the camp.* She didn't draw breath but went on: *And there are rats, big blighters, but one of the boys has made a trap so don't worry. As for what's next, we're not sure. We can't understand why Hitler hasn't made his move yet. I can't tell you exactly what I'm involved in but I'm with another couple of lovely lads on our missions which we hope are doing the trick.* And then he says: *love to Teddy, Dora and Rhoda and dear old Auntie Kit (ha ha) and look after Sybil. I miss you all but hope I can get some leave soon if things stay calm. Have a lovely birthday, Mum. I wish I could be with you. Love William x*

Teddy listened but didn't feel as happy as his mother seemed. Or perhaps she was showing happy. Taking things day by day.

Later, after he'd finished his homework as well as he could in the time allowed before his parents interrupted him, Teddy was issued his first chore of the evening.

"Fix the blackouts, will you, there's a good lad?" said his father.

As he took the blackouts and wedged them into the window frames in the scullery, he thought what would happen if he were ever to say: *No. Do it yourself.* He would never; but it didn't stop him thinking it. How would his father react to being stood up to? He wouldn't risk it. After all, he had to consider his father's nerves, his mother told him often. *He's been through a lot, your father,* she'd say. That was probably true; but he kept his war close to his chest. Though he kept a leather strap hanging, too, on the back of the kitchen door, he'd never used it. But the story was that his father had a strap on the door which he did use.

But he'd seen others who'd been through his father's war lose control. Some of them had come back and were teachers in his school, constantly on a short fuse. He thought of Mr Pritchard who was about the same age as his father, who hurled chalk and board rubbers like missiles across the classroom. He'd already witnessed him in the woodwork room, berating Charlie Morgan for his cheek, and dragging him by his ear across the room to the woodwork bench. There he'd wrenched the boy's head and forced it into a vice which he screwed tightly and, with the boy's ear then facing the ceiling, had poured oil into it through a metal funnel while cursing to anyone who would listen while the boy sobbed.

Not long after the blackouts were in place, Arthur arrived via the side entrance. Teddy could hear him before he saw him, his peculiar one-sided gait echoing on the tiles in the upper yard before he came into the scullery.

"Light a couple of candles, Teddy," instructed his father. "Save the light."

His mother glanced at the single, naked light bulb that hung over the table. Teddy understood the look.

"Get Arthur a drink, Teddy," said his father. "He looks like he needs one."

Teddy took the whiskey bottle that stood on the kitchen cabinet and filled up three of the tumblers that had been placed ready on the table, along with the best ashtray with the grooves to hold the cigarettes, and a deck of cards. Then all four of them seated themselves around the table.

"Happy Birthday, Mary," said Arthur. "Iechyd da."

And they all raised their glasses and said Iechyd da in unison, Mary laughing as always when she tried to pronounce the Welsh words which she said were full of spit.

"Okay, now down to business," said Jim. "Teddy, you can deal, and Arthur, if it's alright with you, tonight we'll trick-take for a penny a point."

"Alright by me, Jim," said Arthur, putting a pile of coppers in front of him.

Mary and Jim stacked their pennies likewise, and Teddy went out of the room, returning a minute or so later with his piggy bank which he emptied on the table.

Teddy didn't have to be told what to do next. He shuffled the cards and dealt clockwise, thirteen cards each. He watched as everyone concentrated, their faces intent on getting a trick, trying to outwit their combatants. He watched as they lit up and smoked, and his mother – for her party piece – blew smoke rings that drifted up towards the ceiling which was yellowed despite the forgiving candlelight. He watched them all resting the cigarettes in the ashtray as their turn came around. He watched as his father's cards shook in his butcher's hands just like Mr Pritchard's, and he watched as his mother noticed him looking. He didn't say much, just kept his head down and performed his role as card dealer in Fagin's den, wondering how it was possible for his father to throw away his hard earned cash on whiskey and fags and horses and cards rather than getting him a new pair of school shoes. He was literally walking in William's shoes. He thought about the teacher who had told him he could go anywhere in this world if he put his mind to it. And he fleetingly saw those words rise, float away, and disappear like the smoke rings in the gloomy scullery.

CHAPTER 27

JIM

January had seen only the rationing of ham and eggs, but now in March the North Atlantic convoys were getting hammered by the Kraut's U-boats and food supplies were decimated.

In the shop, Jim tutted more, aware that he was talking to himself, muttering under his breath about the fact that he would be working twice as hard for half as much money for the war effort. He began not to care whether his customers saw his expression reflected back in the mirror.

In they trudged, miserable buggers, delving in their shopping bags for the ration books they'd been issued in order to register for meat with him.

"You can either have less of the expensive meat or more of the cheap meat. Makes no odds. But you can't exceed your weekly ration per person," he began to explain to each one, as they thrusted their ration books across the counter to receive the official stamp that filled each little square.

How many times would he have to repeat this until they got the hang of it? It wasn't difficult. The sums were simple. They could have as much offal and sausage as they wanted as these items weren't rationed. But he couldn't bend the rules on the meat. One shilling and tuppence per person, per week. As the words spewed out on repeat issued from his terse lips, he realised that there was no profit to be made on any of this. He stamped each book with a force that was quite unnecessary.

This frustration was just the nudge he needed. He justified it to himself as he went on and on explaining the rules to the customers. He couldn't take much more. In the great scheme of things, wanting to provide for his family wasn't a crime, was it? Needs must. This government deserved it for what they were doing to his boy, William, and millions of boys just like him. Just as the government had pulled the wool over the eyes of lads like him back in the first big lie. He was like Robin Hood, he told himself. A rebel with heart. He would procure a few extras for those that needed it – and would pay for it – and in doing so, make a bit on the side for himself and his family. By God, they deserved it. He got a perverse pleasure about getting one over on the government. They were robbing everybody blind. Money. And hope. It was a small risk, worth taking. He had put his ruse to Morgan Beynon when he delivered the poultry before Christmas. All he needed was a reminder. He'd give him a ring.

Jim didn't waste time. For weeks, at night, in the dark, he plotted out how it would work. Mary couldn't see his mind working if the light was off.

By April he was all set up and took delivery of the initial pig. Morgan pulled up in the lorry outside, just as the slaughterhouse delivery driver from Eton Road would normally do on a Monday afternoon. Jim was waiting at the shop door to welcome him, keeping an eye on any front doors opening or any movement in the net curtains opposite. Nothing much was said: the dressed pig was hefted in across Morgan's shoulders and hung snout-down off the giant iron hooks behind the glass door to the passage.

Jim had ensured that Mary was out of the way for what came next. He didn't think of it as lying to her; after all, it was for her benefit in the end, for her own good.

"Why don't you give yourself a bit of a break?" he'd said earlier. "I can manage. You do enough around here."

"This isn't like you, Jim Froom… what are you doing that you don't want me to know about? Not betting again, are you?"

"No. I promise. It's just that I don't like to see you going hell for leather all the time. Not…"

"Don't you ever say, not at my age, Jim. I feel bad enough that I was forty-four in February. But I expect you've forgotten how much it got to me?"

"What do you take me for?"

"My lawful wedded husband. That's what I took you for. For

all the good it's done me."

"Don't say that, Mary. I'm doing by best."

"I know you are," she said, as she pecked him gently on the cheek. "I'll be off to town, then. I'm going to have a nose around Snell's in the arcade and see if I can get myself some new sheet music. We could have a bit of a sing-song sometime again. Get the neighbours in?"

Jim had told her that it seemed a good idea. Inside, his guts had turned over. The thought of Mary finding out. It was true, she'd have his nuts. And he winced. Squeezed his thighs together.

"I'll be off then," said Morgan. "Same time in a month. Hope you shift it all. Keep a note and you can settle when you see me next."

"Okey dokey. It'll all be jotted down in here," said Jim pointing to his little black book.

"Aye. Just make sure Mary doesn't get wind of it. Put it somewhere safe."

"Will do. Have just the place."

And with that Morgan was off. Heading for the border, he said. Back to Gower and God's own country.

Jim listened for the lorry to pull off, bolted the door top and bottom, and made sure there were no gaps between the sheets of greaseproof paper. He opened his black book and wrote down the day and date: Monday, 8th April and continued to write: took delivery of dressed pig. I owe MB cost of pig, plus delivery and his half share in profits. Next delivery, Monday, 6th May. When he'd finished writing, he put the pencil behind his ear, and the notebook in his trouser pocket.

He then walked to the hook and heaved the pig on to his shoulder and carried it to his block. Even though it was fully dressed, it felt heavier than normal. Like a soul, guilt probably had its own weight. He slammed the carcass down on to the block and set to chopping and trimming and slicing and weighing and wrapping and labelling the constituent parts ready to be flogged off. The sooner the better. He trusted his instincts. He knew who he'd ask, knew who'd put themselves before the good of the community and who'd keep their gob shut.

He reached under the block and lifted the steel meat tray onto the counter and went about filling it with the plunder: legs, fillets, loins, belly, chops, cheek, chump, ribs. As he did, he saw the pounds, shillings and pence before his eyes. But then Mary's face replaced them and he was overwhelmed with terror.

He bent and lifted the tray and wedged it on his stomach between his hip bones and walked across the shop and along the passage. No-one would ever think of this, he thought to himself as he lumbered across the top yard, down the steps, across the cobbles and into the old stables.

Once inside, he lowered the tray onto the floor and rummaged through the paraphernalia until he came across the old military chest. Good. He'd estimated it perfectly. It was the right size. The key, he'd taken from the dark recesses of the wooden till in the shop: he now placed it in the brass lock and turned. He lifted the lid. It was full of stacked tins, and underneath, a couple of parcels, concealed in brown paper. He felt nauseous, a momentary whiff of rum filling his nostrils. He started to whistle as he reached for the tray and placed it to rest inside the chest. And then he brought down the top of the chest, and turned the key.

He came out of the old stables and felt the cold air on his hot cheeks, his bowels turning to water. He got to the privy just in time. And after he had, in a way, unburdened himself, he sat on the wooden bench seat and got himself together. He did a lot of thinking in the tŷ bach as the old women called it in these parts. The question was how he'd get the joints from the old stables to the customer without Mary seeing or knowing. It would have to be a Tuesday. He'd have to get Mary out of the house for another day. She'd smell a rat, surely. Jesus. It would be Tuesday tomorrow. He'd have to think on his feet here. Frank Morgan. The runner. He'd promised he'd take anything that was on offer. Had a list of takers as long as him arm. Could dish it all out in the Gate House. Probably hoping that he would pay him over the odds in bets that would never come good. Jim vowed he'd have to discipline himself not to do this or there be no point in any of it. No point at all. He'd get on the phone to him before Mary got back. And then he'd have to devise a scheme to get Mary out of the house again to coincide with Frank's arrival. He'd also have to alter the notes in the little black book to note that the profits would now be split three-ways. Shit. He'd keep some meat from the tray back, get rid of it himself 'under the counter'. He'd have to itemise what Frank took and what he kept back. Christ, it was getting complicated already and it hadn't even started.

Jim made himself decent and whistled his way back into the house, retracing his steps through the kitchen and along the passage. He turned left into the middle room and walked towards the piano. Looking up at the wall behind, he took a swift glance at Mary's home-made warning sign, created with a mixture of menace and humour. *AT YOUR PERIL*. She wouldn't think this funny. She'd have a bloody fit.

Slowly, he eased open the lid of the Townly and glanced down at the void below. It would be safe here in the black space between the strings and the wood casing. Taking his pencil from behind his ear, he made the necessary alterations to the notebook. And then he placed his little, black book inside and shut the lid.

CHAPTER 28
MARY

Mary had come back from her shopping trip happy with her purchase. She'd met *the* Mr Music at Snell's in the arcade and he'd sold her a piece she'd heard on the radio called, *We'll Meet Again*. There were lots of patriotic – or jingoistic – songs around suddenly, but she preferred to concern herself with the time when it would all be over and back to as normal as their life in the butcher shop ever was. Or, life with Jim, who was, unknown to most people, not what you'd consider normal. He played a good game, did Jim. Not many people knew him like she did.

She was going to practise the new score when she had a minute, she told Jim, and that it would be good if they could have a sing-song soon, to brighten up the interminable weather. She wondered why Jim didn't jump at the suggestion: he always liked to have Arthur and Graham and their families over for a little get-together. Instead, he started whistling, and walked over to the Rayburn, lifted the lid, and put the kettle on.

"What's got into you?" she asked.

"Nothing. I thought you'd like a nice cup of tea after you've been on your feet all day."

"Don't go overdoing it, Jim. You'll have me thinking you've got a fancy woman or something."

"Don't be daft, Mary. You know I'd never wander."

And that much was true.

Mary took over the operation when she heard the steam hissing from the kettle. Jim seemed to have forgotten all about it.

"Sit down, Jim," she said. "It'll boil dry with you in charge."

She got everything back under control, took two scoops of tea and placed them in the teapot and poured the boiling water on top. Then she placed one of her tea-cosies over the pot and took it to the table, placing it on the oilcloth. While Jim sat silent on the settle in the corner, she walked to the kitchen cabinet, picking up the slop basin and the tea strainer and coming back to the table. She poured Jim a cup, milk first, and then two sugars. She took hers exactly the same.

"So," she said, stirring both cups and trying to instigate some conversation. "You had a good day?"

"Same as ever. Nothing to write home about," he said, picking up the cup and putting it to his lips.

"And on that subject, Jim. Your son hasn't been writing lately – not to us anyway," she said.

"He's probably using up all his ink on Sybil," said Jim. "He's fine. We'd have heard if something was amiss. Bad news travels fast."

"I suppose so. I just like to have his letters drop through the door. It keeps me going."

Mary felt Jim's hand on hers, tightening its grip.

"Do you believe in hell?" Jim suddenly asked.

"Good God, Jim. What is this all about? You sound like old Granny Weidenbach. And no, I don't believe in hell, or heaven, for that matter as places to go when you're finished up here. There'll be no one standing at the pearly gates with a big key when you go up, or a Devil with a pitch fork and a fire-pit with licking flames when you go the other way. It's here on earth, don't you think, Jim? Heaven? Hell? It's what you make of your life while you're living it. That's what you'll be judged on by others. That's what you'll have to live with yourself."

Mary watched Jim raise himself from the settle, picking up his cup and saucer and taking them to the sink. He rinsed them under the tap and put them to drain.

"I think I'll go upstairs for a spell, Mary, if that's alright with you. I've got a bit of a dicky belly."

CHAPTER 29
JIM

It seemed like business as usual the next day but Jim hadn't slept much overnight, going through in his mind how everything would play out the next morning. He was shocked at how lying was coming so easily to him. First one little fib and then that would lead to another and then another. He worried he'd forget the sequence and drop himself right in it.

He got up rather than thrash around in the bed. He'd leave Mary lie in. Get in her good books by clearing the grate and lighting the range ready for her when she came downstairs.

In the living room, he knelt down in front of the range and riddled through the ashes. He then rolled the newspapers into balls, laid the sticks on top, and covered them with ashes and a few lumps of coal. He hadn't lost the knack. He realised he'd assumed Mary would do it all these years without complaint. Why did he assume so much? He wasn't much of a man. After all these years, what did he amount to?

Hand shaking, he lit a match and set the paper alight. The sticks caught and soon the fire was going strong. He added the coal, lump by lump, and stared into the flames. There was little comfort in his own hearth. He saw everything ablaze again, heard that huge roar, smelled the stench of fumes and smoke and death as the conflagration raged. And it was raging again now and it would keep on raging, engulfing Cwmbwrla, Swansea, Europe, the world, consuming everything and everyone in its advance, as it had done the first time around.

He looked at his hands and saw that they were trembling again; even though there was warmth in the grate, he felt cold, his brow clammy, his mouth dry, and he realised that with his meat scam he was making things a whole lot worse. And he longed that he might allow himself to weep and finally douse the flames; and that there was something, or someone, who could help him because he knew he couldn't help himself.

Still on his knees, facing the fire, he heard the living room door open and knew by the shuffle of the slippers across the linoleum that it was Mary. He turned to the touch of her hands on his shoulders, the feel of her lips on the thinning patch of his crown. He rose and hugged her, taking out the grips that had been holding sections of her hair in the hope of curls overnight. With the metal gone, he drew her closer and kissed her on the cheek. She still smelled of sleep and their old double bed, and he breathed it in, this unusual early morning communion between them.

No sooner had she eased into his embrace than she withdrew, smoothing down her hair and her dress as if to get the morning back on track; a sign that Jim had interrupted the rhythm of her life not only with the lighting of the fire, but with uncharacteristic displays of affection.

"There's nothing to rush off for, Mary," he said. "Kids are still asleep. Have five minutes."

"I don't know what's got into you, Jim, but I've things to be getting on with."

"It can wait. I'll give you a hand in a bit. Just relax."

"Relax? There's no time to relax. Wives and mothers don't relax, Jim. Haven't you noticed? When I'm working in the shop, I'm worrying I'm not being a good mother, and when I'm trying to be a good mother, I worry that I'm not doing my sixpennyworth with you. I bet you don't have this battle going on in your head all the time."

"Don't be like that," said Jim, trailing Mary down the stone steps into the scullery. "I have my own battles."

He watched her as she took her paisley print, cross-over pinny off the warming plate of the Rayburn, tying it around her waist, encasing herself in its cotton, like armour. She dragged her slippered feet to the settle, lifted the lid, and pulled out her lace-up brogues. Then she closed the lid and sat on the bench, bending down ready to put on the shoes.

Jim sank to his knees again and picked up the left shoe, easing her foot into it with the shoe horn that hung on a piece of string next to the settle. He didn't say a word as Mary allowed herself this unusual pleasure. Instead, he picked up the right shoe and had more difficulty placing this on her right foot. He used his thumbs to knead her ankle in an attempt to rid her of the water that was accumulating there. Finally, he placed the right shoe on her foot and then laced-up both shoes, tied bows, and double-knotted them.

"I feel like Cinderella," she said.

"I wish it were like that, Mary," he said. "I'd magic a golden coach and a fine frock for you to go to the ball."

"I know you would," she said, stroking his hair. "But we don't live in fairy tales, do we? Now come on, there's work to be done."

"I can cope here, Mary. I'd really like you to have the morning off. You'll have to have Rhoda with you, but how about you go to Monica's and have your hair done? A perm, or a set, or whatever they do there."

"Monica's? We're not made of money. Christ, Jim. What is wrong with you? Me off to Snell's one day, hairdressers the next?"

"It's not every day, Mary. It's only once a month. You shall go to the hairdresser on Tuesday mornings. As long as you're back before the clock strikes one to get my dinner on the table," he teased.

Later, Jim stood outside the double, wooden gates that opened from the cobbled yard into Beattie Street, and waved Mary and Rhoda off. It was hardly a long journey on foot through the untarmacked lane that connected Beattie Street with Gwilym Street, but Jim felt compelled to keep on waving until they were out of sight. Monica's was the name given to the front room of the first house at the end of the lane that Monica had turned into a hairdresser's shop. He knew it would be a long job as Mary hadn't made an appointment. By the time it was her turn to go to the sink for a wash, and then back to her chair for a trim, and the permanent rods were rolled and secured in her hair, and she was put under the dryer for an hour or so, finished off in front of the mirror, he'd have plenty of time to deal with the pork and Frank, and do what he needed to.

At ten o'clock the yard was empty.

Frank was coming at ten-fifteen. They'd fixed it on the phone the previous evening when Jim had rung through some bets for the next day's fixtures. He'd stood in the passage, listening for Mary, ready to revert to talk about horses and form should she have come through the door at any minute. But she hadn't.

He had fifteen minutes to take what he needed from his stash in the trunk to sell through other dubious means in the shop. Not a lot. But he'd keep this operation out of the equation with Frank and Morgan. This was his and his alone.

He retrieved his key from the till, turned the sign on the door from OPEN to CLOSED. He could always cover himself with anyone who asked – including Mary – that he'd been caught short and had gone to the privy. He left the shop and marched quick tempo to the old stables where he opened the trunk and took out a leg, a fillet, some chops. Not too much. He gathered them up into his arms and ferried them back to the shop, tucking them out of sight under the counter. He knew who to ask. Who the takers would be. The ones who wouldn't ask questions. When he'd done this, he went into the middle room and walked toward the piano. He looked up at Mary's warning on the wall and made the sign of the cross before opening the lid, delving deep to retrieve his little, black book in readiness for Frank, whom he could hear reversing into the yard.

Jim hot-footed back outside, where Frank was getting out from behind the wheel. He greeted Frank, and Frank touched the rim of his hat in response.

"All ready, Jim?" he asked.

"All ready. Wrapped up and priced."

"Good stuff," said Frank, "I'll give you a hand."

"No need. Where d'you want it? Back seat?"

"That'll do fine. I'll push mine forward a bit so you can get it in."

Jim walked to the stables and returned with the tray. His heart was racing and there was an acid taste in his mouth. He leaned into the car with the load and placed it on the leather seat. The smell of the polished leather was strong and he felt queasy. He didn't show. He would never show. He backed his body out of the car and straightened up, rubbing his hands together as if he was trying to shake off something that was stuck to them. Then he took out his little, black book and Frank signed for delivery. He didn't know he wasn't signing for the leg, the fillet, the chops. And then Jim shook hands with Frank. The deal was done. So far so good. And it wasn't even ten-thirty.

Jim stood in Beattie Street, guiding Frank out through the gates, Frank's eyes visible in the rear view mirror, until he saw Frank swing the car round and drive away, the exhaust fumes rank in the air of an April morning that had turned cold again. The stench went straight to Jim's stomach and once again the acid rose into his mouth. He turned quickly, drew the gates and bolted them fast. And then he bolted to the privy and retched until there was nothing but burning bile he felt might strip the lining of his stomach. He felt better once he'd been sick. A penance of sorts. He was ready then to go back into the shop, open up again, and carry on with business as usual.

CHAPTER 30
MARY

Mary told Jim that she felt like a new woman when she got back home from Monica's. She wondered if he'd notice as she buzzed around the kitchen, fussing to get his dinner in front of him as soon as he came through from the shop at one o'clock.

"No need to feel guilty for gadding about for days on end," he joked, as she stood at the gas stove crisping up the weekend's left-over vegetables in a frying pan.

"Don't make me feel like that, Jim. Bad enough I'm serving up bubble and squeak again. Catch-as-catch-can, when you've been busy at it."

Jim watched her dish up for the three of them, making sure that Rhoda had the crispy bits before she started on one of her hissy fits as she did on rice pudding days.

"She's done a lovely job on your hair," said Jim.

"D'you like it?" she said, touching the even roll of pinned-up wave at the back of her neck. "Everyone who's anyone has this style now, Jim."

"You look beautiful, Mary. Really lovely."

"I've had a marvellous couple of days, Jim. I feel full of energy; rejuvenated."

Jim ate as he listened to Mary.

"Well, you never guess who I saw in Snell's yesterday, Jim. You wouldn't believe it. I couldn't either when I saw him, but he was standing right in front of my eyes next to the sheet music. Richard Tauber. We saw *the* Richard Tauber, didn't we Rhoda? And he looked just like he did in the films. Fine looking man. I was going to ask him for his autograph, but then I said to myself: 'Mary, you're going on forty-five not fourteen, not a star-struck girl.' But Mr Snell must have sensed I was too embarrassed to ask myself so he said to *the* Richard Tauber: 'Would you mind signing the music for Mary? She's a good customer of mine, Richard,' as if he was a best friend of his. And that's just what he did, he took his silver pen out of his jacket pocket and wrote: *To Mary with best wishes, Richard Tauber.* And I could hardly get the words out, but I said, 'Oh, thank you, Mr Tauber,' and he said, 'Don't call me Mr Tauber, call me Richard'. Nothing stuck up about him at all. He's been on at the Empire in a concert because he can't do the opera now because of the war. I told him about our William, too. That he'd been a boy soprano and won a scholarship to London and how he was away in the RAF. Made my day, it did."

"Go easy, Mary. You haven't come up for air," said Jim.

"You're not jealous are you, Jim?"

"A little bit, if I'm honest. I'm sorry I'm not *the* Richard Tauber."

"You daft, old fool," she said.

"It's lovely to see you enjoying yourself, Mary. It suits you," he said.

"Well, anyway. That's not all," Mary went on. "Guess who was in Monica's?"

"Go on then, tell me before you choke on it."

"Mrs Bowen. Having a perm. Well, we got chatting and it seems Sybil isn't in good form at all. Probably explains why she hasn't been coming over to see us recently. She's been having dizzy spells and has even had time off from the china department. They're good employers, like that, when there's sickness, Ben Evans' store. I asked if she was a little anaemic as I said I used to be anaemic until you got me eating liver, if you remember, Jim, and she said she didn't know as she didn't want to go to the doctor. So I said that it might be that she's missing William so much, and a breaking heart can make you feel like that. All that missing comes out in the body as well as being hidden in the mind…"

"You're right there, Mary."

"But that's not all. She's having a letter from our William almost every week, which is a darn sight more than he's writing to us – but I didn't tell her that, of course – but I did say that they must be serious. And she went quiet after that."

Mary poured a cup of tea for Jim and herself and watched as he poured some of his into a saucer for Rhoda and blew on it.

"Take time with that, Rhoda," he said. "Leave it cool. Don't want you burning yourself. You too, Mary. You're going to run out of steam if you carry on like this. I'm exhausted just listening to you."

"And you won't believe what she told me when she did start talking again, Jim. You're going to die laughing."

"Go on then. Fill me in," he said.

"She asked me if we'd heard about the goings-on at the other end of Carmarthen Road, at Fforestfach Cross. And I said, 'No, what's been happening there, then?' And she said, in broad daylight, mind you, the police had stopped a hearse that had pulled up outside the funeral directors next to Huw Evans' butcher's shop, and when they opened the door, and wedged open the oak coffin, you'll never guess what they found inside, Jim?"

"I reckon a corpse, Mary. What else would it be?"

"A pig, Jim. A flippin' whole pig. They couldn't believe their eyes. They'd had a tip-off about some illegal shenanigans. Mrs Bowen thought that Huw Evans was involved but she doesn't know for sure. Just hearsay. But the hearse driver owned up when the policeman got his book out to say that he was making a delivery for some Gower farmer. Apparently, they're both going to be in a lot of trouble – the driver and the farmer. Mrs Bowen said there was talk of them doing time. But she's prone to exaggeration, I know. Serve them right, she said. There was a war on and people were dying and others like them lining their pockets on other people's misery. She said they'd have their comeuppance and their judgement come the day. She was surprised that I knew nothing about anything, you know, as you knew Huw Evans, and I said, I'd ask you if you'd heard anything, because if you had, I'd be surprised that you hadn't shared it with me."

CHAPTER 31
TEDDY

By mid-April the weather was full of promise. The nights were drawing out and on the rare occasions when Teddy was not summoned for duty in the shop, he and Raymond could enjoy evenings like they used to.

They cycled through the village of Cwmbwrla, and on along Gors Road which was ablaze with gorse alongside the Bwrlais brook. Teddy and Raymond would often dismount here and lie on the bank and talk about what they'd do when the war was over. Mostly they missed the beach, cycling along the Mumbles Road to the Slip and going through the stone arch to the sand, and on to the sea to have a quick dip of an evening. Or speeding along the Mumbles Road to Oystermouth, where they used to jump off the wall into the sea at full tide. They'd be glad when the barbed wire was snipped and they'd be free again.

On the surface not much had changed: The Tivoli cinema near the railway bridge still showed the latest films. They'd chip in to buy a bag of broken biscuits from the Star grocer's shop in the Square before taking a seat on the windowsills for the Saturday afternoon film – all for a tanner. The graveyard at Babell that separated Raymond's cottage below, from Teddy's house, above, was still overgrown and as uncared for as it had always been. The headstones were toppling over, but the flat stone slabs were useful tabletops for playing jacks. Zanetti's and De Marco's, the Italian cafés, on the main road were still full of steam and the hiss and aroma of frothy coffee; but the boys noticed the cafés weren't as full of customers as they used to be. There was talk that Italy would be joining Germany. It was said that soon the Italian male owners would be interned just as was happening to the German men. The boys reckoned it would be the women who would be keeping the businesses running then, just as they were keeping a lot of things going in this war, but it didn't seem to be mentioned much.

The talk drifted from women to the pretty Italian girls who worked in the café and Raymond casually asked Teddy if he was interested in girls. He put the emphasis on *interested* and qualified it with, *in that sort of way*. Teddy said that he wasn't at all *interested* as he had enough of girls at home, and if Rhoda and Dora were anything to go by, he'd keep it that way for ever. And anyway, he doubted he'd ever have time for girls what with all the chores he had to do for his father. Raymond said that Teddy would change his mind when he started to grow up…

Teddy felt himself shrink. Raymond, unlike himself, was tall for his age, and soft hair was starting to show on his upper lip and cheeks. *Bum fluff* he called it. A few pimples had appeared between his eyebrows which he seemed quite proud of. Teddy was surprised at that, as he was when Raymond told him he had actually kissed a girl and hadn't needed to stop to take a breath for almost two minutes and that he'd probably do it again soon. It was a lovely feeling, he said, and had made his John Thomas tingle and move of its own accord inside his trousers.

"Not all boys like girls, though," said Raymond, as if he knew all there was to know about the world. "Not in that sense."

"What d'you mean?" asked Teddy.

"Well some boys like boys. They're called homosexuals."

Teddy blushed. He'd not heard the word before and now he was considering the conversation.

"And some girls don't like boys, either," Raymond went on. "They're called Lesbians. And my mother thinks your sister, Dora, is a Lesbian. *One of those*, she said she was when she was telling my father when he was home on leave."

Teddy felt more than a blush then. It was a hot rage that spread from the pit of his stomach up through his neck and across his cheeks. He wanted to punch his best friend for saying this. He didn't understand. What was he saying about his big sister? But he was in the café and so he had to keep the feeling inside him, not show his anger or his confusion about something he didn't even understand.

"My mother saw Dora with a girl at the Plaza," continued Raymond.

"So? She often goes to the Plaza with Sybil, or a friend from work. There's nothing wrong with that. Girls have friends who are girls."

"But this looked like a very *special friend*, my mother said. She'd seen them in the double seats at the back of the stalls at the Plaza – very *close*, she said they were. She said her *friend* was very glamorous – looked like a theatre type. Dressed up to the nines."

"I don't want to hear any more," said Teddy, putting his hands over his ears. "You're like an old woman spreading gossip like that. And you shouldn't have been eavesdropping on the conversation, anyway."

"I'm just saying, that's all. It might explain things."

"What things?" said Teddy.

Teddy went quiet then not wanting to really hear any answers. But he wondered if it did explain a lot about Dora's private life that she didn't seem to want to share with any of them at home. Her work life in the hospital with the other nurses, and the Kardomah café she frequented that was often talked about in Swansea for the *arty types* that went in there; her life with the cycling club; the fact that she never talked about boys – or brought them home. And she was always with Sybil. Or was Raymond and his family assuming things, putting two and two together and making five?

Teddy might be only thirteen but already he knew you shouldn't put people into boxes and judge them. You never knew how they might be struggling in their lives the way he was with his in his own peculiar way. People all had their own stories. It wasn't right. He thought of poor Granny Weidenbach, about the Italian men serving the coffee, and then he thought about Dora. And inside there was a rumbling that he didn't know whether he'd be able to control and he felt smaller than ever, fearing that his best friend would be growing away from him very soon.

CHAPTER 32
JIM

Everything appeared to have gone without a hitch so far. Jim had cleared the whole lot of pork without any hiccups. He was finding it easy to operate two sets of books despite leaving school barely able to count. But that didn't mean things didn't prey on his mind.

In fact, his old condition was back with a vengeance. Mary called it the *skitters*, and the way she pronounced it with a lovely Hampshire r hid the fact that he was back and fore to the privy all day. As he sat rooted to the lavatory, it took him back to when he'd had the first bad bout back in early 1918 and he'd found himself spending hours in the latrines. As he reached across yet again to the nail on the back of the door that secured the cut-up newspapers, he wondered if his burning arse was a punishment from a God who might exist after all.

In the shop, Mary held the fort every time he got the call, telling the customers that he wouldn't be long, it was just when you had to go you had to go. Every time he returned she'd connect, eye to eye. She didn't interrogate him, but he felt it was more of an accusatory look than one of concern. A look that said: *Don't get sick, Jim Froom, I've got enough to do as it is.* A look that said: *You need to try and relax and try not to get so worked up about things.* A look that said: *You need to find a hobby, a distraction, something that occupies you when you've finished up in the shop. Like mending the settee for example.*

She was right about most things, Mary: he couldn't relax. Although he moaned about being a butcher, having to put up with the miserable customers, he couldn't *not* do it. He wasn't lazy in that respect and when he was working he felt calmer. It was when he stopped that the bad feelings flooded in. He couldn't settle on anything. He didn't have the *oomph* as Mary called it. He felt it had been all sucked out of him.

He couldn't actually explain to Mary what it felt like: it was a constant churn in the gut; a whirling head full of black thoughts and a racing heart that sometimes made it difficult to breathe. Sometimes he felt remote, as though he was acting out a role in a world he didn't feel part of. His brain felt as if it was in a constant fog. At night, his past flashed back in nightmares and he sweated until his pyjamas were soaked through. He cried out in his sleep. And then there were the shakes and now the skitters. He wondered if she knew how he must be suffering with something they didn't have the name for. If she did, she never said. Perhaps if it had a name it would make it easier. It would prove it existed. And if it existed, then it could be treated. Perhaps she didn't believe it existed or that he might be a victim of it, because most of the time he tried not to show. It seemed it was only when he was physically ill – had the shits or looked poorly – that she appreciated that he was in any way really ill. He realised that it might be something more intense than just nerves.

He hated Saturdays. The thought of an empty afternoon and a whole day the next day with nothing to fill his mind was his idea of hell. He paced around the kitchen not knowing what to do with himself apart from rushing to the lavatory and allowing his head to fill with the fear of being caught out in his black market operation. He reckoned he was more afraid of being exposed by Mary than he was of a court of law. Then he veered to thinking that it might be better if he was found out, tried, and found guilty. Perhaps the punishment – behind bars, rather than by Mary – would be more lenient. He'd be glad when he was back in the shop on Monday, but for now he sorted the orders for Teddy's Saturday deliveries, finding a fleeting calm in the routine. A little like polishing shoes, or a fag, or a glass of whiskey, or placing a bet. But when it was done, there was an emptiness that was nothing like calm.

CHAPTER 33
TEDDY

Teddy rode his bike from the old stables up Beattie Street and around to the shop front. It was manageable when he was pedalling, but when he came to a stop, his legs were too short to reach the ground from the saddle and so he spread his legs either side of the cross-bar and aimed to keep his balance with only the tips of his shoes. No wonder they were always scuffed. Hand-me-down shoes were bad enough but at least they fitted him now without newspaper stuffed into the toes. But the hand-me-down bike was huge for him. Like his teeth. Froom teeth which his little, freckled face hadn't yet grown into.

He dismounted and leaned the bike up against the window sill. The greaseproof papers were already down and he could see his father through the window at the block, trimming fat and throwing bones down into the waiting meat tray. Some customers begged his father for a bag of bones for their dog while for others, the bones were enough to make a soup to feed a family.

His father turned his head towards him and pointed to the clock on the wall. He couldn't hear what he was saying through the glass, but it was probably, *what time of day do you call this? Get a lick on, Son. The army'd sort you out!*

Teddy could see that his deliveries for the morning were already packed and waiting on the counter top.

"All ship-shape and Bristol fashion," said his father, as Teddy came in, meaning that each individual meat order had been wrapped in newspaper and the name of the customer and the address, written on the corner. There was a number given to each so that Teddy could deliver it in a logical route without having to double back on himself.

Teddy loaded up the basket, mounted his bike, and set off up

Middle Road, standing tall in the pedals with his backside off the seat, as he struggled with the incline. His father had done the arranging this morning and the Rundles were first so he took the short cut to Maes Glas Road, turning right off Middle Road and cycling along the dirt and stone lane into Cwmbwrla Park.

It was here he saw a car parked up near the entrance: a black Morris 10. At first he thought it was Arthur's as he sped past over the bumps, but when he looked back over his shoulder, he could see there were two men seated up front. Men he didn't recognise. Men in dark suits and ties. Perhaps they were spies. Perhaps it was true what people were saying about the Italians. Perhaps these men were looking for evidence. Perhaps informers. He picked up pace on the bike and went hell for leather along the tarmacked park path that led to Maes Glas Road. He could feel his heart thudding in his chest which he didn't put down solely to the effort of cycling. He wished Raymond was with him. Raymond would know.

He dismounted at the Rundles, leaning his bike up against the wooden fence of the pocket garden of their small two-up, two-down house. He looked around for signs of the car and the two strange men. Nothing. He wasn't being followed then, nor likely to be hauled into the back seat to be blindfolded and interrogated. He sighed and walked up the path to the Rundle's front door and hammered the knocker.

Mr and Mrs Rundle took a while to answer. Teddy didn't usually get impatient that they were old and doddery, but that day, felt bothered by something that he couldn't explain. A sensation that he needed to get going. At last they came smiling to the door and he handed over the meat and they handed over the cash along with a small tip. Good as gold, they were. Never forgot to tip.

It was then that he heard a car pull up outside. He stretched himself up to his full height of four foot ten, strutting back along the path. *Never show your fear*, his father had told him many a time. *Buggers can smell the stench of it a mile away.* He secured the gate and walked up to his bike, not once giving the two strangers eye contact.

But that didn't stop them turning off the engine, and getting out of the car, and walking towards him. He'd play it cool. Polite. No cheek.

"Weights and Measures," said the one who'd been in the driving seat, speaking for both of them, and clarifying their roles in the Ministry.

Phew. They weren't spies after all. But what did the *bloody Weights and Measures,* as his father called them, want with him?

"You delivering for Mr Froom, the butcher?" asked the other man who'd so far remained silent.

"Yes, Sir. My father."

"Don't mind if we check a few things, do you? Just to make sure?" said the driver man.

"No," said Teddy, pointing to the basket and stepping back.

But the men didn't move forward as he expected.

"Back at the shop, we mean," said the driver man again, in a voice that was firm and without emotion.

Teddy got on his bike. If he pedalled like hell, he could retrace his route and take the short cut back through the park and speed down the hill to warn his father about the men from the Ministry. Teddy hoped that his father hadn't been doing anything underhand with the meat, the meat that was in his basket now ready to be unwrapped and put on trial on the Avery scales.

Outside the shop, Teddy unclipped the basket from his bike. As he did, he noticed the two customers inside turn their heads, as did his father. His father's expression was initially one of concern: Teddy read it as, *Are you alright, Son? You're not ill, are you? Haven't had an accident, have you?* Through the window, Teddy gave him the thumbs-up sign which allayed those initial fears but instigated new ones. And then he entered the shop with the meat.

"I'm alright, Dad," he said, walking around to his father's side of the counter and placing the basket on the small chopping block. "Weights and Measures are on their way."

Teddy noted his father's face blanche, his lips losing colour. His father didn't say anything, but carried on slicing liver and then taking it to the scales to be weighed. As he did, the men from the Ministry pulled up outside. Teddy wondered why his father was so worried. Surely not. Not his father, who dealt curtly with the liver customer, bidding her good day before she left the shop. She nosed into the car and looked back over her shoulder to watch his father, as though she was relishing the thought of some drama in the row, a chance to gorge herself on some unexpected gristle.

As his father was serving the single remaining customer, Teddy watched the men get out of the car, the one in the passenger seat reaching into the back seat for his brief case. They meant business. There'd be paperwork, everything would be noted, go down in the book. You didn't mess with the Ministry. They stepped into the shop and made eye contact with his father and stood silently at the back, under the empty meat hooks, and waited until the last customer had left.

"Good morning, Gentlemen," said his father, as he walked to the door, turned the sign and drew the bolt.

Teddy stood, silent witness, at the block, while the man with the brief case explained to his father that it was just a routine check, that they trusted, that he, like them, had a duty to ensure that the letter of the law was being followed especially in times such as this when there was never more of a need for upholding standards and ensuring fair shares for all.

"If you'd be so good as to weigh each of the individual items in your boy's basket," said the man with the briefcase, opening it up and extracting his book and pen.

Teddy took the first parcel and handed it to his father. He could see that his father's hands were shaking as he unwrapped it so that the Ministry men could see the two lamb chops inside.

"Place them on the scales, if you would, Mr Froom," said the man without the pen and notebook.

His father did as he was told. The men said they had to make sure things tallied. That the price per pound equated with the cost of the order which was written on the newspaper corner. His father picked up an appropriate brass weight and placed it on the empty balance tray and together everyone assembled watched the arrow point to the price. So far, so good. Two lamb chops at 1s 6d per pound weighed up perfectly: 8 ounces in total weight came to came to came to 9d exactly. Teddy watched the men note it down in their book and saw his father relax slightly. The sums added up in terms of him not short selling weight wise and came within the legal ration limit of 1s 2d per customer.

And so his father worked his way through all the orders: breasts and necks of lamb, minced beef, stewing steak, all the cheaper and slow-cooking cuts that the neighbourhood preferred now that the ration had to stretch. Teddy wondered if it was the same in the west of the town, whether the boys in his class at school and their families – the lawyers and the dentists and the surgeons – were on the cheap cuts yet. Perhaps the war was a leveller but he expected some weren't following the rules. There were always those that thought themselves different from the rest. He was glad that his father was following the rules and couldn't understand why he'd looked so taken aback when he'd told him about the imminent inspection.

As his father was weighing the last order – some pork belly – his mother appeared with a cup of tea in her hand. Teddy watched as she stood still and looked at the scales along with all the others and waited for the arrow to stop.

"All seems in order," said the man with the notebook. "We won't trouble you anymore, Mr Froom. Thank you for your cooperation. Good day to you."

Teddy set about re-wrapping the orders, while his father walked to the door and pulled back the bolt to let the inspectors out. After they'd gone, he slid the bolt back again to locked.

"What the heck's been going on here?" asked his mother as she placed the cup and saucer on the counter. "You look like you've seen a ghost, Jim."

"It's all in order, Mary," his father replied, "But customers will have to have a bit of patience for a while. Nature calls."

CHAPTER 34
JIM

[handwritten: Where Dada was]

Things settled down again at 141 after that episode, including Jim's stomach. When the men from the Ministry had invaded his shop, he'd thought the game had been up. Be just his luck for it to be over before it had hardly begun. But since he'd been officially absolved from any wrongdoing, he'd convinced himself that he'd continue to get away with things. He had an air of invincibility about him. Mary had called him cocky, said that he had a swagger about him that she didn't much like. A smugness even. *Be careful, Jim Froom,* she'd said. *The higher you think you are, the further you fall.*

While Mary was out getting groceries one day, he lifted the lid of her piano, and did his sums in his little, black book. He'd never be a rich man. But he wanted to believe he could keep a household and prove his bloody sister Kit wrong. Her and her bloody brightly burning gas light! Bit by bit it would surely come if he took things steady. A little win now and again on the horses and a few bob on the black market and he'd get there. Give Mary and the kids the life he hadn't been able to offer them so far. This war could go on for years. In a way he was glad it hadn't been over by Christmas as some had predicted, as the longer it went on, the more chance he had from profiting from it. It was strange the thought that there were all these privations on the home front when nothing at all seemed to be happening in Cwmbwrla. Though there was talk afoot that Norway was going to be invaded at any minute and Jerry had made another air raid on Scapa Flow and that awful weasel of a man, Chamberlain, had been on the wireless again with some nonsense that Hitler 'had missed the bus' by not invading Britain earlier. So perhaps they would get it hard soon enough. All of a sudden he was shocked at the person he was and his capability for wrongdoing and deceit. Then he thought of William and his legs went wobbly.

It turned out to indeed be true that Huw Evans and the Gower farmer were under investigation. The story made the inside page of the *South Wales Evening Post* on Friday, 3rd May and Mary took relish in reading the article out to Jim as they sat in front of the range that evening. 'POLICE DISCOVER PIG IN HEARSE' it shouted in bold lettering, which she enunciated with equal drama and foreboding.

"Well, well," she said. "Huw Evans. Who would have thought, eh, Jim? His poor wife and kids having to read this. The shame of it all."

"It's not certain yet, Mary," he replied. "Everyone is innocent until proven guilty, remember."

"Come on, Jim, the driver's already owned up. It says here he's been charged – and the farmer, Mervyn Pritchard from Rhossili – and that it will go to court, but it is unlikely that they'll go to prison, rather that they will receive a hefty fine…I suppose the Law has to make an example of them. Profiteering like that. Disgusting, don't you think?"

Jim nodded but didn't reply. He was thinking of Huw's wife and kids – their standing in the community. How Huw would ever build his business back up, he didn't know. He thought he was the only one up to no good and it seemed the whole bloody butchery and farming business was up to their necks in it all.

To divert himself, and avoid conversation for a while, he picked up the *Daily Sketch* and turned to the back pages. It was a big weekend for racing. The Two Thousand Guineas was on the next day at Newmarket. He'd always fared quite well at Newmarket. And he felt good about this one. He studied the form and was drawn to *Diebel*. The French thoroughbred was having a reasonably good season but more than that, he was fascinated with the jockey: Charlie Elliot. He was a feisty fellow and had started off as just a groom's son, so it was a rags to riches story. A little like Cinderella. He thought of that day in the kitchen when he slipped on Mary's shoe as gently as he'd been able and had wished life could be a fairy tale, complete with a happy ever after ending.

And he thought of Teddy. It still hadn't quite gone from his head the notion that his son could make it as a jockey and make them all a fortune if he didn't grow anymore. But that was what it was. A notion. He'd have loved to have been some toff on a racehorse back then. He had to try and let go of the past and concern himself with the present. And his son's future.

He took the pencil from behind his right ear and circled a line around *Diebel* for the three-thirty. He'd go for an accumulator on all the favourites for the three races that went before the big one. A half-crown, which wouldn't break the bank. The stakes were high but he looked at what he was risking with his reputation anyway and convinced himself that his luck would run with him. He'd ring Frank in the morning and send Teddy around with his stake money. If he came good, he'd win a fair few quid, make Mary happy and say goodbye to any more pigs and worry. He was well overdue a big win.

CHAPTER 35

MARY

Next day, while Mary stood at the sink washing the breakfast dishes, she looked out into the back yard. It was a sunny, early May day, just the odd fluffy white cumulus and no apparent threat of rain. She was hopeful she and Jim would have a brisk morning in the shop and finish up early, in the hope that they might even take Rhoda out for a walk in the belief that she'd sleep well at night. Perhaps they could have a little Sunday lie in too if they were lucky.

She watched Jim standing in the bottom yard swinging his wooden clubs. He hadn't felt like much to eat and had gone outside instead to get some exercise and take advantage of the weather. Whenever he picked up the varnished clubs, his repertoire was the same, juggling like a tired circus performer. He caught her eye and smiled. She hoped his mood would last and she'd be having a good patch.

She leaned across the sink and put the window on the latch to let some of the precociously warm air into the kitchen. It would seem that spring had not only seeped into her and Jim but also the little robin whom she could see, as well as hear. She'd thought up until this moment that robins only cheeped their spring song from concealed perches. A fat chance of that at 141 where there wasn't a tree or a bush in sight. This little robin must have felt at home as it was there, in full sight, on top of the metal holder around which she wound the washing line on the post.

Jim had never failed to look after this tiny bird all through the winter and now it looked as though it was singing just for him. A wistful song, its trill notes descending quickly from high to low. Mary filled up when she saw Jim stop his club-swinging, looking at her to see if she'd noticed his little chum. He was nothing more than a child himself sometimes, wanting to be acknowledged for something he'd done right. Though he smiled, there seemed always a deep sense of sadness in his eyes, as though he were constantly living his life in the minor key. She could see why he and the robin made good friends. Momentarily, she felt the same. Despite the years, and the trials, and never being out of each other's sight or from under each other's feet, they were in tune with each other. And it was amplified by the sound of spring that the robin announced in their ordinary back yard, until a cloud temporarily blocked out the sun, the robin ceased to chirp, and Jim turned and walked down to the old stables to take his clubs back before opening up the shop.

Mary kissed Jim on the cheek as he came back and through the scullery.

"What's got into you?" he asked.

"Spring. That's what's got into me, Jim Froom. Let's try and make the most of it this afternoon. Have a change," she said, as he walked away from her, shutting the door into the passage behind him.

Behind the door, Mary stood listening. She could hear him stop at the telephone and take the receiver off the cradle, dial the operator and ask her for the exchange to put him through to Swansea 2391. Frank, she thought, knowing full well that Jim was at it again. Hardly a day would go by without him having a flutter. It was like an illness he couldn't save himself from. She heard him list his preferences for Newmarket, heard him telling Frank that he knew in his blood that these punts would come good today. And then she heard him tell Frank that he could pay him when he'd call on Tuesday. He replaced the handset then and made his way into the shop, whistling with every step.

After what seemed like the right time, she made her way into the shop and started to unhook the greaseproof papers from the window. As she did, she couldn't stop herself:

"I couldn't help but overhear you just now, Jim. On the phone to that bloody Frank again. You know how I feel about the betting, but it's why you said to him, *when he'd call on Tuesday*. It sounded as if it were a regular thing, him calling on Tuesdays.

A habit. Like your bloody betting."

"He doesn't call on Tuesdays, Mary. Why would he? It's just that I feel so certain about today's bets coming good, that it's automatic he'd come Tuesday to hand over the winnings to me," he said, helping Mary unpick the hooks, and paying her back with a kiss.

"I don't like you cocky, Jim. Perhaps even less than when you're jittery. I'd like you to be just somewhere-in-the-middle Jim, if that's not too much to ask."

"I do try, Mary. Honestly I do. But that's the truth."

"I'd hate you to lie to me, Jim."

Jim looked at the clock. Nine o' clock. On the hour. He walked to the door and opened up, glad that their irritating customers would take the intensity out of the conversation and shift her focus for a few hours.

After lunch, Mary told Jim to get himself scrubbed up and changed. They had the afternoon to themselves and little Rhoda.

Jim and Mary walked along Weavers Avenue, each holding one of Rhoda's little hands. Whenever she gave the instruction, they swung her into the air, her shouting, *and again*, each time. Mary realised that although she constantly moaned about how Rhoda took it out of her at her age, she knew she wouldn't have many more moments like this. With every swing, she felt all her children, each in their own turn, enjoying this simple pleasure, mother and father on either side, in step, a peculiar family rhythm.

As they turned left through the alley and into the expanse of the park, she felt the sun on her face. This same sun, would be warming William's face wherever he might be. She wondered why, when everything was so perfect and so beautiful – the sunshine, her walking with her husband and her daughter, people she loved, people who loved her – it somehow made her melancholic. Perhaps it was too perfect. Too beautiful to last. Just like the fairy tales that started 'Once Upon a Time', things only happened once and then they were gone in a puff, like the fragile head of a dandelion clock.

It never ceased to amaze Mary that in the midst of the labyrinth of almost identical grey, terraced houses, was the park.

Even though the top field had been taken over by anti-aircraft lights and barrage balloons, there were still acres of green spaces where people thronged in their hundreds, all with the same idea of enjoying the first days of spring in the open air while there was still peace in Cwmbwrla. But when she looked, really looked hard, it was the absence of young men she noticed. Instead, the men around Jim's age were dressed up in their whites and playing cricket near the pavilion, where a few older men urged the teams on. The sound of the ball on willow was soothing, as if nothing was going on in the world to disrupt the patterns of British life.

"Never thought of taking up cricket, Jim?" she said.

"Cricket? Me? Not enough excitement, Mary."

"Exactly. That's why I thought it would be good for you. And you'd have the company of men of your own age."

"I prefer your company, Mary."

"Don't soft soap me, Jim. Don't ever soft soap me!"

"Let's have an ice cream, then, if the kiosk is open. Cool things down."

At the mention of ice cream, Rhoda was shouting for a Walls as she knew the little cart that used to come around the streets with *stop me and buy one* written on it. The ingredients were still getting through and luckily, the kiosk was open so Mary got in the queue and bought three cornets. They walked across the grass, licking the melting vanilla from the wafer cones, until they found a spot to sit under the trees near the Old Age Pensioners' meeting hall.

Mary took out the old blanket stuffed in her shopping bag and spread it on the ground, the three of them sitting down to finish off their ice creams. When they had, Mary took a cotton handkerchief tucked up her sleeve and spat on it before wiping around Rhoda's mouth and chin. Down the years, she'd wiped away the mess from all their children. Rhoda'd be the last she'd see to like this. Who would Mary be then? She looked at the mucky handkerchief, the M monograph stitched in blue in the corner and she wondered what it stood for: Mary? Mother? Martyr? She was all these things. But who could she have been? Who might she be in the future or was it already too late? She put away the thoughts along with the handkerchief which she stuffed up her sleeve again.

She vowed she would live in the present for a couple of hours, enjoy what she'd been blessed with. She told Rhoda to pick some daisies and to make sure they had long, juicy stems. She watched her little girl bend in earnest to do so, coming back to her with a smile and a handful of daisies. Mary then instructed Jim to do the honours, by which she meant make a chain with them that could be used as a coronet, a bracelet, a necklace, anything and everything that Rhoda would need to make her a princess for an hour or so. Mary watched Jim try to be as delicate as he could, using the nail of his left thumb to make an incision in each fragile, green stem without damaging it and threading another daisy through until he was done. Mary didn't want to break the spell by talking, but she was thinking that Jim was a lovely father and that she could have done a lot worse.

When Rhoda was done with the daisies and bedecked in white petals, Mary turned to the buttercups.

"These can tell lots of things about you," she said to Rhoda, holding one of the golden flowers under her tiny chin. "See. You like butter!"

"How can you tell?" she asked

"Your neck is glowing and golden. You can't see; but I can."

"Do it to Daddy," squealed Rhoda. "See if he likes butter, too."

Mary winked at Jim and held the buttercup under his chin.

"Am I glowing and golden?" asked Jim

"You are indeed. I can tell you like butter. I can also tell you like betting. This flower speaks the truth."

Rhoda strained to see if she was able to see what her mother said she could.

"Mummy's teasing," she said to her father.

"I don't think so; but I won't argue today," he said, laughing. "Which reminds me. I need to check the time."

Mary looked as Jim reached for his pocket watch. She knew he was thinking about the horses, wondering how they were getting on as it was coming up to four o'clock. Whatever was going to happen had happened by now.

The world might have been in a state of flux, but the mood of the afternoon in the park was carried back home to 141. Mary had actually enjoyed her time with Rhoda, make-believing with the flowers. These moments of joy would be gone in a flash. She even allowed Rhoda to drag a chair to the scullery sink for her to fill a couple of empty milk bottles with water. She was going to make scent she said, by unpicking the petals of the daisies and buttercups and dropping them into the water. Mary felt calm. Maybe she wasn't such a bad mother after all.

Jim, on the other hand, had headed straight for the phone. Mary thought it unusual that he'd left the door open, as if he didn't care a jot that she might be eavesdropping. Perhaps he was trying to show how confident he was in his belief that today would be the day he'd come good on the horses. Mary wished she could believe it too and that he – and they – wouldn't come a cropper.

She needn't have worried. As soon as the handset was placed back in the cradle, she could hear him actually singing, *pack up your troubles in your old kit bag,* and then turning, she could see him, and hear him, marching quick time across the lino in the living room until he came to a halt on the scullery steps, where he saluted and said, *Presenting and ready for duty, Ma'am*, and clicked his heels.

"What are you so pleased with yourself about?" she asked.

Jim relaxed his pose and rushed towards her, lifting her off the ground.

"I told you, I'd do it, didn't I?" he said.

"What? You mean you've actually won?"

"Won? We're quids in," he said, kissing her on the cheek and spinning her around. "This calls for a celebration."

"Are you telling me the truth?"

"Cross my heart and swear to die," said Jim, crossing his heart. "Open the whiskey, Mary. Let's get Doreen and Graham over. And Arthur. Have a bit of a sing-song."

"D'you know, Jim. I'd rather it be just you and me tonight. We had such a lovely afternoon and I don't want to break the spell."

Jim pulled her into him and she breathed in the moment and the distinctive smell of him, fearing that in this cocky state, when he thought the gods were with him, he might already have given the nod to reinvest the winnings.

Later, with Dora out for the night, Teddy down at Raymond's

for the evening, and Rhoda out for the count, Mary placed the whiskey and two tumblers on her knick-knack table in front of the range. They would have a quiet evening, just the two of them. Not as parents. Not as workers in the shop; but simply as Jim and Mary. Jim had wanted to get the news on the wireless but Mary had been firm and said, *No. Not tonight.* It was nothing but bad news coming down the airwaves these last few days: Norway not holding, Jerry about to go into France and the Low Countries. Even Chamberlain it seemed wouldn't hang on much longer. Tonight they'd talk. She wouldn't even pick up her knitting, she promised, as long as Jim gave her his full attention and promised not to study racing form on the back pages of the *Sketch*.

The evening ticked by, Mary topping up Jim's glass as it became empty, making sure she paced herself. It was warm in front of the range and she didn't even bother to put on a light but just let the glow of the fire make the room rosy. She and Jim enjoyed their own little living room and the simple pleasure of each other's company, until she could see that he'd nodded off, his glass held precariously in his hand, chin to his chest, mouth open and snoring. She took the glass away without him waking. She let him sleep for a while and sat in the warm silence looking at him, thinking about the day and the fact that life wasn't really that bad after all. Sometimes she thought there was more intimacy in this comfortable silence of years than there'd ever been in sexual intercourse.

She finally told Jim that it was time for bed, but he snored on. She shook him gently on his shoulder, though there was hardly any response. Well and truly half-cut. She called his name over and over, urging him to stand up, knowing that she was going to have trouble getting up the stairs. She placed her right arm against the small of his back and her left under his elbow and strained to pull him upright. Then she linked arms with him and supported him across the living room and along the passage, leaving the warmth of the room and the evening behind her. *I love you, you know, Mary Read*, he kept trying to mouth, her telling him to shut up and reserve his energy for what came ahead. She counted him up the treads of the stairs, him repeating every number after her like a small child. She supported him along the landing and got him on to the bed, where he lay back on top of the covers.

"Let's get you undressed, you drunken idiot," she said firmly as she tried to get her breath back.

"Come here and give us a kiss," he said.

Mary ignored him and knelt down and unlaced his shoes, slipped them off one at a time and placed them together neatly at the side of the bed. She peeled down each sock, arranging each, side by side and then making them one by folding them over at the tops, popping them inside one of his shoes. Then she leaned across the bed, undoing his tie, and opening the buttons of his shirt, struggling to remove it, one arm at a time. She watched his chest rise and fall above his vest where his once red chest hair was turning white and wiry. She ran her fingers through it gently; but he did not move. His leather trouser belt, she undid easily, smiling that it was on the last notch now, remembering how once it had been on the first. She unzipped his flies and tugged his trousers down his legs so that they fell around his ankles. She laughed to herself at the sight of him lying there like that. She wished she'd had a camera. That would sort his vanity. She pulled them off and then, with both hands, raised his legs and swung them on to the bed. She couldn't budge his head on to the pillows nor get him under the covers; he was like a dead weight. So she took the spare blanket from on top of the wardrobe and placed it over him, leaving him there for the time being while she went back downstairs to tidy up. He was going to be a sorry state in the morning.

She stood at the sink again just as she had done at the start of the day. With the blackouts up, she suddenly felt sealed in, her chest tight. She washed the tumblers in soapy water and rinsed them under the tap, then picked up a T-towel and started to dry them. As she did, the silence in the room became strangely charged, a thick pressing silence as if it had some sort of texture.

She could feel her scalp tingling, noticed the fine hairs on her forearms standing up. She felt chilled. She turned and placed the glasses on the table and folded the T-towel and placed it on the Rayburn rail to dry overnight. She felt she wasn't alone, that there was an invisible something in the scullery. She thought for a minute that it might have been the drink, but she felt stone cold sober as she walked and sat down on the settle to get herself together and try and warm up.

It was then that she heard the familiar strains of her best loved song, her elder son's soprano voice singing, *O for the wings of a dove*. She was wrapt in the music and wondered whether the words and haunting melody which filled the room were a sign from above, some strange portent meant for her ears only.

CHAPTER 36
TEDDY

Something woke Teddy out of his deep sleep the next morning. He came to with a start and wondered what it had been. Then, he remembered what day it was: Sunday. 5th May. Good. No school. No need to rush. Whatever noise it was that had roused him initially was no more. The house was still silent. It couldn't have been anything much as no-one had moved. He turned over and thought he'd go back to sleep for a while. As he did, he heard the knocking on the front door.

There was no sign from his parents in the front bedroom and then he realised it must be his sister Dora coming back early after a Saturday night at her friend's house again. She'd probably forgotten her key. Judging by the state of his mother and father last night after they'd hit the whiskey, he imagined they wouldn't have heard a thing. He'd let them lie in. It was their one day of rest after their week long slog. *Go on Teddy, there's a good boy*, said the little voice in his head. He checked the time. 8 o'clock.

With bare feet, he crept along the landing, down the first three treads and paused at the dog-leg just to make sure he hadn't disturbed anyone. Then he carefully negotiated the steep run of twelve stairs, and tiptoed across the tiles in the passage. Opening the half-glass door, he stepped into the front porch, stretched slightly to turn the latch on the solid wooden front door, and opened it to the pavement.

The boy was standing there on the other side. Teddy didn't have to be told. He knew by the blue uniform and the cap and the leather pouch attached to the belt and the telegram that was held in his hand. The messenger couldn't have been much older than he was himself; they were about the same height though they'd dressed him up in long trousers for his role. Not even old enough for a motorbike, his red-painted push-bike was leant up against the shop window. Teddy looked the boy in the eyes and the boy told him that he was sorry to have to deliver this news and simply passed the thin, typed paper from his hands into Teddy's, picked up his bike, and was gone into the rain that had arrived unexpectedly overnight.

Teddy stood in his pyjamas, rooted to the doorstep, knowing in that moment, that everything was changed for ever. He felt both a fearful child and a sudden adult with the knowledge only he possessed. It was there, he knew, in the unopened telegraph that was shaking in his hands. *The Air Ministry regrets to announce that your son Wireless Operator and Gunner, William Peter Froom, has been killed in active service. Letter to follow.*

He would have liked to stay where he was and make it all different. He wanted not to have heard the knock, wished that the hands on his bedroom clock could tick backwards, to make everything not have happened.

He walked onto the pavement, the wet stone cold on the soles of his feet, the dank rain drizzling on his head and his pyjama top. He stood in the road and looked up to the two sash windows above the shop, the curtains still drawn. He felt a lump in his throat and swallowed hard. He was a boy who still wore short trousers but he had to do what boys in long trousers did, what the messenger boy had just done.

He went back into the porch, and pulled the door as quietly as he could behind him. He stood shivering there, a shivering of the sort he'd never experienced before in all of his thirteen-and-a-half-years: from the inside out rather than the outside in.

He went to the scullery to make tea for his mother and father. He'd heard from somewhere, at some time, that he had to put plenty of sugar in the tea for shock. He didn't know what he was going to say or how he was going to break the news. He'd heard his mother and his father talk often enough about not knowing what to say or not being able to find the right way to comfort people when they had lost a loved one. He knew then the reason why. Sometimes there were no words.

With the telegram tucked into the breast pocket of his striped pyjamas, he carried the tray with the two cups and saucers along the passage, the tea slopping into the saucers. It didn't matter. Not now. The meat hook hanging from the ceiling that kept the glass door from the passage to the shop slightly ajar, confronted him. Being a Sunday, no dead animals were hanging from it, but he remembered all the things he'd seen hanging from that hook in the past: William's dirtied RAF regulation, sausage kit bag stuffed with Christmas presents when he'd come home on leave at Christmas like Santa Claus; his cocked air-force man's hat; his empty great coat; sides of beef, carcasses of lambs, pigs hanging snout down – all merging into one another.

He thought about his brother being identified as just one part of a whole, a cog in the machine: Wireless Operator; squadron number 59; serial number 619761, the numbers and ranks that would label him in the telegram or in the letter to come just like the way his father would categorise the cuts of meat in the diagram on the wall behind his block to make it easy for his customers: forequarter, hindquarter, topside, rump, fillet, brisket, breast, belly, loin, scrag, knuckle, best end of neck. He wouldn't be able to explain the connection in his train of thought if someone had asked him. It was just the tightness in his tummy and an acid taste that kept rising into his throat from an empty space inside him. His nineteen-year-old big brother had been reduced to the telegram he carried in his pyjama pocket, and it didn't appear to him here on the home front that the war had even started yet. To the customers passing the time of day in the shop, it was the phoney war.

Why he chose to knock on his parents' bedroom door that morning, he didn't know. He never usually bothered. In fact, he rarely went in there at all. It's where his parents went to have some time to themselves, and it was a sort of an unwritten rule at 141 that no-one disturbed them. Especially when they'd let themselves go for a few hours on a Saturday evening.

There was no response, so he picked up the tray, turned the brass knob and went in. With the curtains still pulled and the greyness of the day outside, it was dim in the room. And it smelled: his father's sweet-stale whiskey breath still hung in the air and they were both still out for the count. His mother had obviously managed to get herself into bed and lay under the covers, but his father was positioned diagonally, facedown on top of the eiderdown, his bare legs visible where he'd kicked off the blanket.

Teddy called softly to his parents in the hope of easing them as much as was possible into the day they would have to face. He stood there at his mother's side of the bed, repeating *Mum? Mum?* and shaking her shoulder gently. He thought he'd have more chance of waking her, judging by the look of his father. He also thought that she would be the one who could stand the news better. He imagined it would be his mother who would have to tell his father when she managed to rouse him from his stupor.

"Teddy?" she said, coming round and raising her head from the pillow. "What's the matter?"

He couldn't answer. The words were stuck somewhere between brain and mouth. Putting the tray on the floor, he bent towards her, and tried to encase her in his little arms.

"Oh Mum!" he said.

He could tell by the way that her shoulders rose and her body tensed that he didn't have to say anymore. He sat down on the counterpane and reached for her reading glasses on the little table at the side of the bed. Her eyes still heavy with sleep, he eased the glasses gently onto her face, adjusting the arms around her ears.

And then he reached for the telegram in his pyjama pocket and handed it over to her. He placed his small hand on the top of her arm and rubbed the Wincyette sleeve of her nightgown gently, as if by rote, the way she'd rub his tummy when he'd have an ache. He watched her read the message, once, twice, three times, and then she folded the paper and placed it on the table. She didn't cry. She didn't shout. She simply said, *You'll need to hold the fort today, Teddy. Just until your sister gets home. I'm going to have to break the news to your father. He's going to take some tending to.*

"I've made some tea, Mum," he said. "Three sugars."

"You're a good boy, Teddy. Leave us alone now though. Close the door on the way out."

"Shall I open the curtains?"

"No. We'll leave them shut today."

Teddy turned and left his mother sitting up in the bed, his

father at her side, snoring and oblivious.

Teddy was relieved that Dora was not yet home. He went back into his room, and lay on the bed. He just wanted to be on his own for a while. It was then he started to cry. He'd never cried like this before, it was almost without sound, just the feel of tears pouring down his cheeks as he lay on his side with his knees tucked up to his chest like a little ball, trying to make itself smaller and smaller. He gazed at William's empty single bed. Thought of the last time he'd seen him there at Christmas. How long he lay like this, he couldn't tell.

He heard a sound coming from his parents' room that didn't sound human. It was the sound of a discordant wail, two primitive beasts howling into the early morning, a sound he'd only ever heard before when he'd been taken to the slaughterhouse with his father.

CHAPTER 37

JIM

Jim didn't dress: the need to just didn't enter his head. He just about managed to throw on his dressing gown and place his feet in his slippers.

He sat back on the bed where Mary was sitting, fully dressed, all buttoned up in one of her better dresses. Her hands were clasped in her lap and she seemed as still as death herself, staring into a space that was unfathomable for them both. Yet she'd dressed, as though the dress would stop her falling apart. He put his arm around her and realised that as ever, it was as much for the strength that he hoped would seep from her to him than for the support he could offer her. He always let his feelings get the better of him, but he realised there on the bed, that he was a self-pitying creature and had brought about most of the so-called tragedies that had befallen him so far in life on himself. Was this the same?

Mary didn't respond to his touch; she was stuck somewhere he couldn't reach. He rose and went out of the bedroom, shuffling along the landing as though his legs too were stuck in the slime and sludge of the past that was always with him, dragging him down. In the bathroom, he cleaned his teeth as his mouth felt like the bottom of a bird's cage, and wiped his face with a flannel. His reflection told him he should shave. Never a day passed when he didn't feel compelled to shave. Never be seen on parade unless clean shaven, was the rule. But this was a day like no other and even though he looked gaunt and the red and grey bristles made him look older, he couldn't muster the strength. A man would be disciplined for this. He stared at his reflection and he felt it respond: *It's your fault. You killed him. You and your pathetic, bloody useless war against the government.*

It must have been gone eleven by the time he and Mary ventured downstairs. He'd lost all track of time and everyone already together downstairs must have decided to let them be. Teddy had obviously let Louisa know and she'd dropped everything as she always did and come over the wall to help as Rhoda was now plonked on her lap having, what Louisa always called, a cwtch. Teddy was going over the rug with the Ewebank and Dora was in the scullery as he could hear pots being clattered. His belly turned at the smell of frying onions. She was obviously trying to do her best, but he doubted he'd have the stomach for anything.

Dora charged into the living room, breaking the silence that he and everyone else seemed scared to do. *Mum? Dad? What happened? What did it say? How do you know it's true? There might have been a mistake. There are often mistakes. When will they write and tell you more? Sybil will have to be told. Are you going to tell Sybil today? She needs to know about it. I'll come with you to tell Sybil.*

It was like someone had turned the tap on full when she spoke. The words kept gushing out and Jim wanted someone to find the bloody stopcock and turn her off at source. She was usually so restrained and self-controlled. Yet she was only voicing what he was thinking, that there'd been a mix up and it would all be clarified and undone when the letter came. She'd come home from her night at a friend's house to this on the ordinariness of a Sunday morning in Cwmbwrla. Like him, and most people around here, the bloody war hadn't even started yet. It was somewhere else. The phoney war was suddenly not so phoney after all.

"Dora, please!" begged Mary. "Calm down. I know he's gone."

"How do you know for certain, Mary? Dora might be right," said Jim.

"He came to me last night," she said, in a matter-of-fact statement. "I'd just finished the washing-up and I was sitting on the settle and I felt him near me. And then I heard him singing, telling me in his own way. That's when I knew."

Jim watched Mary say all this and he looked at the others sitting there listening and he knew it to be true. Before the war he wouldn't have perhaps believed her. Her canny intuition. But the war had somehow made everyone's emotions chime with things in a way that often defied logic. It was as though they were all wearing invisible antennae that sensed things they couldn't see with the naked eye.

Jim watched as Louisa got up from her chair and hugged Mary for she understood what it was like to lose a child. Jim watched Teddy and Dora and he knew they understood the enormity of it, each in their particular way. And Rhoda. Even little Rhoda understood that something big had happened as she burrowed in deeper and deeper to Louisa's ample chest.

CHAPTER 38

MARY

By the evening, the trough of low pressure had pushed through and the sunshine was back. As she came out of the house, Mary stopped for a couple of moments: the sky looked over-bright, as if it were mocking her. The neighbourhood was deserted. She'd forgotten it was Sunday until she heard the two bells at St Luke's ringing out for Evensong. And then she thought of William in his cassock and his white surplice, the picture she proudly had hanging on the living room wall of him as a chorister on the trip to Canada. Why the hell would a boy who'd done that want to join the Air-Force without having to be called up? Perhaps he did though. He was never going to be the one to stay home and be a butcher's boy.

She crossed the road and walked along the pavement to 122. She said she'd do this on her own. Jim hadn't offered to come with her: *I just can't Mary. I can't bear to break it to the girl. You're good at things like these.* At least Dora had some back bone and had begged to come. But no. She had to do this her way. She walked up the steps and paused to get her breath back and herself together before she'd have to knock the door. She looked back across the road: the row was in shadow.

She didn't feel she had the strength to do what she had to do; but someone had to do it. And that someone was always her. She wondered whether one day, she'd suddenly collapse under the pressure of all the years and all the events she'd had to manage and juggle. When she was dead herself, would someone take a stick and poke at her, to see if she really was, because they had something they needed her to do? But for now she had to keep going. She breathed in. Set her jaw. Knocked the door.

"Sybil?" she said, surprised that in fact it was indeed Sybil who answered the door. She'd expected Mr or Mrs Bowen, but then remembered they'd be in chapel at Babell, praying for everybody's souls. "Alright if I come in?" said Mary.

"Excuse the state on me," said Sybil, ushering Mary along the passage. "I've just washed my hair and had a bath ready for work tomorrow. Is everything alright across the road? I'm sorry I haven't been over lately, I've been a bit up and down with my health."

Mary could tell by Sybil's non-stop gabble that she anticipated what was coming. She kept talking so she wouldn't leave a space where the news could get in. She was no more than a child, Sybil, dressed in her housecoat and a white towel turned into a turban around her hair, her face paler than she thought healthy.

Sybil showed her into the parlour on the right, where she asked her to sit down in one of the armchairs on either side of the fireplace. Sybil took her place opposite her. The sun streamed through the front window and the rays of light fell on her turban and she glowed like some strange ethereal creature.

"Sybil. I think you know why I've come over, don't you?"

"William?"

Mary nodded before getting up and going towards her. She knelt on the rug and pulled Sybil into her, wrapping her arms around her shoulders and drawing the girl's body into hers. She could feel Sybil shuddering, but no sound came out. It set off a similar implosion in her, beneath the surface, her body heaving in sympathy.

"Oh, Mrs Froom. What are we going to do?" Sybil cried, raising her head, the turban coming undone where she'd tucked it in at the neck, the damp towel, resting on her shoulders, her wet dark hair making her look crazed.

"It's Mary, Love," she replied, stroking Sybil's wet hair off her forehead. "I don't know what we're going to do, but we'll do what we have to do, because there's no other way."

"I only had a letter from him on Friday – look," she said, reaching into her dressing coat pocket and taking out the familiar thin-papered, censored envelope. "He said that he hoped he'd be getting some leave soon if Hitler didn't spoil his plans. He said he'd be writing to you soon, too."

Mary hoped he hadn't written, anticipating the dread she would feel if his letter came along with the one from the Ministry.

Mary got up from her knees and sank back in the armchair, wanting something to come over her that felt like a long, long sleep.

"Mary, I need to tell you something. William wanted to get married when he was home on leave next. We'd talked about it in the letters we sent back and forth. He was going to tell you when he came home and, of course, come and do the right thing and ask my father for my hand in marriage."

Mary reached for her handkerchief, as usual, tucked up her sleeve, and dabbed her eyes. All those dreams, wiped away in a jiff.

"But Mary, I need to tell you something else. We were going to get married sooner than I'd wanted to because…" she said, shifting forward in the chair and looking directly at Mary. "Because – and please don't judge me – I'm pregnant."

Mary twisted the handkerchief in her hands. It felt as if a grenade had been detonated and was swallowing her whole into the chasm it had created. But she could believe it when she looked at Sybil's wan face, looked at her dressing gown which she was almost filling, could believe it when she recalled Dora making tea while she and Sybil were chatting in the middle room and Dora telling her that Sybil wasn't herself and was having to take time off work. Of course it was more than yearning.

"Oh Sybil," said Mary,

"I couldn't not tell you, could I?"

"No. You couldn't. And there are more seven-month babies around Cwmbwrla than you'd believe. Sometimes it's best the arithmetic goes awry. And there'll be more. There's a war on, after all. You're young. And if it's any consolation, I had a seven-month baby with our Dora – not that Jim would ever own up to it, mind you. It was when he came back from the war. Yes, even we were young once… And William? He knew?"

"Yes, he knew."

"Good," said Mary, strangely comforted. "I'm glad he knew… but what about your mother and father? What have they said?"

"Nothing. As yet. I don't know how much longer I can keep it secret. Not until September."

"And Dora? Have you told her – I know you're almost joined at the hip."

"Yes, I've told her, and I asked her to keep it to herself. No offence, Mary."

Mary dabbed her eyes again, realising that there was such an imperceptible shift between despair and elation, and that even in the midst of sorrow there were moments of a strange kind of joy, as if to prove to her that she was alive, that she would go on living despite everything.

"What do you think your parents will say?" asked Mary,

"Well, they won't be happy and that's putting it mildly. You know how they think. According to them, it's a sin. I mean, what would their chapel friends say?"

"It won't be easy," said Mary. "And there's your health too. I mean, I don't think you've been going to the clinic and seeing a midwife, have you? You'll need to do that, Sybil. You really will."

"Dora's been keeping a close eye on things and looking after me. She is a nurse, after all. But yes, I will have to tell them at some stage. But as for my parents, shame is what they'll feel, Mary. Humiliation in the community. They've always told me that if I brought trouble into the house, I could pack my bags and they'd have nothing to do with me. I don't think there's anything I could do worse than be pregnant and bring a baby into the world."

"I'm sure we could get our heads together and come up with a list of things that are worse than having a baby. How about starting a war? But our door will always be open, Sybil. You need to know that. We're your family now, too."

"But what about Mr Froom – Jim?"

"Jim? Don't worry about him. I'll take care of that. I mean, he's got no leg to stand on when it comes to judging."

"I'll break the news to my parents about William tonight when they get back from chapel. Not about the baby, though. Not yet."

"He'd have made a wonderful father, our William. He was a good boy," said Mary.

"I know that, Mary," said Sybil, placing her hand on her abdomen. "That's the awful pity of it all."

By the time Mary got back home, Dora had put Rhoda to bed, and was standing scouring at the sink. Mary could tell by the vigour of her actions that Dora was on pins, anxious to find out what had played out between her and Sybil.

"You look terrible, Mum," she said. "All pale and puffy. It must have been awful for you. And Sybil."

"I'm alright. And Sybil will be too. I know about the baby and I know you know too, so stop going at those pans and sit down. You're not going to shape the future by scrubbing and scouring. Don't turn into your father," she smiled.

"It wasn't my place to tell you, Mum. I'm sorry."

"I know that, Love. Sybil was keen to tell me and to say it wasn't your fault that you were keeping it quiet. It's lovely to see you and Sybil so close. Friendship is a wonderful thing."

"Yes, Sybil's like family."

"And if it's any consolation, Dora. I'm in no position to be shocked by such things. And your father shouldn't dare pretend to be when the time comes. You're good at arithmetic. You know when your father and I got married. Remember you saw our certificate? You know your birthday. Sybil won't be the first or the last. As I said to her, there's nothing more natural than having a baby. It's about love in the end don't you think?"

"If only life were that simple," said Dora coming to lay her head on Mary's shoulder. "I'm so tired, Mum. Drained. I can only imagine how you're feeling. I'm going to go straight up to bed if you don't mind. Leave you and Dad to talk."

"Go you. I won't be long myself. I doubt whether your father will have much talking in him, you know what he's like. And you couldn't have got much sleep last night either, gallivanting wherever you were after a long shift. Anyway, I hope you manage to get some tonight. There'll be tough times ahead."

After Dora had left the scullery, Mary stood at the sink, unable to believe it was only the day before when she'd stood in the exact same position and her world had been a very different place. She thought about the park, the daisy chains, the buttercups, the ice cream and she felt a wave of guilt sweep over her that while she was out and about gadding, whatever had happened to her son was happening. Or had already happened. It was the not knowing the when or the where or the how or anything that made it worse. She would have to wait for the letter. And she had to talk about it to Jim. It would be like pulling teeth, the way he went in on himself.

She turned and made her way back to the living room, sidestepping the shoes that were lined up on the step, polished and buffed as normal, ready for the next day. But despite the routine and the apparent pattern of ordinary life that showed itself in the scullery, Jim was still not dressed nor shaved. He was sitting at the drop-leaved table at the side of the room, one leaf opened out, his marble-covered sales ledger and cash book open, his cash tin at the side. He always did his books on a Sunday. Even though they'd lost a son, it had to be business as usual. There were bills to be paid. Stomachs to be fed. There was never any let up when you were in business for yourself.

Mary went over and stroked his hair and he turned and kissed her hand.

"She knows now, Jim. It's all so real when you tell someone."

He didn't reply, but turned and put his head back in his books, totting up columns and then counting piles of coins and bundling pound notes and ten-shilling notes together. Later, he'd total up and curse as he did every Sunday evening, about there being no money in meat, and bloody customers. And later, Whiskey, the cat, would dash from the fireside to find safety as Jim shouted: *Scarper. Bugger this bloody cat to hell* and lift his leg as though he were going to boot him right up the arse all the way to Timbuktu.

Mary sat down in her place in the corner and picked her knitting up off the table. It was another pullover that she'd been underway with for William. The body of the sweater was complete, the sleeves too, ready for sewing up along the seams. The stitches around the polo neck would need to be picked up. Mary looked at the loose stitches enclosed in four, large safety pins ready for her to finish; but she couldn't make a start. What was the point?

In turn, she opened each safety pin looking at the looped stitches just hanging there. And then she took the end stitch and pulled, watching the pullover unravel and lose its shape, row by row, the plain and the purl, undoing. She increased her pace with every row, the navy jumper shrinking, disappearing before her eyes, until nothing but a long and tangled length of navy 3-ply wool lay on the rug at her feet. *There*, she said. *It's all come undone now.*

She could see Teddy over the top of her glasses, looking up from his homework that he was doing on his lap on a tray. The same tray that he'd brought the tea on earlier. Bless him.

"Have you got a minute?" she asked.

Teddy put the tray aside, and got up out of the chair and took a little three-legged stool that sat tucked in the corner and brought it close to Mary's feet. He eased himself down on to it, and facing her, held out both his little arms.

Mary took the wool and looped it on to the rigid fingers of Teddy's left hand and then on to the fingers of the right, over and over and over again in silence until she made a skein of wool in the figure of eight. Then, she reached over and removed the skein and placed it out of sight in the brass knitting box below the knick-knack table. The cast-off wool would come in handy again someday.

"I'm going up, Jim" said Mary, later.

"I'll be up in a bit," he said. "I'll just finish off down here."

Mary undressed and put on her nightdress, draped her goodish dress over the chair. It would do for the next day as there'd probably be lots of people coming in and out once they'd heard the news. Thank God it was Monday; not ideal, but better than having to open up the shop and try and put on a brave face for the customers. Jim would have to do the cutting up in the shop as per norm, poor bugger; but he'd be behind the greaseproof paper. She'd have to cope on her own when they'd come.

She sat in front of the dressing table mirror, unclipped her hair and began brushing it with the surprise brush that Jim had bought her for Christmas. It seemed like so long ago. She wondered if Jim had had an inkling. If he had, he never would have said. On she brushed, images flashing in and out of her head as she did. Her arm ached and she didn't know if it was from the time she had spent brushing or the picture she saw of William disappearing round the bend in the train on Boxing Day morning, her waving and waving until he was long gone. She felt her heart was actually breaking in her chest and she wondered if it were true that you could die of a broken heart. She didn't care if she did for a moment, and then she thought of Rhoda, Teddy, Dora, Jim and now Sybil. She couldn't die. She didn't have the luxury of dying. She was needed.

There was no need to turn on a light. The room was darkening and warm with the curtains having remained closed all day. She got into bed, put her head on the pillow in the hope that sleep would come and ease the pain. But sleep evaded it her. She heard Jim come into the room but she didn't speak and she knew he thought she was asleep. She could tell by the way he tried to be quiet when in fact he made more noise in trying.

"It's alright, I'm awake," she said.

"Sorry," he said, as he got under the covers.

Mary felt his side of the bed sink as he did. The feather mattress had come with them to Middle Road and it fitted them, held their bodies in its shape, dipping in the middle with the years. Mary was on her left side facing the wall, and she could feel Jim turn the same way, drawing closer to her. She didn't move towards him, or away from him, but just allowed him to nestle closer. She was cold. Cold with grief and shock and she needed the warmth of his body as she would a hot water bottle. She felt his right arm around her waist as he pulled her into his body. She let her body go of its own free will. She could feel his knees in the back of her thighs, his chest up against her back, his face burying into the neck of her nightdress as though he was a lost, little puppy looking for a stroke. She placed her hand over his and squeezed it. It was enough for him to know.

He raised her nightdress with his left hand and stroked her bare backside. She could feel his hardness pressing against her and she didn't resist. It was a strange feeling, not so much his desire for her, but an overwhelming need of her. It was if he was physically connecting to her in his grief in a way that he couldn't with words and she was surprised with herself that she needed him, too. It was an odd act, she thought. Functional there in the dimness. Him grunting for a few minutes, then soft and stilled, her shedding a few tears. It was as if they were trying to recreate the beginning of everything when all of it was ending. She couldn't explain the feeling. *Necessary,* was the word that would come closest to it. It didn't last long, and when it was over, Jim pulled her nightdress back down and said, *Sorry, Mary,* and she said, *It's alright Jim. It's alright.*

Later, as she lay on her back when Jim had fallen asleep, she was thinking about funerals and how there wouldn't be one for William, and the phrase, *in the midst of life we are in death* kept repeating over and over in her mind and it felt that she – he – they – perhaps shouldn't have had intercourse and how the Bowens might have thought it to be a despicable sin and wholly inappropriate and they'd be struck down by a God looking down on the sad comical pair of them in the feather bed. But at the same time she was thinking, *in the midst of death we are in life* and God, Jim's warmth was like oxygen, and how she needed him so much when the whole world was upside down and back-to-front. In all the upheaval there was one thing she knew for certain and that was it could never be right to bury a child before you, and she didn't know whether they'd ever get back in kilter after this. Sybil, the baby that she still was, had put it into words better than she could ever express it: the awful pity of it all.

CHAPTER 39
JIM

Jim woke up tired. His grief was debilitating, and he could see no end to the hollowness of this mental anguish, because there was no end. From now on he was a father who'd lost a son. There'd be many fathers who'd be feeling how he was feeling as he tried to face the day. But he believed he must be the first in Swansea to have lost an Air Force boy to the war, as none – to his knowledge – had been reported in the paper so far.

Downstairs, Mary was in the scullery making some toast. The normally welcoming smell of it browning under the grill turned his stomach over, but he knew she'd force feed him and tell him that he wouldn't get by on an empty stomach. He wondered if she was right. He had more chance of getting by without the burnt bread than without Mary. He felt so close to her, as close as he'd felt in years; perhaps ever.

He sat with her at the kitchen table while she cajoled him into some toast and a boiled egg at the same time as chastising him about being unshaven again and that he'd feel a little better if he had a good wash and a shave. She was tough with her love, Mary, as though she was trying to bring up another child. He'd try and step up. He owed it to her.

He was hacking the top off the boiled egg shell when Mary asked him if he'd be alright cutting up on his own in the shop. It was then he remembered. It was Monday. Jesus Christ he'd forgotten all about Morgan coming with the pig. Ellis has been part of his routine for years and he expected him as much as he did rain, but bloody hell, Morgan. One month wasn't enough to establish a routine. Morgan wasn't yet part of the automatic fabric of a Monday at Middle Road. In the shock of what had been happening in the last twenty-four hours, Morgan hadn't been on his mind at all. He considered whether he had truly forgotten, or had deliberately chosen not to remember. Knife in hand, he stood staring at the decapitated shell, the runny white of the egg running down the eggcup.

"You alright, Jim?" asked Mary. "Try and force it down."

"Sorry, Mary," he said, pushing the uneaten egg on the little plate into the middle of the table. "I just can't."

What the hell had he opened up? Look where his deeds had got him. A dead son and a wife who was soon going to find out about his antics. There was no possibility he could let Morgan know. He'd have left the farm by now and God knows how many drop-offs he had with other butchers before he got to him. Jesus, Mary would have his guts for garters. He'd rather face a judge and jury and get banged up for a few years, than face the wrath of Mary. Perhaps he should confess now, over his uneaten toast, claim insanity, instead of being outed later.

But he couldn't admit. He was impotent to alter the course of fate. He'd allow time to pass and inevitably come undone in front of Morgan and Mary, take the humiliation, accept whatever might ensue, and suffer his just desserts.

As usual, for a Monday, Ellis had dropped off Jim's meat order from the slaughterhouse. Jim stood at the block, chopping, skinning, sawing, and slicing; it might as well have been him spread out on the block, Mary standing in his shoes, dissecting him as he was dealing with the meat. Bloody hell. This might come to pass.

Every couple of minutes he looked up from his work, peeping though the gap in the greaseproof paper to look out for Morgan. Every so often, Mary put her head around the glass door to see how he was holding up, bringing him a cup of tea every time she made a pot for the neighbours who were popping in and out via the front door. Poor, long-suffering Mary. How could he have ever thought this was a good idea? In the middle of all the agony they were going through together, he'd *done this*. He felt it would sever them.

Louisa, as good as her word, had come over the wall to help. She was preparing lunch which Jim declined. He said he was queasy and didn't want to risk it. He wished she wasn't there in the scullery. He feared he'd be getting a public humiliation later if Louisa was witness to all that was going to play out. In minutes the news of his wrong-doings would spread like an incendiary bomb around the neighbourhood.

He was sweating then, wiping his brow with the sleeve of his white coat, wondering how much longer he'd be a butcher, that once proud sign outside the shop, torn down by his own foolishness. What would he – they – do then? He wanted it – everything – over and done with. And he thought of Huw Evans and his family, and Mary's face and her horror when she'd read it from the *Evening Post*. He saw his name in print. Everything was out of proportion. Morgan wouldn't shop him, would he? That would be suicide for Morgan, too. And Mary? What would Mary do? She'd keep it to herself if she could, wouldn't she? Or would she pack her bags and be off with the kids? He was in her hands. She'd mete out justice on her terms.

At the sound of Rhoda's little shoes on the wooden floorboards, he turned from the block.

"Bye, Daddy," Rhoda said, waving at him. "Auntie Louie is taking me to the park. I'm going on the swings."

He felt his face colour.

"Louisa's taking her off my hands for a couple of hours, Jim. That's good of her isn't it? I'll be in to give you a hand clearing up. I don't like you in here on your own. I'll close the front door. I'm drained with all the neighbours. They mean good, but it's exhausting."

"That's kind of you, Louisa. How long will you be?"

"How long do you want me to be?" laughed Louisa.

"I thought long enough for Mary to have a little lie down. She's exhausted."

"Don't even think of it, Louisa," said Mary. "I'll be fine with Jim, here. You come back when you can't stand it anymore. Take the pushchair. With a bit of luck, she'll have forty winks."

And with that they were off, leaving Mary in the shop with him. He looked at the clock: coming up to two. It was around this time when Morgan had arrived last month. But Mary had been at Snell's then. It had been a precision manoeuvre. Jim was counting down. Waiting for a bloody, big mine to go off.

CHAPTER 40
MARY

Mary really didn't have much to do in the shop. She just wanted to be close to Jim. She busied herself by wiping down the marble slabs in the window. She felt better when she was occupied like this, making herself useful. She felt sure Jim was glad that she was there with him, steadying his nerves. Especially after the closeness of the night before.

At the sound of a lorry arriving outside, she looked up. The engine was idling; the distinctive sound of the handbrake which was being wrenched into position.

"That's Morgan's lorry, isn't it, Jim? I didn't know you'd told him, already," she said.

"I don't know how he knows, Mary," said Jim, not looking up from the block. "I haven't been in touch with him for ages."

"Anyway, let him in Jim. I'm up to my eyes here in hot water."

Jim put down his knife, wiped his hands on his apron, and sidled up to the door. Mary heard him break wind as he passed her. He drew back the bolts, top and bottom, and opened up.

Mary took a loin cloth and dried her hands as Morgan came into the shop. He and Jim stood like mute sentries inside the door.

"Mary? Didn't expect to see you here today," he said, shifting his gaze from her to Jim.

Mary could tell by the expression on his face that Morgan was unaware of the news about William.

"You don't know do you, Morgan? About our William? I thought that was why you'd come. That you'd heard the news."

There was no answer from Morgan. No interjection from Jim. They looked like two overgrown kids, standing there, side by side: two naughty schoolboys who'd been summoned before the headmistress. Something was rotten here. It stank to high heaven.

"Well, come on, you two? What brings you here on a Monday in May, Morgan? Jim?"

Morgan was never short of words, but for once he was silent, looking at his partner in crime to show him the way. He loosened the tie around his neck, as if it were a noose, and stretched his neck and jaw. She'd never noticed he had a tic before.

"It's alright, Morgan. I'll explain," said Jim. "I'll settle what I owe you for today but keep it on the lorry and then you'd better be off. I'll be in touch."

And then Morgan was out the door and gone in a flurry of exhaust fumes.

"I think I'd better sit down," said Mary, when they were back in the scullery. "What's going on, Jim? I'm in no mood for a sob story so spit it out and have done with it."

Nevertheless, Jim started with an apology and how sorry he was that he'd ever considered the black market and a criminal way of making a bob or two. It was that he wanted to do it for her and the children, he said, as he felt a failure and always had done, ever since his sister, Kit, had accused him of being a hapless husband. And he never wanted them to be as poor as he was as a child. It was something he couldn't throw off. He didn't want Mary to have to scrimp anymore and he thought he could make life better. That was why he did it.

And he wanted to get even with the government – cheat them – the way they'd cheated him, and now his son, out of the youth that kids should have as a right. That was the truth. And now he couldn't believe he was putting her through all this when they were already going through the wringer.

Mary listened. *I'm all ears*, she said to Jim, not without a hint of anger. But there was no slanging match. She was too irate for that. There were no words that captured the mangle of emotions she felt. Duped. Used. None snared the enormity of it all. How dare he treat her like this on top of what else was happening? She didn't know how much more she could take. It was as though someone had set light the fuse to a stick of dynamite and she was watching it spark ever closer to the point of explosion. She couldn't explode. She didn't have the energy to explode. Imploding she was. Going in on herself.

"I'm really sorry, Mary. I really am," he kept repeating.

"For what, Jim?" she asked, flatly, "for doing something behind my back or for being found out? And is there anything else you want to put on your confessional list while you're in the mood?"

Jim hung his head like a scolded puppy. She feared he might wet himself at any moment. She continued to listen with disbelief as he unburdened himself adding the fact that he hadn't been going to Fire Watch meeting in the Old Bakery, well, he'd been going there, but he'd also been trying his luck on gambling and if truth be told, he'd lost a fair bit.

"You've lost more than a fair bit, Jim," she said.

She knew his unburdening for what it was: as usual, it was to make himself feel better, rather than do true penance. He was speaking at speed, words spewing from his lying lips. Those same lips that only last night in bed, she'd allowed to nuzzle her neck. She felt like a whore; some nameless, faceless woman of the night who had been paid off and then abandoned.

"So," she said, her insides shaking but her face expressionless. "So what are you going to do about it all, Jim?"

He vowed that he'd ring Frank, because Mary should know that Frank was involved too, and tell him that the deal was off and not to come next morning. And no, he wouldn't owe Frank anything for the meat because he'd write off the debt by foregoing his winning on the horse, so there'd be no *dirty money* as Mary called it coming into 141.

"I want you to ring him now, Jim. I'm going to stand over you like a Sergeant Major while you tell him, because you know, Jim, I don't trust you anymore. Isn't that sad? To think I thought we were a team and that you'd actually been thinking of me when you'd coaxed me to go to Snell's or have myself a little fillip at Monica's. What did you take me for?"

She put the kettle on and made a pot of tea and brought it to the table to let it stew for a couple of minutes. Her husband keeping secrets from her. Her dead son and Sybil keeping secrets from her. Dora holding things back, too. What else didn't she know?

"I don't like it when you're this calm, Mary," said Jim. "You frighten me."

"You frighten you, Jim. Don't put the blame on others," she said pouring them each a cup.

"And where did you hide everything?" she asked.

"In the stables, in an old chest."

"And the tallying? What about the book you were obviously running?"

"In your piano, Mary."

Mary closed down then. She felt physically violated. She'd never thought of him abusing something that was so personal and meant the world to her. How could he make her feel so sullied? It was like him admitting to being unfaithful with another woman. In the midst of all the sadness, he was heaping on more, tearing her apart.

"Will you tell the children, Mary?"

"No, Jim. They've got enough to deal with. And anyway, I think they know who you really are more than you do. That's your punishment. My God, to think I read out the article about Huw Evans and his family and you just sat there…"

"Can you forgive me, Mary?"

"I'm not God, Jim. If you're looking for forgiveness and absolution, I suggest you contact him. Go to confession, inhale the incense or whatever they do there, say three Hail Marys and get down on your knees or prostrate yourself and weep. Perhaps some time in the future, I'll accept. But for now I've got a son to grieve and a marriage that's as good as dead."

"I'll move into the back room with Teddy, then?"

"Yes. Do that Jim. That's a good idea. And by the way, if there's anything else you feel compelled to confess, I suggest you get it off your chest soon. I can't put up with this. Remember, Jim, I'm sitting here listening and responding to this because I'm not giving up. I'm strong, not weak. Don't you ever forget that."

Mary walked out of the scullery then and up the stairs to the back bedroom. Exhausted, she slumped down on William's empty bed and pulled back the counterpane exposing the bedding and pillow cases she hadn't changed since he'd left on Boxing Day. She had the urge to get into the bed, snuggle down, and pull the sheets up over her chin and breathe in the scent of him. She felt like a child again, reaching for her comfort blanket, the illogic of grief battling with the logic of her supposedly adult self. Instead, she stopped herself and picked up the pillow, clutching it close as she walked along the landing to her own room. She replaced Jim's pillow with William's. She'd take Jim's to the back bedroom where he'd be interned for as long as she deemed necessary. Meanwhile, she'd place her head on her son's flannelette pillowcase, impregnated with his particular smell.

Just as the telegram had stated, it was Thursday that same week when the official letter came from The Ministry. Mary was washing-up when she heard the postman push it through the letter box, second post. She didn't have to ask Jim – she couldn't bear to talk to him after his so-called confession – but she heard the armchair creak in the next room, and him groan loud enough so she'd hear, as he got up and made his way along the passage. She carried on wiping, glad for the small mercy that, as it was a Thursday afternoon, the shop was shut. She wouldn't have to put on a show and play a public game of togetherness.

Jim slouched down the steps to the scullery, as though he was depleted of all the oxygen his lungs needed to keep him going. He'd surely aged ten years. His face looked saggy and as cream as the envelope he handed to Mary who wiped her hands on her pinafore and went to sit on the settle, leaving Jim standing near the sink.

She picked up a knife from the cutlery tray on the table and sliced open the envelope. She pulled out the typed letter, reading it silently to herself and then out loud, as best as she could, to Jim. She owed him this:

"Dear Mr and Mrs Froom,

We offer our sincere condolences on the death of your son, Wireless Operator; and Gunner, William Peter, RAF, squadron number 59; serial number 619761, William Peter, along with two colleagues, were undertaking a night training operation into enemy occupied territory and after a successful mission, their Blenheim aircraft, overshot the runway on return to base, at Poix and crashed and burned.

Our thoughts are with you at this time…"

She couldn't bring herself to finish it. It was only by seeing it in print and reading it to Jim, that it hit home. She handed Jim the letter, but he gestured to her that he couldn't, so she rose, enclosed the letter in the envelope again, walked into the living room and put it in the letter rack along with all the others.

Jim trailed her like a needy child and she wanted to swot him away out of her sight as she sometimes had the urge to do to Rhoda, though she never did. They were about the same mental age, it seemed.

Mary watched him as he sank back into his chair at the side of the range, his hands on his lap, his fingers laced together, stretching and squeezing, back and fore, in agitation as though he was playing the game of 'here's the church and here's the steeple' that the children had long outgrown. He looked down at the mat; she knew he didn't have the balls to look at her eye to eye. She'd never felt so much like wanting to be held close in all her life, but she knew the man in the chair didn't have it in him. And anyway she wouldn't allow him even if he could muster up the courage.

"I think they must have been dropping leaflets. Propaganda," he said, looking up at her with imploring eyes, like a dog wanting to be stroked after it had chewed a slipper.

"An accident," said Mary. "Not even bloody Jerry."

"It's never the big things that get us, is it? Remember Granny Weidenbach hanging out of that window? And us thinking that she'd fall out at any minute. But she didn't, did she? She slipped on nothing more than a patch of unseen of ice."

"A tragic accident," said Mary. "But doesn't make it any easier to deal with, does it? Harder somehow."

"We won't be able to say goodbye, you know that, Mary, don't you?"

"Yes, I know that. But when this bloody war's over, I'm going to France to visit his grave wherever they decide that will be. I'm going to join the British Legion. I'm going to help raise funds for victims of war: men and boys and widows and families and everyone who's left behind to try and make our boy's death mean something. And I'm going to help the people in our community right here. The victims – the Germans, the Italians – people like us, Jim, who haven't done anything wrong and get sucked into it all. They're mourning their sons just like we are. I'm going to try and put something right."

There was too long a silence before Jim took his turn again in the conversation.

"It's all my fault, Mary. I killed him."

"No you didn't Jim, that's just your usual guilt and self-pity. Save me from it now."

"The betting. The black market. Sins of the father…"

"What d'you mean, *sins of the father?*" she said sharply. "For God's sake, Jim. What *else* is there I don't know?"

CHAPTER 41
JIM

Jim looked up and caught Mary's gaze, drilling him over the top of her glasses. She was silent. That meant trouble. He would rather have her vent her wrath about the betting, the lies he'd told about himself and Morgan and Frank and the pigs. Would rather have the decibels rise and her spit to have wet his face with the force of her shouting and her humiliation of him, than nothing.

He decided this was the time. Life couldn't get any worse, surely. Better to do it now so that there wouldn't be anything more to confess. He'd take it on the chin like he had done in the ring back in Tredegar. Wipe the slate clean so that perhaps he could start anew.

"I'm a fraud, Mary. Nothing but a pretence of a man. Perhaps you should have listened to your mother. She saw through me. She knew you could have done better. And she was right.

"You thought you were marrying a sergeant, didn't you? A man who'd been rewarded for his character. Perhaps his bravery. His ability to take responsibility and lead men, boys even, through all that horror. Boys like our William. Kids away from home for the first time, not knowing where they were and what they were doing. That's why I asked William about what kind of man his sergeant was before he went back, because I was afraid he'd have one like me. I hope he didn't. I hope he had someone who looked out for him, was prepared to die for him.

"Don't get me wrong, I mean I was a sergeant. It was a proud moment when they put those three stripes on my arm that Christmas Day. But I didn't deserve them, Mary. I let them down. All of them. The men. The boys. The Army. Myself. And you.

"It wasn't long before the end of the war. Early 1918. We'd been marching for days up through France with supplies for the Front.

We were headed for Flanders, not far from enemy lines. We were knackered. On our knees. Our feet raw and bleeding from the blisters. The stench of fungus between our toes. We'd been kipping in hay in abandoned barns when we had the chance. We tried singing – you know, the usual ones from my repertoire, the ones you say are stuck in my head – but we were beyond that. It had been a long four years, Mary. I'm not making excuses, but unless you'd been there, had seen what I'd seen, sights that weren't fit for any human being, especially a woman, you wouldn't have believed it. That's probably why I never wanted to talk about it with you. It was beyond words.

"Anyway, the songs weren't doing anything to lift our spirits. I think some of the boys would have been whimpering if they hadn't been singing. And so we just marched on trying to keep in step, swinging our tired arms, left right, left right, one, two, three, four, one, two, three, four.

"And on the tenth night, Mary, just before dusk fell, we reached this Belgian town. Or at least what was left of this Belgian town. Ypres. Wipers we used to call it. Nothing but rubble and dust. Desolate. Not a person in sight. The stench of charred buildings all around. And dead animals. Dogs. Cats. It's how you'd imagine your hell on earth, Mary. My small group of men – we were around twenty by then – were out on their feet and we needed to rest up.

"It was then I saw a ruined inn and I went to have a closer look. Well, you would do. And there was a cellar, Mary, steps leading down to a cellar. You could smell the liquor in the air. I'll never forget that mix of booze and dust and smoke in my nostrils, on my tongue. I led the way, Mary. A sergeant taking boys play-acting as men down the stone steps to the cellar. It was dim there, but we could see the wooden barrels and casks and smell the rum. What was I supposed to do, Mary?

"'Relax, boys,' I said, and they turned the taps on the barrels, and the rum ran free. I instigated it, Mary. Was the ring leader and willing part of it all. One lad, had his head under the tap, letting the liquor gush into his mouth, the way we let Rhoda drink the water from the fountain in the park. I'll never forget his smile. Or those of the others. Turned into pack animals with the booze.

Coarse. Sweating. No stopping them. Or me, Mary. We drank ourselves stupid for hours and hours until I must have collapsed into a drunken stupor, because I don't remember anything much after that. Until the morning, that is."

Mary was still silent apart from the occasional sigh. Jim wished she'd butt in and chastise him, but he felt as though she was enjoying seeing him suffer, being brought to this. Perhaps he needed to.

"It was a cold morning, Mary. Bitter. I've never felt mornings like that before or since. I'd gone to sleep on the floor and woke up aching, my bones stiff, and wondered where the hell I was. I came-to sharpish, the terror filling me as I looked around and saw the sleeping bodies: men still blotto, the air rank with their breath and sweat and the sound of loose snoring.

"But they weren't all there. That's when I felt my insides turn to water. Where the hell had they got to? And in that state? I left those that were still asleep and went up the stone steps to street level. In the freezing fog, the town looked like hell, all the tones of grey you could ever imagine. It was difficult to see far in that visibility, but in the near distance, coming along the road that separated what was left of the houses on either side, I saw my half-dozen missing men, flanked on either side by men in uniform – army uniform from our side, Mary. They were forcing my men to march at pace. I could hear their shouts: Faster. Come on. Quick march, quick march, and as their boots thudded as they drew nearer. They were almost out on their feet, their faces the colour of death itself. But it was the look in their eyes, Mary: fear, guilt, and I knew then I was for it without having to be told. Then one of the men – boys – retched and was sick all down the front of his uniform. I can still smell that, the poor lad's belly spewing terror and rum. And then he shat himself, Mary. That young boy stood there and filled his army pants. Why don't you say, something, Mary?"

"I'm listening, Jim. I'll speak when I'm good and ready," said Mary, removing her glasses and patting her eyes with the handkerchief she took from under her cuff. "Go on."

"Well, I think you know where I'm leading, Mary. It was terrible what I did. The danger I put those men in. In their cups, they'd gone wandering, oblivious to where they were and what peril they were in. They'd staggered their way through the streets and out from the town and found themselves within yards of enemy lines when the two sergeants who were roughing them up a bit coming towards me, had seen them. And when they'd sobered up a bit, and answered the questions, they led those sergeants in temporary charge of them back to the cellar. To me.

"That was the beginning of the end, Mary. I suppose I can count myself lucky that I wasn't taken out and shot at dawn as some poor bastards were. It was all kept quiet, strictly hush hush. Top Brass didn't call for an external Court Martial but took it upon themselves to deal with me. Within the regiment. So that was the end of my sergeant days and my brief days of glory when I thought I was someone for once in my life and I'd earn a good wage and be able to keep a wife. A wilful disregard for duty, they told me. They were right. So how could I tell you, Mary? You surely would have walked away from a man whose stripes were ripped off him. A man who was served discharge papers and left the army demoted and ashamed and at the lowest rank, earning a bloody pittance – the paltry sum of 1s 2d a week plus 1d for every year I'd served. A bloody Private I am. Private Froom. Your sham of a husband. Now say something, Mary. For Christ's sake, speak. Skin me alive. Put me out of my misery."

CHAPTER 42
MARY

Sitting upright in the chair, her back straight, she felt suddenly much taller than Jim. She remained calm. What was the point? Anger had never solved anything. Just look at the state of everything in the world. She wasn't going to give Jim a clean slate: he didn't deserve that for what he'd done with the business of the pig and how it had put her whole family at risk. But what he'd just confessed explained a lot that she'd pondered over the years. She felt that his admission of what had happened back then was perhaps a sign that he was prepared to change – if he could. Good Lord, things couldn't get much worse and perhaps he – and she – had to go to these depths of painful honesty before they could rebuild.

At least he was talking about it. A man like Jim – perhaps most men – found this hard. Deemed it weak, even. Unmanly. Without truth in a relationship, however difficult that truth might be, what chance did husbands and wives have? She didn't want things to be concealed from her 'for her own good'. She wasn't a child. She didn't want to be treated like an inferior, one that was cosseted or perceived as too delicate to face reality. She was an equal. For God's sake, they'd worked in meat, day in, day out, for the last seven years. She was made of strong stuff. And even if her mother hadn't been right about all things, she was right about always talking through problems and that a trouble shared was a trouble halved. She'd put it in Jim's hands. Allow him to come to his own decisions on what he thought he should do next, now that everything was out in the open.

"Well, I trust at least you feel better for telling me that, Jim. For getting it off your chest. Of course, I knew there was something that was troubling you deeply, but I couldn't help you unless you were prepared to help yourself. And admitting it is the first step. That's very honest of you. But it's only a start, Jim. And you can't blame all your weaknesses on that, because some of them have nothing to do with it at all. But I know how much you have suffered – are suffering. You don't sleep with someone for over twenty years without wondering what is causing their nightmares – the ones in the night and the ones that spill over into the day. So where do we go from here?"

"We go to the old stables, Mary. Just you and me, while everyone's out and Louisa has Rhoda. I want to show you everything," said Jim.

Jim disappeared into the shop for a few minutes and when he returned, he held a key in his hand. She followed him out of the living room, past the broken settee with the propped up leg, and out of the scullery through the yards into the stables. There they passed yet more unused things: their redundant bikes and the neglected garden tools hanging sadly on the walls. It was as though her life had been on stop for ever. It couldn't – and wouldn't – go on like this. It had to start up again one day. In what way she didn't know, but she wasn't about to end up redundant like those bikes.

Jim bent down at the old military chest and turned the key in the lock.

"I thought you said it was your illegal meat you kept in here?" she asked.

"I've kept a lot of things in here, Mary," he said delving through the tins, to bring out the brown paper package tied with string.

She watched him as he unknotted the parcel, pulling back the brown paper to reveal the contents: there they were, the discharge papers, faded now with time, and his sergeant's cloth chevron. All the insignia and paraphernalia of who he'd once been.

"What shall I do with them, Mary?"

"Well, what do you want to do with them, Jim?"

"I never want to see them again."

"We'll burn them, then. Take them inside and chuck them on the range."

"No. I don't want to tempt fate, take trouble into our home."

"It's a bit late for that, don't you think? And you haven't caused anything to happen, Jim. It doesn't work like that; life."

"I'll set fire to them, outside."

Mary went first, Jim steadying her as he gave her a leg-up over the wall to Louisa's. He followed with the pitch fork that he'd taken down from the wall in the stables. At last he was finding a use for it, thought Mary, even though it was disproportionate to the size of the task they had in store. In physical terms at least.

They stopped near the compost heap close by the wall across the end of the garden. There wasn't much space now that the Anderson shelter was in place, and the rows of vegetables and canes for the runner beans.

"You do it," said Mary. "It will be good for you to do it yourself. Proof, if you like, that I can witness."

Jim searched the dried ground for some tinder and kindling, picking up a few dead branches that had fallen over from the house next door down. He crumpled the brown paper, and placed the length of string on top, carefully adding the dried twigs after he'd snapped them into small pieces across his knee. Then he reached in his trouser pocket and pulled out his little petrol lighter and flicked it alight. Mary saw his hands shaking as he cupped the blue-yellow flame and took it to the corner of the paper. There was a feint whiff of petrol and it caught first time. In the strong, dry breeze, the paper singed and burned and soon the twigs caught light and crackled in the May afternoon.

It was the discharge papers that Jim fed to the fire first. Mary watched the flames gulp them, the damning print disappearing into nothingness. Jim picked up the pitchfork and stabbed the fragile remains. Next were the chevrons, which shrivelled in the heat, before being swallowed into the roar of the little fire. Jim, attacked the burning material with the prongs of the fork, his face red, not because of the scale of the fire, but with the intensity of the emotion. And when he'd done that, he stepped back, put down his fork, and rubbed his hands together, as if there was something that was stuck to them that Mary was unable to see. *There*, he said, quietly. *All done.*

It wasn't *all done* as far as Mary was concerned. Far from it. She was prepared to forgive – or at least, accept – what he'd done in his anguish and his cups in the more distant past; but the way he had ridden roughshod over their current partnership in life and work and violated her piano, wasn't as easy to accept. She knew it would always be there, that it couldn't be undone. Ever. It was what she'd do in response that concerned her. Life was all so raw at the moment, and when she'd most wanted to turn to Jim for support and, he to her, they couldn't do it. Each of them had to suffer the grief of what had happened in their marriage, and the immeasurable loss of their son, separately.

No sooner was the conflagration over, and the flames died down than Jim had asked – begged, even – to be allowed back into the marital bed. *But I need you, Mary,* he'd said. *You don't deserve me, Jim. You can't just click your fingers like a magician and make everything all right.*

So Mary told him that she would stay in their bed while he remained in the back bedroom with Teddy, until enough time had passed and she was ready to have him back, for have him back she would. She made it clear that she'd didn't expect miracles in Middle Road, but he needed to know that there would be conditions attached and she would expect a willingness to try at least to put his life in order and take responsibility for some of his own actions. She felt a little like a politician and wondered if she might have done something like that if her sex hadn't prevented her so far. She was good with people, she'd been told. For the first time she felt that she was only forty-four and not almost forty-five and the way she looked at that could make a heck of a difference when all this mess was over.

The mood in 141 that week mirrored the mood of the row, of Swansea, of Wales, Britain and of course, the Low Counties. There was a charged feeling of expectation, of waiting for something for so long that you began to feel perhaps that it might never happen. As if the whole world might silently explode. But the worst had already happened for her and Jim and their family. Yet not for the neighbours. Not yet for the country. And that sense of disarray pervaded and an uneasy calm hung heavy in the air in the ordinary terraces of Cwmbwrla and in the government at Westminster where that weak man Chamberlain was drawing out his own political death. And Mary realised that she was perhaps keen on drawing things out for longer than was necessary too, so she wouldn't have to face up to telling Jim about Sybil. For all her bluster and her talk of being an equal, was she, after all, nothing but a weak woman, scared of standing up for another woman, perhaps all women, and even herself?

CHAPTER 43
JIM

It was a long week, that week leading up to the Whitsun weekend. On the Friday afternoon, Jim stood at the block, boning legs of lamb for those awkward customers who preferred them that way. *The flavour's in the bone,* he wanted to tell them, as he had for years. But he couldn't be bothered anymore.

He wanted them to be gone so that he could put up the greaseproof papers and shut himself inside with Mary and the family so they might try and grieve privately. There hadn't been a chance. He knew they all meant well, the neighbours who'd kept their front curtains closed, up and down the row, all week in respect. The neighbours who'd endlessly trailed in carrying homemade sponges, Welsh Cakes, Bara Brith, slabs of bread pudding in trays, and jugs of stew covered with T-towels, to save him and Mary having to fend for themselves. It was love food, prepared with the thoughts that couldn't be expressed face-to-face: *Sorry for your loss,* seemed the hardest words to say and the hardest thing to accept when there was no physical body to say goodbye to.

As he dealt with the meat, he realised that the neighbours had more chance of saving him and Mary's souls from sorrow, than the men of the cloth who had put their faces in that week, too. They hadn't seen them for years, but in they trooped, Glyn Richards, the Minister from Babell chapel, and Vicar, Tom Griffiths, from St Luke's church, with their white collars and condolences, hopes for life everlasting and their offers to say prayers for William. But Jim didn't hold with any of their mumbo jumbo. His horses were a more certain bet and that was saying something.

He looked at the clock. Closing time couldn't come soon enough. He was wrung out: as though he'd been put through the mangle and couldn't begin to contemplate how he could stand much more. He longed for Mary to let him back into her life, if not back into her bed. He'd never felt more alone in all of his almost fifty years.

CHAPTER 44
MARY

"I've come to give you a hand," said Mary as she entered the shop at closing time. "Not that you deserve it. And don't take it as a sign."

"Thank you, Mary. I won't push my luck. I know where I stand."

"Good. Now we'll finish up, then have a cup of tea and some of the blessed cakes that are filling up the scullery, and sit outside. It's a lovely evening."

Everyone in the neighbourhood seemed to have the same idea. The days were longer mid-May, and the sun shone onto the gardens opposite. The little oblong patches of lawn were neatly mown and the edges clipped, roses opening out in the borders, and alyssum and lobelia in bud, as if nothing could possibly be wrong with the world. Mary wasn't a jealous woman, but she envied those on the other side, their little manicured gardens, that buffer between the pavement and the front door. And the fact that they got the sun in the evenings.

The whole row was out, sitting on their little walls, legs dangling onto the pavements, front doors left ajar behind them. Mary couldn't hear what was being said, but there was a buzz of conversation, animated faces, serious expressions. What now? she thought. What had she missed?

Dragging Rhoda by one hand, and holding a tin of Welsh cakes in the other, she crossed the road to 142. Graham and Doreen were there chatting to Louisa, little Joan sitting on the grass. Good. She'd be company for Rhoda while she had a grown-up conversation with people that wasn't about meat. She plonked Rhoda down with Joan, opening the tin as an offering, and took her place on the wall.

"Have you heard, Jim?" said Graham.

Mary bristled at the way the talk of politics and issues she knew about and concerned her deeply, was seen as the territory of men only. She already knew something was amiss by her exclusion. She didn't like being on the side lines while the men talked.

"Been up to my eyes in blood and guts all day, so don't know what you mean. Graham," said Jim.

"He's gone in," explained Graham.

Mary didn't need to hear anymore. She knew this cryptic code as well as any man. Knew who the 'he' was; knew what 'gone in' referred to. Why didn't Graham include her and the other women in the conversation?

"Bastard," shouted Jim, who then said sorry to the women if he'd offended them, but that bloody Hitler was a bastard.

"*We* haven't had the wireless on," said Mary. "*We'd* have heard otherwise. And don't watch your mouth for us women, Jim."

"It was on the six o'clock news. Home Service. Apparently he went in at dawn. On all fronts. France, Belgium, Luxembourg and the Netherlands," continued Graham.

"Jesus Christ," said Jim. "Kept them – and us – waiting long enough. I really thought perhaps he'd not take the risk after all. Beginning of the bloody end, this."

Mary watched the women pale. Everyone knew what this meant. The phoney war was finally over. Look out, now, Cwmbwrla. It will be your turn soon. For a fleeting moment, she thought that William would be in the thick of it. And then she realised that he was gone, and wouldn't take any further part in what horror was to come. Perhaps, that was a strange blessing.

"And that's not all," Graham added. "His number's up, too. Gone to the palace to see the King."

Again, Mary knew who the 'he' was. Couldn't come a day too soon as far as she was concerned. You couldn't make a pact with the devil as he'd tried to do. Lily-livered Chamberlain. At last the government had lost confidence in him. The people had a long time ago. Good riddance.

"Will it be Churchill, then?" asked Mary, getting herself vocally into the debate.

"They say so. He's on his way to the palace, too. He'll be Prime

Minister before the day's over. Wouldn't like to be in his shoes now, poor bugger," said Graham.

"Is he any relation to you, Jim?" asked Louisa, knowing that the C in JC was an abbreviation for Churchill.

Mary laughed out loud at Louisa's quip, almost choking on the currants of her Welsh cake.

"No, he's no relation to Winston," said Mary. "Churchill was Jim's mother's maiden name. She wanted to keep it in the family, carry on the line. But you never know, they might share some things – determination, bravery, grit. We'll have to wait and see."

CHAPTER 45
TEDDY

Teddy's meat round was busier than normal on the Saturday preceding Whit Sunday. The basket felt heavy and so did his legs: his calves ached and his thighs strained as he cycled up Middle Road. They'd felt like this all week ever since he'd opened the door to the messenger boy. His mother had told him that it was probably down to growing pains; though he knew it was more to do with William, something that he couldn't explain. He also knew he wasn't growing much anyway and had given up measuring himself daily, marking off his height on the back of the bedroom door.

He guessed the neighbourhood was going to make the most of Whitsun with a special Sunday dinner, before they got bombed to smithereens. It could be any day now. Everyone was getting prepared again after what had been a time when people didn't really believe it was going to happen. Not ordinary people, in Cwmbwrla, far away from what was happening *over there, on the other side.*

The ARPs were out and about again, sandbags everywhere, buckets with the stirrup pumps standing ready on the street corner. He felt his stomach go over, and wished that he'd brought his gas mask, just in case, but he'd forgotten it on purpose because he couldn't stand any more load on the bike.

It seemed everyone had heard the news about William, as when he knocked the doors on his round, people looked at him sadly and without exception, said: *Sorry to hear about your brother, Teddy. Terrible business. Please send our condolences to your mother and father.* And without exception, they tipped him more than usual, most giving him a sixpenny-bit. The coins were too many for one trouser pocket, so he balanced them out evenly between the two, the fabric sagging like saddle bags either side of him. He reckoned by the time he'd finish up his errands, he'd have about ten bob in loose change which he couldn't wait to show to Raymond. He'd share it with his friend: they'd spend it on whatever they wanted rather than slot it into a piggy bank. He was surprised this was out of character for him. Reckless thinking. And he guessed it was because the war was happening now and who knew what would happen next.

After he'd wolfed down what there was for dinner, he left 141 in a flurry of excitement, his mother shouting after him, *Make sure you're home by dark*. Since he'd finished his chores for the day, and counted his money, he felt lighter somehow and the bike easier to pedal.

It was downhill to Raymond's anyway, and he sat back in the saddle and stuck his legs out either side of him, let go the handlebars, and let the momentum carry him past the cemetery at Babell. He felt the rush of air in his face as his hair was being blown back and he didn't care one jot about the rhyme his father would always say to ward off cavalier behaviour on the bike:

> *Look at me, no hands*
> *Look at me, no teeth*

With a screech of breaks and a scuff of the soles of his already nearly worn-out shoes, he came to a halt outside Raymond's. Raymond's mother opened the door and Raymond appeared in the passage, wheeling his bike through. Teddy felt all his limbs and his insides loosen. He felt safe with Raymond, as if none of the things that had happened to him this last week, would defeat him. Raymond looked even bigger than he had done a week ago. How was that happening? His hair was slicked back like the images of men on the front of his mother's knitting patterns. He could smell Brylcreme like his father used. There was another smell too as he came closer and bumped his bike down the small step onto the pavement. It was the smell of sweat. Grown up sweat. Armpits and stale jumper. BO, his mother called it. Teddy knew he didn't have that smell yet, and as unpleasant as it was, he envied Raymond it; that, and the long trousers he was wearing.

Together, Teddy and Raymond, freewheeled down the remainder of Middle Road, taking the bend at speed, and pulling up just past the Gate House in Cwmbwrla Square. Teddy balanced the bike standing on tiptoe and looked at Raymond, whose both feet were planted firmly on the ground. For a few moments they just stared and said nothing, unable to take in the scene properly.

"What's going on?" said Teddy.

"It's both of them," said Raymond.

They dismounted their bikes together and pushed them slowly towards what was happening in the Square. Leaning the bikes against Willy James the newsagents, they edged ever nearer the throng on their side of the road. Outside De Marco's café, a crowd of about a dozen men were shouting, baying and shaking their fists at the De Marco men who were sweeping up broken glass covering the pavement. Teddy looked across the road to see a similar crowd doing the same thing outside Zanetti's café. He looked at Raymond for an explanation.

"C'mon," said Raymond. "Let's take a closer look."

Teddy was nervous now but also angry. As they approached the scene, he was hot with emotion seeing the way the seemingly ordinary looking men from Cwmbwrla were jeering at the Italian men. *Bloody Fascists*, they screamed, *Fuck off back to where you came from*. As far back as Teddy could remember, the Italian men had always been from around here; this was where they'd made their homes, where they belonged, running the cafés, making the coffee, being nothing but nice to him and Raymond when they'd go in for an ice cream. There was venom in the crowds' high pitched voices, and evil in the way they were pointing their fingers as though jabbing their very eyes. Teddy felt things were getting out of control and that someone was going to get hurt soon and he didn't know why this drama was playing out before his eyes.

"It's 'cos the Italians declared war on us yesterday," explained Raymond.

"I didn't know that. Bloody hell," said Teddy. "What'll happen now, then?"

"They'll take them away and lock them up, I expect," said Raymond.

Teddy looked past the crowds towards the white police box

near the Tivoli. The sergeant and the local bobby were coming out, putting their hats on as they walked towards the affray.

"But they haven't done anything wrong," said Teddy.

"People don't care about the facts in war, Teddy," said Raymond like a politician. "They just see what they want to see. Spies. Informers. Infiltrators. People who they want to think are not like us living in our midst."

Teddy watched the two coppers approach the crowd, begging them to take it easy and go home. They didn't look as if they were going to arrest anyone. Not yet. The crowd stilled for a while, but didn't disperse, remaining standing there, arms folded, defiantly watching the spectacle of the Italian men brushing up the shards of glass that had fallen from the smashed front windows of their cafés, watching them bend down and sweep the debris into a pile, watching them pick up the large pieces, placing them into a barrow.

Teddy and Raymond walked closer still and could see through the broken window into the café inside where the Italian women and girls of the family were cleaning up as best they could. There were no customers. Not anymore.

"I can't stand this," said Teddy, feeling a lump in his throat and a sense of something taking hold of his body, making his legs tremble. "It's not right."

"That's war for you," said Raymond.

"Well, I can't stand back just looking and doing nothing. I'm going to help."

"You can't do anything, Teddy," said Raymond. "It's beyond our control now."

"I can do a little bit and so can you, Raymond. Come with me. Quick!"

From somewhere, Teddy had the energy in that small body of his to drag Raymond by the arm, back along the side of the road to Danny Bell's Emporium opposite the Gate House. In they dashed, through the gaps between the tables and chairs, further into the depths of the little store, through the space where the paraffin heaters and dustbins were stored, and further still to the where the garden tools were stacked alongside the garden brooms.

"I'll take two of those," said Teddy to Danny Bell, pointing to the brooms that were nearly as big as him.

Danny Bell picked up the two brushes, brought them to the counter for closer inspection, and Teddy nodded in approval and said, how much, then? as though he'd been bargaining all his life.

Teddy was aware of Raymond wondering where the heck the money was coming from to pay for this mad-brain idea.

Teddy put his hands in his pockets, stood on tiptoe, and turned the fabric of the pockets inside out so that the silver coins spilled out on top of the counter. He watched Danny Bell press the keys on the till, saw the drawer slide open and him place the coins one by one in the compartments.

"Keep the change," said Teddy in a high-pitched, boy's voice that he was failing to lower. "Spend it in the cafés when they have the windows put back in."

Danny Bell pushed the drawer shut and handed over the two brushes to Teddy.

"Well, are you with me or against me?" said Teddy to Raymond as they came out of the store. He didn't know quite where this pluck had come from. It had been building up inside him for days, months, perhaps years. Teddy handed Raymond the brush and Raymond put it over his shoulder and Teddy did the same. Together, Raymond towering above him in stature, at least, walked in step, like two soldiers carrying pikes, back to the cafés. They'd do the De Marco's first and then they'd cross and do the Zanetti's. Even though it might be stupid, even though it might be dangerous, Teddy vowed he'd ignore the crowd and do what he had to do and what he could do. For the first time in his thirteen years, he felt he could make a difference What's the phrase people used? Yes, he was taking a stand.

CHAPTER 46
MARY

Mary fought her corner calmly in an invisible boxing ring throughout the rest of May. She wasn't actively making Jim do his penance by hollering or issuing him with a list of instructions, but was mentally ticking off a list of conditions she had set for him. It could only come from him if he were truly penitent. She didn't have the energy anyway, as if the emotional bombs that had ripped her life apart had knocked the stuffing out of her. But she wouldn't show.

The settee was first. On the Saturday evening following the invasion they'd spoken about on the wall, she watched Jim down on his knees; in his hands, the tape measure he'd taken from her knick-knack table. He worked in silence, his tongue sticking out between his lips in deep concentration. He measured one of the remaining three legs – height, width, depth – and jotted the inches down on a piece of paper, with the pencil he took from behind his ear. He was trying. But he wasn't what you'd call a do-it-yourself man however much he thought he could be. He might be a master butcher, but with woodwork he was clueless.

"Why don't you make a pattern?" she said.

"What d'you mean?"

"Well, as I do when I'm dressmaking. A template."

"Why didn't I think of that?"

"Because you have me to think for you, Jim Froom. I'll get some greaseproof paper from the shop."

She returned with a large sheet and watched him as he traced around the wooden leg, wishing that it could be as easy to create a template for their life.

"I'll come with you," she said, and together they went down to the old stables. "I like to see you doing something with your hands. It's good for you. And me."

He rummaged through the planks of wood stacked up against the wall, settling on oak with a fine grain. It was too big to work with as it was, so he took down his old saw from the wall. Gently placing the plank on the workbench, Mary watched as he sawed back and fore, to create a more manageable size to work with, the sawdust flaking on to the surface. He wiped the raw edges of the newly exposed wood clean with his finger. Mary sniffed the air, the smell of freshly-sawn timber was to her liking, as was looking at the little muscle close to Jim's right elbow, which formed a dome like the top of an egg, appearing and disappearing with the effort of his work. All the years of chopping meat had done that. It singled Jim out. His defining feature. A muscle that resembled an egg.

Once he'd created the small oblong of oak, he placed it flat on the workbench taking the template, cutting carefully around the pencil marks with a scissors, then placed the outline on top of the wood and drew around it with a pencil. Mary wondered whether he'd have the patience for what came next, but he stuck his tongue through his lips again and placed the wood in the vice and began chiselling away around the edges to reveal the rough shape of a new leg.

"Almost done," said Mary. "Take your time now. Don't spoil it."

"Trust me, Mary. I won't make a pig's ear out of it, I promise."

Mary didn't answer, but just raised her eyebrows.

"I'll just chamfer the rough edges and drill a couple of holes in the top and that's it," he said, picking up the sandpaper and starting to rub down. "Don't want anyone getting splinters."

Mary went closer to inspect.

"Not a bad job, Jim. Be good if you got used to this."

Mary led the way back to the house. Although he wasn't wagging his tail, or carrying his manufactured triumph in his jaw, he reminded her of a faithful gun dog, keeping close to his mistress. She felt they'd taken some small steps.

Later, after Jim had fixed the leg on the sofa, and Mary and him had sat on it together for the first time in years to test if it held their weight, Mary felt some of the tension lift. She felt girlish, childish even, as they sat like a gauche, courting couple, aware of the space between them, but neither moving closer to each other.

"Show us your egg, Jim" she laughed.

He raised his right arm to halfway between waist and shoulder, bent it at the elbow, and clenched his fist, open and close, open and close. As he did, the little egg-shaped muscle appeared, disappeared, appeared, disappeared.

"William used to love you doing that, didn't he?" she said, as she shifted her backside along the cushion and simply placed her hand over his and squeezed hard, "You're still not allowed back in the big bed, though. Not yet."

Mary knew Jim needed some fresh air after that. They walked along the passage and as soon as Jim had opened the front door they could see there were a fair few of the neighbours out again in the early evening. Jim and Mary stood on the doorstep and turned their heads to look at what everyone else seemed to be looking at: in the King's Dock, framed by Kilvey Hill on the left, and Townhill on the right, where scores of boats of all sorts and sizes sat in the water.

Jim put his arm around Mary's shoulder and she did not resist.

"Well, seems like everyone's heeded the call, then, Jim?" she said, realising that no-one would ever be bringing their son home. William was somewhere they didn't know, and beyond rescue now.

"Going to bring our boys back from the other side. Sitting ducks, they'll be. Jerry'll be picking them off from the air."

"Don't be so downbeat, Jim. It might go better than you think. We've got to keep chipper."

CHAPTER 47
MARY

Not long after Mid-Summer's Day, when the air was warm and the days long, and Mary was moaning about the midges that went after her and no-one else in the family, the first physical bombs blasted the Frooms out of their complacency. They'd become immune – almost blasé – to the fact that this might happen. So, when the air-raid siren whined and wailed and startled Mary out of a deep, early-Friday morning's sleep, she assumed it was just a false alarm, turned on her side and tried to get back off. But the warning continued, its high to low monotony eventually hitting a nerve. This wasn't a practice.

As Mary came out of the bedroom, she could see that Jim had already taken Rhoda from her bedroom and was carrying her along the landing. The little girl was covering her ears with her hands and shrieking hysterically. Teddy came out of his room, and followed Mary calmly down the stairs, Jim directing operations at the rear, shooing the whole family ahead of him.

"I'm not going to the shelter, Jim. I said I wouldn't and I meant it. I'll take my chances," said Mary.

"But the kids, Mary," said Jim.

"It'll be alright. Trust me," she said, as she opened the door to the cupboard under the stairs and reached for the flashlight that hung on the wall. "Come on kids. Hunker down. We're going to be fine."

Mary sat Rhoda on her lap and cuddled her in so that she stilled. The whole family was quiet in anticipation of the unknown, sitting bunched up together on the floor. Even though they couldn't yet see what was happening outside, they could hear. The siren had stopped now, and the low-pitched thrum of aircraft could be heard. It sounded as though they were right overhead.

"Those are not ours," said Teddy.

"How do you know?" said Mary.

"Well, ours – Blenheims, Hurricanes, Lancasters, Halifaxes – go like this…"

And he proceeded to approximate the throbs and distinctive togetherness of the engines of British Aircraft with his voice and lips.

"How do you know stuff like this, Teddy?" asked Mary.

"William taught me when he was home. He told me what Jerry's sounded like as well. Like this: whoa whoa whoa whoa," he mimicked, opening and closing his vibrating lips to try and represent the drone. "They're more out of tune. Just like we can hear now."

They all huddled close together and continued to listen. Jim thought it an apt moment to go into circus mode to entertain Rhoda. He placed the bulb end of the torch in his mouth, and she laughed at his blown-out cheeks glowing pink in the dark cubbyhole. It was enough for the time being.

If they'd not been entombed in the fug of the under-stairs cupboard, or the glory hole as Mary insisted on calling it, and if they'd had the nerve to go to the front door, and open it, and peer out towards the docks and Kilvey Hill, they would have seen the flares being dropped from the Luftwaffe's aircraft lighting up the areas of packed terraced houses so they could pinpoint exactly where they'd drop their high explosive bombs.

But they heard the bombs being dropped, that high pitched screech as they were released from the plane, falling to the ground with increased velocity and that explosive boom that shook the ceiling and brought down flakes of plaster onto their heads.

"Bloody hell, that was close," said Jim, between blasts.

"Sounds closer than it actually is, Jim," said Mary, giving him one of her looks to try and stop him making the kids more frightened than they already were.

"Well, some poor buggers are having it," he said, as though her words had fallen on deaf ears. "Just hope they weren't under the stairs."

Yet in the morning, after they'd finally gone back to bed, they woke at the usual time to the normal rhythm of life. Teddy said he'd walk to Dynevor to see if he could find any evidence of the night's bombs, craters or buildings that were blitzed. Jim opened up the shop at nine o'clock to the dribs and drabs of customers who stood waiting outside the window as per the norm. Louisa came over the wall to take Rhoda off Mary's hands for a couple of hours while Mary helped Jim out in the shop, saying to Mary that she'd be buggered if Jerry'd get her out of her own bed again as she wasn't going to endure another night ever in that blessed Anderson shelter, sentiments with which Mary agreed entirely. It would only happen to someone other than Mary. That was the logic. She'd been through enough and it was impossible that anything much worse could befall her or her family.

CHAPTER 48
TEDDY

The nights when the air-raid warning sounded were a regular occurrence in the weeks that followed. Now that the Germans had taken France, they could operate sorties from their air bases at Calais and along the Normandy coast. It was just a hop across the English Channel.

Teddy wasn't frightened anymore and that surprised him. If anything, he was excited about it. They'd got themselves more organised as the bombings continued; his mother would place biscuits in the glory hole and a bottle of milk and some cups, ready and waiting for when the family would troop down the stairs and assume their positions on the mattress that his father had now somehow or other managed to wedge into the small space. Rhoda would go back to sleep, Dora would snooze and sometimes sketch a woman's face framed by long, wavy hair. It reminded him of someone and after some thinking he thought it might be Sybil. It had a feel about it. Perhaps Raymond's mother was right.

As for him, he would try and make use of the time and read, or do some extra homework. His birthday was in August and he'd been told he was young in his year at school and he didn't want that to be an excuse for falling behind in his studies. He was going to ensure that nothing within himself stopped him from achieving his burning ambition to be a surgeon. After the mission he'd instigated that he'd since renamed *operation two brooms*, he knew he had something in him like the Charlo boy with the football togs, though he knew that the world was a precarious place, and that dreams could be snuffed out by factors beyond his control. His father might be such an obstacle.

Teddy was sick to the teeth of his father sharing the same room. Perhaps that's why he was relieved when the siren would go off. The more it sounded, the happier and freer he was. It was something he couldn't explain exactly and there was no-one to listen to him anyway. How could he even think of telling his form master at school that his father was sleeping in the same room as him because his mother had kicked him out for reasons he wasn't aware of? He knew too, that when mothers and fathers had tiffs in some of the families of the boys in his class, the sons didn't have to bed down with the guilty parent. They had spare rooms. Rooms to sulk in alone. Rooms where boys had peace and quiet to do their homework so that they'd get on in life.

Ever since William had died, he'd felt his father leaning on him more and more: to help behind the counter, or cycle to the hide and skin, or take Rhoda out to get from under his feet, or put the blackouts up, or make up a round for Solo. He did feel so sorry for his father: but he also felt sorry for himself, in that he realised he was now a substitute William, the younger version of his dead brother. He understood deep down that his father wanted to keep him at home, not just for his fatherly selfish motives, but perhaps to keep him safe from any harm that might come his way. He didn't want his little Teddy's second-hand shoes to walk him away from him, the way William's had. But Teddy's feet were itching and outgrowing those shoes. You could tell how tall someone might be, their stature in the future when fully mature, by the size of their feet. Raymond had also told him that you could also tell how big your John Thomas would be by the same measure. Well hung, he called it.

Sometimes, when his father would come to bed, he'd wake him up. *Can we have a chat, Son, if you're awake* (knowing full well that he was asleep) *man to man*? And he would lie there in his single bed, in the dark (which was probably a good thing as his father couldn't see his face) while his father would chunter on about the things that were pre-occupying him. *I know you don't want to be a jockey, Son – your mother has knocked that idea out of my head, and anyway, I reckon you're going to get too big because I've seen a change in you recently – and I know you said something about being a surgeon, but when you think about it – logically – there's not much difference between being a surgeon and a butcher, you know, the precision of it all. There's as much skill in being a butcher. Take it from me.*

And he would lie there in the dark already knowing from the experiences of life that he had already learned in his first three years at grammar school that there was indeed a lot of difference between being a surgeon and a butcher. Not least the money. Or the status. His father probably knew that, but couldn't say: and how could Teddy tell him? It would destroy him when he was already almost destroyed. His face would crumple there on the pillow, knowing that his father wanted to see him be a version – or a better version of himself – JC Froom, Family Butcher, there in a white coat and a blue and white striped apron, standing behind the block, JC Froom and Son, now proudly painted on the red wood outside. His father would tell him that it was a good business he'd built up, and it had the potential to be even better. There'd be a good career for him just waiting to be handed to him on a plate. *All yours, Son,* he'd say. *Your mother and me can take a back seat then and leave it in your capable hands.* For who knew what the world would be like when this war was over. There was security in what you knew. And he'd like to have him around more now, the way things had turned out.

Teddy couldn't answer or even say he'd think about it. But there in the back bedroom, he sometimes saw his dreams deflating the way the air would slowly disappear from a pig's bladder when he and Raymond used one as a football for a kick-about in the park.

His mother had said it was fine for Teddy to invite Raymond to stay overnight on his birthday on 18th August. There would be no exception made in sleeping arrangements though, and Jim would remain in the back bedroom. His mother suggested that Teddy and Raymond have a bit of an adventure and camp out on the mattress in the cupboard under the stairs. They could gab away into the small hours without disturbing anyone. And it meant that she wouldn't have to skirt around any embarrassing lies.

Teddy was awarded a relatively easy day that day as it was his birthday. His mother had told his father to go easy on him and Dora had stepped in for a change as his replacement, offering to cycle the left-over meat down to the cold stores in the Strand, which meant that once Teddy's meat round was over, he was free for the rest of the day to do as he liked with Raymond.

It was a cloudless day, no threat of rain; a good day to be out on the bikes. Teddy and Raymond set out, their knapsacks over one shoulder; gas masks over the other, and cycled into Cwmbwrla Square. It was quiet for a Saturday: a sorry sight now that the Italian cafés were empty and boarded up.

"They've locked the men up," said Raymond. "Interned them. Aliens."

"And what about the girls and the women?" asked Teddy.

"They tried to keep things going but were getting the rough edge of people's tongues. Calling them all sorts of things...I don't know if you know, Teddy, but my mother says that she's heard that your mother has been involved..."

"What? Running them down? Being foul to them?"

"No. The opposite. She's been seen going into the cafés, quite openly, my mother says, with buckets and cloths, and has been helping them clear up and clean through after the damage people had been doing there. I wouldn't have thought your mother would risk that. Not being in business herself. Not with the way things are. I mean, she stands to lose the lot."

"My mother's not afraid of anything," said Teddy, feeling as though he was going to burn from the inside out with the rage that was eating at him. "She doesn't worry about consequences, like some. She knows what's right and wrong. And she isn't a gossip!"

"I didn't mean to upset you, Teddy. I just wanted you to know, just in case. Anyway, it's all a waste of time."

"It's all so unfair," said Teddy, as they cycled past, looking at the filthy language – ITIS PISS OFF, FASCIST SHIT, BLACK-SHIRTS FUCK OFF – that had been daubed on the wooden plywood that covered the holes where the windows had once been. "It's not their fault."

"The only fair in life is the funfair," said Raymond, sounding so worldly-wise and full of knowledge. "That's what my mother, says anyway."

"Your mother has a lot to say about a lot of things."

"I just think she's lonely," said Raymond.

"Is you mother alright? You know, with your dad being called-up?" said Teddy trying to patch up the awkwardness.

"She says she's alright. Says she has to be. I try to be the man around the house now... And what about your mother and father?"

"They're fine, now," said Teddy, wondering if Raymond could see the black fairies dancing on the top of his head. "I don't know what set it all off. Just a tiff."

They turned right near the police-box next to the Tivoli, past Price's garage and headed up past the Bwrlais Brook. It wasn't far, yet another world there: the railway embankment cut through the valley, and there were allotments, but what interested Teddy and Raymond more than anything else were the reservoirs belonging to Jeremiah's Foundry. The locals called these 'the bounds'. Though the water was used in the cooling process for industry, a lot more went on there. Often there were dead dogs floating on the surface. More since the war had begun. Teddy looked at the still waters, and recalled the time when he'd done as his father asked and taken yet another litter of Whiskey's kittens in a sack, tied the bag tightly with twine, attached a brick and drowned them. He hadn't thought it was that awful at the time. It was what people did. But since the cafés' incident, he thought himself changed, felt shocked that he'd been capable of so much cruelty in the past. Why did people have cats if they couldn't afford to look after them? But the answers were probably not that simple.

Without the knowledge of their parents, Teddy and Raymond often went for a dip in the 'bounds' ponds, despite warnings that many children had been drowned there. Teddy heard constant horror stories about the danger of their murky depths, and weeds deep in the mud below that sucked children down.

Teddy and Raymond used a false logic that if the worst did happen to them, then they wouldn't get into trouble and have to go home and face the music. But today, despite Raymond's playful taunts for Teddy not to be chicken, Teddy just didn't want to venture in. He was stripped down to his knitted trunks, but stood as if his soles were glued to the grassy bank at the water's edge.

"I just can't today," he said. "I've got this strange feeling in my belly."

Teddy knew then that Raymond wouldn't push him. He was wise enough to realise that it wasn't the water, more like sadness he had because his brother wasn't around anymore.

"It's alright, Teddy," said Raymond, as he draped his old, striped towel across Teddy's shoulders.

Teddy didn't respond. He was shivering, not so much from cold as the sun was high overhead, but from right inside of him. He'd felt like this the morning the messenger boy with long trousers had knocked on the door and handed him the envelope.

"I'll look after you," said Raymond. "Put your vest and shirt back on and have a sit down. You're not a coward – if it's any good for you to hear, I've felt like this too. When Dad went to the Navy, I couldn't stop being sick. It's like sadness is stuck in your stomach and needs to be spewed out. It will pass. Just because you're a boy, doesn't mean you can't be sad, or not be brave. You can cry in front of me, Teddy."

"I just feel as if something awful is around the corner. All the time," said Teddy, leaning into Raymond.

"Nothing awful will happen to you when you're with the great Raymond Williams. Just remember that," he said, as he patted Teddy hard on the back. "Look, we'll just sit and skim stones and see who can make them jump the furthest. Then we'll have a sandwich and some pop. That'll sort it."

CHAPTER 49
MARY

Mary was surprised to see the boys back home so early. She said that they probably wished they'd stayed out longer as now they were in, she could rope them in for a Saturday evening round of Solo, once she'd managed to get shot of Rhoda and got her off to sleep. Dora was out with her friends again – burning the candle at both ends as it was a Saturday – so that meant they were desperate. She had a lovely pot of stew cooking slowly in the bottom oven of the Rayburn. That would be their reward. With as much bread as they wanted to mop. Then on with the cards.

After everyone had been fed and watered, Teddy started putting up the blackouts without his father or mother having to ask. Jim said that it was a crying shame that the window had to be obscured on such a fine, clear night, and Mary retorted that was a small price to pay. *Some* people didn't have any glass left in their windows. Or any businesses through no fault of their own. She looked at Teddy as she said this and he gave her the thumbs up. And she knew then that he knew what she'd been up to and what she stood for and she felt shoulders rise for the first time in a long time with what felt like pride.

She, Jim and Raymond stood at the window then as Teddy paused with what he was doing for them to take a final look at the stars which were really putting on a show.

"Beautiful," sighed Mary, as Teddy wedged the blackout inside the frame, shutting out the whole world.

"Might be beautiful, but Jerry'll be able to pick us all off a treat tonight. No need for flares," said Jim.

"You always have to spoil things, Jim. Where's your sense of wonder? Of optimism?" said Mary.

Jim started to whistle, *pack up your troubles in your old kit bag and smile, smile, smile,* and Mary told him to zip it. And she slapped him playfully on his arm as they made their way back to the table.

"Do you play cards at your house?" Mary asked Raymond.

"No. Dad didn't like cards and even though he's not there now, Mum and I don't play. Not much fun just the two of us. Though sometimes I play patience – clock patience mostly. On a tray."

"Well that's nice. She won't mind you being in this den of iniquity, will she?" asked Mary.

"No, she's happy to put her feet up, and for me to be with Teddy on his birthday," he said, looking at Teddy.

"Well, Teddy can explain the rules. Don't over-complicate things now, Son, we haven't got all night," she said playfully.

So they played. For matchsticks not money that night: cash was now off limits since the day of the great confession. They didn't want to court trouble and have Mrs. Williams come up knocking at their door accusing them of leading her boy off the straight and narrow. The time ticked by, the clock on the mantelpiece chiming on the hour. At one point Jim got up from his seat and went to the wireless and started turning the dial. The crackle of the needle and the jumble of interference filled the stillness of the room, breaking the mood of concentration around the table.

"What are you looking for at this time of night? It's way past eleven o'clock," said Mary.

"Lord Haw-Haw. See what rubbish he's got to spout tonight. *Germany calling. Germany calling,*" said Jim, trying to imitate the little traitor.

Mary threw Jim one of her looks over the top of the glasses which said, *not tonight, Jim, just get back here, shut up and sit down.* She didn't find Lord Haw-Haw funny at all. She found his nasal voice and his propaganda chilling. Jim found it amusing. And anyway, they'd been advised – though not told – by the powers that be that it would be better for everyone's peace of mind if they didn't listen to it at all. Mary didn't want Raymond to go telling tales. She was so concerned about what people might think and say about her and Jim since the pig episode even though the knowledge of it couldn't have gone any further than the four walls in which she was now sitting.

"Anyway, it's getting late now. You two boys need to think

about getting some shut-eye," she said. "Tomorrow is another day."

Mary remembered glancing at the clock: it was almost one o'clock when the warning siren screamed. She'd remained downstairs clearing up and doing a bit of knitting when it was quiet, after the boys had gone in their cubbyhole and Jim had said his goodnight to her before going to his quarters, as he called them.

No sooner had the incessant howl of the siren ceased than the bombing began. It was close: window panes vibrating; walls shuddering. The sepia photograph of William and his fellow choristers at the choir school trembled on the string on which it hung and when the blast was done, Mary looked and it was all askew. Then the blasts came in quick succession, rocking the house. Jim came down the stairs at speed with Rhoda still sleeping in his arms. She remembered thinking how quickly kids adapted to a new but ridiculous situation, as if it became normal when it was anything but.

"For Christ's sake, Mary," shouted Jim. "Get under the stairs."

Jim turned the knob of the make-shift space they had deemed would give them adequate shelter, opened the door, and urged Mary to hurry up and hunker down.

"Shove over, boys," he said. "This is a bloody emergency."

They all cowered in the cupboard, no-one saying a word. Jim held the torch and Mary could see that everyone's face, apart from Rhoda's was pale with fear. For once, Jim was holding back from being the performer and trying to lift the mood with his jokes and antics. This was not the time.

"This is the closest it's been so far," said Mary. "If I believed in a God, I'd ask him to save us now."

"We'll be alright, won't we boys?" said Jim, looking at them to back him up.

The drone of aircraft and the screech of the descending bombs were relentless, as were the blasts that followed each screech. Some came in rapid sequences, as though they were intent and focussed on a particular target.

"Well, they're a good way away from the docks. Bastards. That sounds like it's the railway line, peppering it all along, taking the whole bloody section out, I reckon, between the embankment and the tunnel. Just pray the ammunition train isn't on it," said Jim.

"How can anyone do this to people? Ordinary people?" said Mary.

"The terrible thing is Mary, we're no better. Probably doing the same thing to them."

"I could never imagine ever doing something like that," said Mary. "I couldn't imagine any woman doing anything like that."

Jim didn't have chance to reply as another screech came sounding as though it was almost within touching distance. Down it whined toward the ground as they were counting the seconds, their hands over their ears to protect themselves from the blast.

But it never came. Their shoulders were raised in tension almost like ear-muffs and they kept their hands held to their ears and looked at each other, realising full well what had happened. Or what had failed to happen.

"That's not gone off," said Mary. Let's get out of here," she said, as the all-clear sounded.

When they stepped out of the cupboard, Mary fully expected to see the high explosive bomb in the passage of 141. She told Jim to hang on tightly to Rhoda as he carried her towards the front door and into the road. She shouted at the boys to stop grinning, it wasn't funny at all. She often wondered why she shouted to show love and concern.

It was the middle of the night, if time and patterns mattered anymore. The local ARP men were grouped at the top of Beattie Street, just outside Morris the grocers on the corner opposite. The smell of acrid smoke hung in the summer air. Mary could taste it. Looking down towards the docks she could see a red glow over what she thought must be the Landore area: the whole town looked to be on fire. With that police cars, fire engines and the bomb disposal people started to arrive, the ringing of bells getting ever-closer.

Mary and the family walked towards Beattie Street and looked towards Townhill. Jim had been right. Looked like the railway line had taken a direct hit, and a train, as the flames leapt high into the sky.

"To think me and Raymond were playing down there today, Mum," said Teddy.

And Mary clipped him around the ear.

As they looked down the street, they could see the commotion at number 3. The Demery's house. Out they came, and up the street, helped by the ARP men: Mervyn, and his two sisters, Lizzie and Marian, both wrapped in blankets despite the warmth of the evening.

"Stand back, please everyone," instructed the ARP man. "Make way."

Mary could see that Mervyn was trembling from head to foot. He'd always had the shakes, ever since he came back from the War, but now he was juddering, his jaw loose and teeth chattering, his whole body wracked as if in some convulsion. In the beam of the lights, Mary could see that the three of them were covered with white dust: in their hair, over their faces, in their eyebrows, coating their dressing gowns and slippers. Their terrified eyes stared out from the ghostliness.

Mary realised that for Mervyn and Jim, and all the women, herself included, this war didn't seem like a new and separate one, but as if the first one had never gone away, was on constant repeat, like the indigestion that was now starting to take hold of her, a squeezing pain in her chest.

The ARP men resorted to megaphones to inform the crowd that was forming and gawping at the Demery family. Jim had been right. The bomb hadn't gone off: it had pierced the roof of number 3, gone through the sisters' bedroom, through the ceiling, and had come to rest in the downstairs passage, next to the cupboard under the stairs where the three Demerys had been shielding. It was what the men explained was a delayed reaction high explosive bomb. *They'd had a lucky escape*, they went onto say. Perhaps they had. But it was all relative now Mary thought as she witnessed the three sorry figures being escorted away from the area which was being heavily sandbagged.

And no-one knew what time had been set on the fuse for it to detonate.

"One o'clock," I reckon, said Mary. "Just when everyone's sitting down to their Sunday dinner."

As instructed, everyone in the immediate vicinity of Beattie Street had to evacuate: *with immediate effect*, was the emotionless language that was used. Jim handed Rhoda over to Teddy while she and Jim darted inside 141 to open the windows facing Beattie Street. They'd been told in no uncertain terms by the bomb disposal experts to *make it quick* as there were *no guarantees*. While Jim went upstairs and dealt with the windows there, Mary went to the mantelshelf in the living room. She removed all of William's letters and put them in her handbag, as though she could keep them and his memory safe inside the leather. She wasn't going anywhere without the letters or her handbag.

Back outside the shop, Mary took Rhoda from Teddy and told Teddy and Raymond to bugger off sharpish to Raymond's house. Tell Raymond's mother not to worry, and that her cottage was far enough away from the expected extent of the blast.

Her indigestion burned her throat as she thought about Dora. Where the hell was she? Who was she with? She could never extract much out of the girl. But she wasn't a little girl and she had to remember and she'd lived in London quite independently for years so she had no right to demand to know the ins and outs of her every move. All she ever got from her in response to her asking where she was going was, *Out. Don't worry.* And now this.

Mary watched over them in spirit as Teddy and Raymond walked down Middle Road in their pyjamas. She watched them pass the graveyard at Babell, the stars lighting their way. She watched as Teddy turned and waved and gave her the thumbs up again, before disappearing down the dip before Raymond's row.

Mary, Jim and now Rhoda who was wide awake and disoriented, shouting 'where are we going?' started to make their way up Middle Road. All they had in the world for the time being was each other and the clothes they were standing in. It shocked Mary to think of how frivolous she could be. Inappropriate even. People would have things of significance to concern themselves with other than what she was wearing. Yet she was pleased she was still respectable to the outside world in her dress. Good job she'd stayed up late.

In their pyjamas, Jim and Rhoda cut sad figures at the side of her. They looked misplaced. She'd seen images of people dressed like this in the newsreel: refugees walking along unknown roads to God knows where, fleeing the enemy on the continent. And now she was one of those people. It was here, right in the middle of the night in ordinary Middle Road, Cwmbwrla. Jim was now being proved right. She recalled what he'd said to her that day that war broke out. She couldn't believe it was almost a year ago. *The world's a small place now and it will be moving in, and people from Cwmbwrla will be moving out, and everything will be on the bloody move again. All over the place,* he'd kept saying. *You mark my words.*

Mary felt she'd marched two hundred miles rather than the two hundred yards to Mrs Stone's. Even though she was carrying nothing but her handbag, with William's letters, tucked within its leather, she still felt weighed down. Physically her calves ached and her ankles were swelling: just because there was a war on didn't mean that everything else ceased to happen. And her periods were still happening on occasion and she was worried that tonight of all nights, when she'd be forced to sleep in somebody else's bed, sod's law it would be the night. Being on the Change was a bugger. Catch men going through it and then they'd have something to moan about. But women didn't seem to moan about it. They just got on with it and suffered in silence.

But her heaviness had been worse since William's death, and then the pig business and Jim's confession about his past. It was a lot to carry. Perhaps she'd made it worse for herself by banishing him to the bedroom, as she was so far down the line into him making reparations, she didn't know when she would call a stop, at what point enough would be enough.

Then there was Sybil and the baby. And now she found herself in Mrs Stone's so perhaps this was the moment when the decisions would be taken out of her hands.

"I'm sorry you've all been turfed out of your home, Mrs Froom," said Mrs Stone as she took her, Jim and Rhoda into the back kitchen and made them a cup of tea. "But please make yourself at home for as long as you're here."

Mary looked around the kitchen: sparkling and clean, a kitchen cabinet, a table with a fresh cloth on it, matching cups and saucers. It looked almost unused.

"It's nice to have someone in the house for a change," said Mrs Stone. "It always used to be full."

Mary understood the pristine nature of the kitchen then. It was warm but cold at the same time if such a combination were possible. Mr Stone had never come back from the First War, and the lodgers that she'd taken into her two spare room, had gone off to the Second one.

"The beds are all aired, I like to keep them like that. Ready. And the bathroom's here," she said, opening the door on the landing to show them.

Mary noticed that the lavatory was in there, taking pride of place on a kind of plinth in the room where the walls were white tiled to half-way up and edged with smaller, oblong black ones. God, what she'd give to have a toilet inside. She felt like she'd arrived in a posh hotel, though she'd never been in an hotel once in her forty-four years.

"I'll leave you to it, then," said Mrs Stone. "Hope you get a good night's sleep. What's left of it. We've had a right pasting tonight, haven't we?"

Mary placed Rhoda in the little single bed in the box room. It was snug, and there was a little bedside lamp with a dim light and a shade. Rhoda had fallen to sleep again in the kitchen, her little cheeks were rosy in the glow of the lamp, and she'd reverted to sucking her thumb. Mary wouldn't take it from her mouth. Not tonight. She tucked Rhoda in, kissed her on the forehead, left the lamp switched on, and the door slightly ajar, and went to where she was to sleep with the man who had become a stranger to her in bed.

Jim was sitting on the eiderdown. Mary looked at the poor sod there in his pyjamas waiting for her, knowing that he'd like to get under the covers, but not daring.

"It's alright, Jim. I think you've done your time," she said, "Help me with the bed."

She took one side and Jim the other and they pulled back the eiderdown and turned down the flannelette sheets. Jim took off his slippers and placed them neatly under the chair at the side of the bed and got under the covers. He didn't say a word, but lay on his back, his head on the two plumped-up pillows and waited.

Mary felt like she had when they first married and officially shared a bed together. She took off her glasses and put them on the little table at the side of the bed and she unpinned the waves in her hair. She placed the grips alongside her glasses, ready for the morning. She knew Jim wasn't looking at her. He was staring at the ceiling so that he wouldn't. She unbuttoned her dress and raised it over her head, closing her eyes as she did so that if Jim did catch a glimpse of her, she wouldn't see. Her hair sparked with the static and her fingertips tingled with slight shocks as the fabric passed over her hair. Her petticoat she kept on, but she rummaged underneath it and unclasped her corset and slid it to the floor. She unhooked her brassiere and eased the straps down over her arms, one at a time and drew it up through the neckline of the front of her petticoat. Sitting on the edge of the bed, she rolled down her stockings to her ankles and then sat on the edge of her side of the bed and gently pulled them from her feet so that she didn't ladder them. Her knickers she kept on. They felt damp. And then she knew why. She picked up her handbag and took out a couple of her spare cotton handkerchiefs embroidered with M, she always kept in there. Just in case. She folded the handkerchiefs to make a wadge, placing it as best she could in the gusset of her knickers. It would have to do.

With Jim still not speaking and remaining staring at the ceiling, she pulled back the sheets, turned out the little lamp at her side, and got into bed. As if by rote, she reached out her right arm towards Jim as he reached out his left to hers. He interlaced the little finger of his left hand, with the right little finger of hers. Love-knotted they used to call it when they were young.

"I've missed you, Mary," he said softly. "The touch of you. Your smell."

"Me too, Jim. It's good to have you back."

"New start now."

"Yes, new start. No more secrets. Ever."

"No. No more secrets. I promise, Mary."

"That's why I need to tell you something, Jim. Something I haven't told you and I should have. It's about Sybil."

CHAPTER 50
TEDDY

Teddy had said he'd give Raymond a hand with the weeding in his garden the next morning. It wasn't a chore especially when the reward would be one of Mrs Williams' Sunday roast dinners. As he hoed between the rows of carrots, to stop the chickweed and fat-hen from taking hold, he could smell the cooking seeping out of the back kitchen window, which Mrs Williams had left on the hasp because of the weather. Lamb. He knew the smell. His stomach groaned.

He rested his arm on the hoe for a moment and looked at the garden. It was more like a farm. Since Raymond's father had been away, Raymond had managed this all by himself. Taken responsibility. He'd told Teddy that before his father left for war, that he's have to step in his shoes and be 'the man of the house'. Teddy looked at the farm his friend had created where everything was coming good all at once and in abundance: rows of carrots, beetroot, lettuce, shibwns, peas staked on twigs, broad beans, and the kidney beans Raymond was now picking ready for dinner. He didn't even have to reach anymore to pick them from the top of the canes. Teddy felt Raymond was growing so fast he'd be gone from him soon.

Teddy wished they had a garden at 141. Even though he tended what was left of Louisa's next door for a tanner a week, it wasn't the same. His father would enjoy gardening again if he'd give it a try. The feel of the soil on his hands, the satisfaction in sowing seeds and seeing them come to fruition, would be good for him. He'd have to encourage him when he got back home. Be more like Raymond and take the initiative. It seemed Raymond even had the weeds under control.

Teddy turned to the sound of Mrs, Williams' voice coming

through the opened window.

"Be on the table in half an hour, boys. Raymond – hurry up with those beans. Haven't got all day. And then don't forget to wash your hands before you come to the table to sit down."

Teddy watched Raymond hand his mother the beans through the window and then walk back towards him.

"Time to down tools for the day, now," instructed Raymond.

Teddy held his hoe upright and scraped the clods of earth off with the sole of his shoes. His father wouldn't be happy about that when he went to polish them up that evening. If indeed they did get to be back in 141 later. Then he walked along the neatly mown path at the side of the vegetable rows, thinking how ridiculous he must look to Raymond as he was still in his pyjamas with his lace-up shoes. But Raymond wasn't laughing, but held the door of the shed open for him, and they both hung up their gardening implements and went back outside.

It was as they neared the kitchen that the bomb went off. Teddy turned and looked at Raymond and then towards the source of the blast. Everything was in slow motion: the roofs of Beattie Street being blown high into the blue sky, hovering there for what seemed like minutes – slates, chimney pots, lead flashings, gutters – held there, frozen before his eyes, as though a frame had stuttered to a halt in a Pathé Newsreel, before the debris came floating, slowly, slowly, soundlessly free-falling, until the disparate parts that had made up people's homes hit the ground, and a billowing cloud of dust rose, obliterating everything. And then there was a long drawn-out charged silence unlike the sound of any silence he'd ever heard before.

Teddy stood motionless in that strange stillness. Beattie Street had been blown sky high. But it wasn't the end. He was still here standing with Raymond in the garden. In this moment, he felt he'd had some sort of revelation, that despite the pressures of the war and his father, it wasn't inevitable that he'd follow in his footsteps, was it? It was an odd sign, but it was as if the explosion was telling him something. For a split second he felt it might be William close to him, whispering to him, but that was daft. As stupid and impossible as it seemed, there was a powerful voice that was not his own inside his head: *You need to chase your dreams, Teddy. You've changed a lot since you were fourteen and you're going back to Dynevor, this term and next term. This year and the year after that. You might be the boy with the hand-me-down jumpers and the stupid home-made woollen trunks with a chevron, but you're bright enough to know there's a really big difference between being a butcher and a surgeon. Step into the surgeon's gown, not the striped apron. Stand your ground, Teddy.*

Teddy felt his insides shivering, again.

"What time is it?" he asked Raymond, after a lag of time he couldn't determine, his croaky voice breaking the stillness.

Raymond looked at his wrist watch.

"It's one o'clock," he replied. "Dead on."

CHAPTER 51

MARY

Mary had thought the family might be out of their house for a good while; but it was later in the evening of that same day, when the area had been deemed safe, and the dust had settled, they were given the go-ahead to return.

She walked back down Middle Road, hand in hand with Jim and Rhoda looking like refugees among the grey ordinariness of Welsh terraced houses. Mary couldn't believe it was still Sunday, less than twenty-four hours since they'd been evacuated. So much had happened. So much had changed. Barriers were now in place to cordon off Beattie Street – or what was left of Beattie Street – and she paused with Jim and Rhoda on the legal side of them and stared, unable to voice what she was witnessing.

"Why's it all gone?" asked Rhoda, Mary having no idea how she could ever answer that apparently simple question.

It was foreign territory: the familiar made unfamiliar. The whole row had gone up; there were mostly just external walls at either end where the Burmans and the Richards had lived, and in between, odd rows of broken bricks to indicate where the walls that separated each house had been. In all this destruction, Mary was amazed that the debris hadn't spread further, as most of the rubble seemed to be within the footprint of each house. But that might have been because of the teams of men who seemed to be everywhere, busy shovelling and carting bricks to the waiting lorries. One of the men told her that they were making the bomb site good; that's all they could do for the time being. There was no way of knowing when the houses might be rebuilt and their occupants could return.

It was then that Mary realised that there was never any going back to the way things were: for the residents of Beattie

Street or for her family. Everything in the wider landscape of Cwmbwrla had been changed forever. She considered whether this same truth held when it came to Jim. Or the kids for that matter. Little Rhoda? Teddy? Dora?

Dora, elusive Dora, she didn't know what would happen with that one. She didn't divulge much about her nursing or her private life. She was what Mary's mother would have called, *a dark horse*. She seemed to enjoy the nursing and Mary knew it would make a good career for her. It was a passport to work anywhere she liked. Perhaps she'd stay in Swansea and get digs with some of the friends she spent so much time with. Perhaps, after this war was over, she'd return to London. After all, what was there in Swansea to keep her? She'd love Dora to take her in her confidence and tell her what she was thinking. She knew her daughter well enough though, to know that just because she wasn't including herself and Jim in her decision-making, didn't mean she wasn't still planning. Mary was old and wise enough to know that just because things weren't talked about, or out in the open, it didn't mean they were simmering under the surface. The unexploded bomb at the side of the stairs of Demery's was proof of that. And now look.

Mary hadn't forgotten about Jim's duplicity either. His bare-faced lies. Just because she'd allowed him to share the double bed out of necessity, didn't mean that she'd given him the absolution he craved. He'd come clean, and knowing Jim, that made him feel better. But now she carried the burden of his repentance as well as her own disappointment. She'd accept; but she didn't know whether she would ever forgive. It would be different. No going back. Just like the poor buggers from Beattie Street would have to stay in temporary housing until it was time for them to come home. It would be in the same place but it would be unfamiliar and wouldn't be what they had and loved before because that had been taken away from them through no fault of their own. It was all so bloody unnecessary and tragic.

But she would cope. She'd rise out of the ashes of her grief and her almost doomed marriage and her broken dreams. It would be a new world when all this was over. She surely wouldn't be too old to be the woman she was capable of being. To have a role. Perhaps be a nurse like her daughter. After all, she'd only just turned forty-four. But realistically, she might be too old for that, all the energy you needed to stay on your feet for such long hours. But she cared for people. And she wanted that care to be practical. Not like the religious types that got her goat, spouting platitudes, but active Christianity of the practical kind. Believing in people. All the politics she'd been steeped in as a young girl, all the stuff of life she'd learned since, all the mechanics of Parliament she read about in *Hansard*. She could do that. She wouldn't go for Prime Minster straight away, she laughed to herself. She'd start little and local, and having a business she knew she'd have a bit of an advantage even if she were but a mere woman. She could be a Local Councillor in the Cwmbwrla Ward. She'd show them how to get things done rather than sitting around a wooden table and talking about it. She'd make it better for the women – and the men – the people of the area, including the Italians and the Germans who'd have to be bedded in again hoping to find a new way forward once all this hell was over. But for now she'd have to put this dream on hold as local council elections had been suspended because of the war. Suspended was a good word for how she felt right at that moment.

Some things were more certain in the meantime: Jim would have the meat delivered the next day as usual and would stand at his block and cut it up. He would continue to moan about the customers, continue to bet and continue to whistle because he couldn't help himself. On Sundays he would shine the shoes on the steps in the false hope that it would be enough to ward off further catastrophe. It was part of his condition, and that wasn't his fault. That was what war had done to him. Especially when he'd put the stopper on the effects of the first one for so long. But she was adamant that he'd have to shape up about the things he could do to help himself and in doing so, help her. And she'd help him all she could, because she knew that would make her life better too. He'd have to muck in and support her be the person she wanted to be before it was all too late.

If she was honest, she was delighted that Rhoda would start school next month as planned. That seemed as certain as anything could be in life anymore. She needed the discipline and the friends as the bright little things was raring to go. Mary was looking forward to it. She wondered if most mothers felt like this and she guessed they did but didn't have the nerve to say.

As for Teddy, she feared he'd be another victim in all this upheaval. Teddy had to stand his ground. He was a good boy. Too good if there was such a thing. He was a boy who'd do as he was told always to the detriment of himself. Of his dreams. She realised she'd leaned on him too much over the years. She hoped Teddy would have the resolve to realise his dreams of being a surgeon, rather than doing his duty, doing what was expected of him and succumb to his father's weakness. There was strength in weakness sometimes, she knew that from experience. She didn't know for sure what the outcome would be but prayed Teddy's shoes would take him anywhere he wanted to go just as his teacher had told him. He was fourteen now. He could officially leave school. Wear long trousers. This would be a big year and only its passing would tell how it would play out.

Time would tell a lot of things, but she wouldn't let things just run away with them all as though she was powerless to direct the course of action. Their life had been shattered, but it wasn't in complete ruins. She would rebuild what might be left of her family to go forward in new ways. Because she did have a choice. They all had choices.

Dora would be home later. Teddy would be summoned back from Raymond's. For now, they would go inside and get out the dustpan and broom and mop and bucket and dusters and polish. It wasn't much; but it was a start.

CHAPTER 52
JIM

Jim was glad that he'd been the one to decide that they had opened all the windows facing Beattie Street. They hadn't lost a pane. It was one thing he'd done right and it felt good. Of course, the house had gained about an inch of dust in every room, apart from the shop and the upstairs front bedroom, which had remained sealed tight as those rooms faced Middle Road. He grinned and stroked his chin as though in deep and serious contemplation telling Mary that she needed to realise that it was a sign that the gods might be looking down on him for once, and she could at least allow him to reclaim his territory in his own bed for that night.

"All hands on deck," he shouted, as every one of the family now safely back home, set about cleaning up.

It was late but they all decided that now was the time so that everything would be fresh for the week ahead. Jim said he'd be in charge of this mop-up operation.

They scrubbed the bathroom until it shone and then worked along the landing and down the stairs into the passage; it wasn't too bad, considering. Until, that was, they reached the middle room door and looked at Mary's piano, completely coated with fine, white dust. Jim stood back, silent, not daring, waiting for instructions.

"Don't you dare touch," said Mary. "You can read the sign. It still applies."

Jim didn't argue but turned on his heels and told the family to evacuate and leave her to it. She had a lot going on with her time of the month. Together they would sort out the rest of the house so it would be good and ready for when Mary finally emerged. When she did, she came into the living room and ran her index finger along the mantel shelf, inspecting operations.

"Well, have we passed, boss?" asked Jim.

"It'll do for now," said Mary, reaching for her handbag on the chair, taking out the letters from William and placing them back in the letter rack on the mantelpiece.

CHAPTER 53
MARY

It was quite dark outside by then so Mary took the flashlight while Dora picked up the mat from in front of the fire which Mary had told them all had not been cleaned to her satisfaction. Mary unwound the rope and let the washing line down for Dora to hang the mat over it.

"You hold the torch," said Mary. "And make sure you direct it on the yard. Don't want anyone shouting, *Put That Light Out*, not when I've got things to do."

Mary walked to the old stables and came back with the rug-beater which hadn't been used in years.

"Stand back," she said to Dora.

Dora did as she was told and sat down on the step.

Mary began to thrash the mat, setting up a regular rhythm, the dust escaping the wool with every fierce beat, particles rising into the warm, dark air and illuminated in the beam of the flashlight. She didn't want to stop, she wanted to go on thrashing this inanimate object until the feeling that was trapped inside her had disappeared.

"Are you alright, Mum?" asked Dora with concern.

"I'm fine. Be even better when I've finished with this bugger."

"You need to calm down, you know."

"I will. Just let me be," said Mary. "Fed up to the teeth with keeping things inside. Always better out than in."

When she'd finally stilled, she sat beside Dora on the step to get her breath back.

"You've had a lot to carry, Mum. I don't know how you do it, really. And yes, you're right, things are better out than in."

As they sat together on the step, Mary felt Dora's arm around her, and her lean her head against her shoulder. The physical presence of her and the rare show of affection made her feel safe and loved. They shared too few moments like this, just the two women together, because that was who Dora was now: a woman.

Mary found it bewildering and beautiful that she had once carried her within her womb – secretly at first – and 'prematurely', given birth to her: the first child. She was ashamed now as she was held within her grown-up baby's embrace, that she'd feared back then that Jim had been hopeful of a son who would automatically carry on the family name. If he did, he'd never let it be known. And now Mary felt an overwhelming feeling of time passing, and with it inevitable change and a pride in this self-reliant human who Jim and her had managed to create and rear. They'd done something right during their marriage. Though she doubted Dora would be one to ever want to see her name in lights above the shop: JC Froom and Daughter had never been considered by Jim, and if he'd considered it, she knew full well this free spirit by her side would reject the offer.

As they enjoyed the moment Mary sat calmly, not budging from the comfort and smell of her grown-up baby. She breathed in the distinctive scent of her, sniffing her thick, red hair, the way she had sniffed her scalp, fascinated by her pulsing fontanelle, when she was a new-born.

"Well?" she said gently, not wanting to ruin the ambience, "I think I know what you're going to say. I'm not daft, you know. Your feet are itching to take you away again, aren't they?"

Mary waited for Dora to respond. It took a while.

"No, I'm not going away, Mum. Not yet, anyway. But in a way that depends on the war, and on you – and Dad," she said.

"You're not ill are you?" asked Mary. "There's not something going on that you're not telling me about, is there?"

"I'm not sick, Mum. Don't worry," said Dora, taking Mary's hand and squeezing it.

"You haven't got yourself involved in any undercover operations or crime, have you? I couldn't take that."

"No, Mum. I'm not a spy but I am sort of living my life undercover."

"Oh for God's sake, Dora, enough of the riddles," said Mary, breaking away from the embrace, feeling a rumbling in the air again.

Mary was quiet then as Dora spoke in measured tones, spelling out all that she needed Mary to know. Mary listened intently, trying to take it all in.

"Mum, you know how close I am to Sybil, don't you? Of course you do – you're not daft – you've seen how we've kept our friendship going through the years: all through the time I was away in London, and since I've been back home. As you and Dad have often said, she's like family, part of the furniture. And she would have been family if William had gone on living. Bear with me, Mum, because this is quite difficult for me to explain... I'd like Sybil still to be part of our family now. With the new baby..."

"Of course you do, Dora, I mean, it's only right ... "

"As you can imagine, when she did eventually tell them about the baby, they didn't take to it kindly. They're keeping her almost a prisoner over there until the confinement. You could say she's been in confinement all her life."

"I wondered why I hadn't seen her for so long – apart from sometimes seeing her peering over the nets in the front room. I didn't want to pry, poke my nose in there in case she hadn't let her parents know. What are they planning for her?" asked Mary.

"Adoption," said Dora, searching her mother's face for a response.

Mary's face was burning now.

"The Bowens? Planning to give a part of my son and Sybil away to strangers? Christians? They're more concerned about being judged as bad parents and having their so-called standing in the community – and in the chapel – besmirched as they might say, than they are about Sybil's predicament and her happiness. It's a baby for God's sake. She hasn't marched into Poland. She hasn't daubed anyone's front door with filth or roughed anyone up. It isn't evil or dirty. For shame on them. Not on Sybil. D'you know, sometimes I think Man created God rather than God created Man so *men* like Mr Bowen can make up rules to keep everyone else in place in order to suit him. Though I'll never set foot in Babell, I can see him there: Mr Stanley Bowen, sitting right up the front in that bloody *Set Fawr* as they call it, where he can be seen to be big and important when he is nothing but a weak and timid little squirt. I'll help Sybil. It goes without saying. We're going to be grandparents just as Mr and Mrs Bowen. And anyway, I can't bear the idea of my grandchild out there somewhere with someone I don't know from Adam. It's all I have left of William to hang onto. I assured Sybil when she told me about the baby that our door would always be open should the worst happen when she told her parents. And that still stands, Love. Tell her that I meant what I said and that she's welcome here anytime. We'll get through this like we've got everything so far."

"Are you sure, Mum? It's a huge commitment."

"I might not go to church or chapel, and get down on my knees, but I know right from wrong, Dora. It's the way I was brought up."

"But Mum, as I said, this is difficult to explain. And make the sleeping arrangements *complicated*," said Dora.

"Spit it out, Dora, said Mary. I can't take anything left in the dark anymore. So what now?"

"Well, you know I said I love Sybil. I mean love as in the way a woman loves a man, or William loved Sybil, and the way Sybil loved William, for I know deep down that Sybil loved him deeply in that special way there is between a man and a woman. You see, Mum, I love Sybil in *that* way. Um, do you understand what I'm getting at?"

Mary said nothing but saw all of a sudden the pieces of Dora's elusive and unspoken-about life falling into a perfect whole.

"I see," said Mary, not knowing at that moment whether she did fully understand the ramifications that Dora was alluding to.

"You see, Mum. It wouldn't be appropriate for Sybil and I to share a room. Not feeling as I do about her. Of course she doesn't know. Or at least she hasn't said so. And I would never tell her as it would spoil our friendship. And it wouldn't be right. I'd be awkward. And untruthful, really. I'd hate that. And I'd never take any risk in jeopardising our friendship by telling her because you know, Mum, I'll never have *that* sort of relationship with Sybil, Mum... Mum?"

Mary knew that the words her daughter was uttering were

rocking the already unstable ground on which she was standing. She realised that Dora could have left them unsaid; but that would be a coward's way out. And Dora wasn't a coward and neither was she. Of course she could withstand what was coming.

"So," said Mary. "Change of plan. I see what you're saying about the *practical* sleeping arrangements. It's hardly Buckingham Palace."

Mary could see Dora's already pale face was white in the low beam of the flashlight.

"It won't be that difficult what with you working shifts. Rhoda will have to stay where she is in what is now your room, with Sybil and the new baby. It might do her good. If you're working nights, you can bed down there in the day when they're up and about. If you're on day shifts, then simple: you'll have to share the back room with Teddy. You can sleep in William's bed. I'd like that," said Mary.

"I doubt whether it will be for long, anyway," said Dora.

"What d'you mean?"

"Well, I reckon women will be called up soon. And I might leave nursing and enlist ahead of that. I've never liked the uniform anyway," said Dora, laughing. "But seriously. I want to do my bit for the war effort. I've been thinking that once Sybil is back on track, I can sign up for the WAFS. I feel I owe it to William. And I think Forces' Life will suit women like me, if you get my gist, Mum. There'll be a lot of women who can't wait to live the life of *camaraderie* the Services offer."

"You must do what you must do, Dora. Be true to yourself. It's taken me until now to realise that."

"Will you tell, Dad?"

"Yes, I will tell your father because there are to be no more secrets in 141. Not anymore."

"Oh Christ, Mum. How do you think he'll take it?"

"It will be what it will be, Dora. That's not your problem. That one's for your father and me."

"I'm so sorry, Mum."

"There's nothing to be sorry for, Dora. I'd have been far sorrier if you hadn't been able to confide in me," she said, as she kissed Dora on the forehead.

"I'm lucky to have a mother like you," said Dora, as Mary ran her fingers through her hair.

"It's not going to be easy any of this," said Mary, realising that she was echoing the words that Jim said around the dinner table that first Sunday war broke out. "But love is love. It's as simple as that when you boil it all down."

CHAPTER 54
MARY

The last weekend in August signalled that the summer was almost over. The nights were already drawing in, and it was cooler in the mornings and evenings. Mary thought back to the previous year: waiting for the inevitable announcement that would be coming down the airwaves that they were at war with Germany. That had been a long, stretched out few days, as if time had been ticking to a different beat.

And the months that followed felt the same. As autumn turned into winter and into spring, there was a drawn out sense of unreality, that a war was going on somewhere, but it wasn't happening to them in Cwmbwrla. Nothing was happening and then suddenly, everything was happening and her son was dead, and the bombs had started to fall, and her husband had been caught red-handed and the revelations had followed, and no sooner than that had happened, there was another revelation from her elder daughter. Life had sped up, gathering momentum like a strange home movie running at the wrong speed.

It felt like that again now: a lull fell over the house, a period of brief calm, when the air-raids had ceased for a while. There was a slow tempo to life in those last days of summer.

Mary knew it wasn't going to last: Rhoda would be off to school on the first Monday in September, Teddy would return the same day to Dynevor, Jim would be in the shop cutting up just as he always had. Mary realised it was more than a lull: it was the anticipation of emptiness: William would never come back; it was unlikely Dora ever would once she had joined-up; Rhoda had countless years in school ahead of her. As for Teddy, she didn't know. For perhaps the first time, she felt as Jim did: she needed her son, too. But she knew it wasn't fair that it had to fall on

Teddy's head to try and heal the gaping wound that had been suddenly gashed into the fabric of their lives.

She felt selfish even thinking this; that Teddy was some kind of replacement for his elder brother, just a smaller version. But it was hard to survive grief and she knew they were clinging on to anything that might save them. It was likely that this was influencing her offer about Sybil, too: that she wasn't perhaps a generous and good-hearted selfless soul but was motivated by self-interest and desperation to take a tiny part of her dead son in the form of a new life and rock it in her arms for comfort. And Sybil, too: there was likely something deep down which wanted to comfort and protect a person who was carrying a part of their son and a little of them.

But she was also adamant that she was going to do something to please herself for the first time in her life and in doing so, please others. Outside the shop. She could see it now. Her future self. When this bloody war was over, she was going to take her place in the gap that was left behind and try to make it whole again. And she was going to do it with Jim's blessing for she knew that it would ultimately be a blessing for him too.

Late on the Saturday afternoon, Mary brought the kettle to a boil on the Rayburn and made a pot of tea. She placed two cups and saucers on a tray, a couple of Marie biscuits on a plate, opened the scullery door, and then walked up the back yard to the side entrance and into Beattie Street.

She couldn't get over the site of the row not being there anymore. It had been a week now since it had gone up, and most of the loose brick debris, wood and glass had been carted away. It was as though no-one had ever lived there though there was a small jam-jar of the last of the summer's sweet peas which was still somehow intact and had survived everything, still positioned unscathed on a little side table not unlike her own knick-knack table. It made her well up. And the gardens still bloomed: they had been proud of their back gardens in the row, and without the houses Mary could take in the sight of hydrangeas, hollyhocks, delphiniums, tall lupins, marigold, carnations and those sweet peas. They were cottage gardens that would give those of where she came from in Fordingbridge a run for their money. And to think the Welsh were not known for their gardens.

The stone walls that demarcated each garden from the next, were still there in parts, and she could see Jim in the distance from where she was standing, toiling away in the Demery's garden. It was good to see him putting his back into something again. It had been a long while.

She walked down the street with the tray and negotiated her way carefully over the uneven ground to join him in the garden.

"Don't stop," she said, as she placed the tray on the broken wall and found a flat spot to place her behind.

He smiled at her and continued with the task in hand, digging out a row ready for planting. He'd taken his old gardening boots that he'd brought with him to Middle Road from Devon, that had lain idle in the old stables for years. When he'd picked them up, a mouse who had taken refuge in the left one, broke free. As was his wont, he'd cleaned them up, inside and out, and deemed they were as good as new. Same with the gardening tools that had hung on the hooks there: he'd cleaned the steel and oiled the wood so that the rakes and the hoes and the spades and the picks were fit for purpose. It was good to see him doing something again. As she looked she wondered if it was as much for his own body and mind as it was for the war effort and digging for victory. She reckoned his personal victories were as important as the national ones.

She hadn't seen him sweat for years and she could see that beads on his forehead, and patches soaking his work-shirt under his armpits. He worked along the width of the garden, the sole of his boot coming down hard on the edge of the shovel, and then him lifting the damp, dark soil and placing it neatly along the trough he was creating. He did everything with precision. With care. It appeared this was a labour of love as well as the practicality of sowing cabbage, kale, onions, marrows, that would come to fruition the next spring and keep them fed at 141. Bloody Jerry might have thought he'd finished off the row, but Jim had other ideas. It would thrive. Regenerate. Come and come again like the veg.

When he'd drilled holes with his wooden dibber, he knelt and planted the marrow seeds, then rose, brushed the earth off his hands, and came to sit next to Mary on the broken wall, resting his spade, edge down, handle up, against the wall close by.

"Looking good," said Mary pouring him out a cup of tea. "Mervyn will be pleased you're keeping an eye on it."

"Well, it's the least I can do, poor buggers to be forced out of your home like that. It's lucky that the corporation can house them until it's all sorted. Not the same though," he said.

"No," she said. "Things change."

"I am trying, Mary. To make things up to you, you know."

"I know you are," she replied, placing her hand on his thigh and patting him.

And then she told him about Sybil and the baby, Mr and Mrs Bowen, and the bits and pieces about Dora and the promise she had made to Dora about Sybil and the fact that she knew he wouldn't mind at all. That was correct wasn't it?

After that, they sat sipping their tea, not saying anything, because there was so much to say that would be better left unsaid. The silence felt comfortable between them there in the garden. Mary breathed in the smell of the warm, turned earth, and the mingling scents of the flowers as late afternoon moved into early evening. She wondered why flowers smelled more strongly at this time of day. And why everything she sensed was more acute since the war: the sight of something beautiful, the feel of sunshine; the depths of her emotions, the intensity of her dreams. It might have been because everything was fleeting and mortality was just around the next bend. She thought back to the scullery, to the night before the messenger had come with the news of William's death. She couldn't find a name to encompass what had happened when she'd heard the singing. A messenger? A premonition? Did it matter anymore because she knew then what it signified even though she couldn't rationalise it, because some things just didn't have logic. And she accepted that now.

"Look," said Jim, whispering to Mary, and pointing to towards the wall. "My little friend is back."

Mary turned to see the little robin, perched on the handle of Jim's spade, its red breast on fire in the lowering sun. It was chirping away quite boldly considering it was in such close proximity to them.

"He knew where to find me, again," said Jim. "D'you know what I'm thinking, Mary?"

"Yes, I do, Jim. And I was just thinking the same thing myself."

CHAPTER 55

JIM

Everything had changed. Yet some things stayed as they always had. On the first Sunday in September, a year to that day since War had been declared, and Chamberlain's voice had intruded into the living room at Middle Road, upending the lives of the Froom family, Jim once again set about to do what he'd done, every subsequent Sunday morning since.

He bent down and delved under the sink in the scullery and pulled out the shoe-cleaning kit. He carried it to the steps and set it down while he took the pages of the *Daily Sketch* that had been dropped through the letterbox by Willie James' paper boy the day before, and spread the paper over the steps and placed the cleaning materials on top. It was good that the text was to be obscured: it didn't make good reading there in black and white: *London blitzed; Battle of Britain continues;* Churchill says: '*never has so much been owed to so few*'. If loss could be translated, it was the feeling he had now in the pit of his stomach. This bloody war had only just begun.

He lined up the shoes as he always did. His and Mary's were the ones they'd had last year and the year before that and as far back as he could remember. They'd make do. A good polish and they'd come up like new. He prised open the tin of Cherry Blossom and pressed his cloth carefully into the polish, using it sparingly on the uppers of Mary's first and then his. He rubbed it gently and evenly into the leathers. He'd let it sink in while he got on with the rest.

He picked up the next shoe in the row: Dora's chunky size 8 and next to it, was a small, dainty shoe. Must be about a size 4, Jim reckoned. Not large like the Frooms' footwear. He took the polish and applied it to Sybil's flat, black slip-ons: first the right, then the left. He looked at the uppers: no sign of wear. Nor on the soles. Despite her being over eight months pregnant, the treads were even. Mary had said she wasn't waddling at all and was carrying very well. He could see that for himself when she'd come to the door with her bag the night before. Mary said she thought Sybil was carrying a boy and she'd got her to lie down on the floor in the living room. Then she'd taken a needle and threaded it and held it above Sybil's swollen belly. Apparently, Mary could tell by the way it hovered and circled, what the sex of the baby would be. Dora had laughed and told her that modern medicine discounted this theory but Jim didn't know what to believe anymore. He was open to suggestion and didn't discount old wives' tales or folklore if it helped give someone the answers they were hoping for and got them through.

He worked his way along the line of shoes: Teddy's were next. Even though they were brand new ready to go back to school, they'd benefit from a good dab of polish. Although Teddy didn't seem to be spurting, his feet were, and judging by their size, Jim thought he'd eventually be a boy of enormous stature – inside and out. He was going into Form 4 in long trousers. He pressed hard with the cloth into the firm, unscathed uppers and wished that Teddy would never leave Middle Road and leave him but he felt the boy had other plans and nothing was going to stand in his way. He'd have to see how it all played out.

Rhoda's shoes were not so tiny now though still little: brand new, black lace-ups that would walk her to her first day at school the next day. He reckoned they'd get some wear; she couldn't sit still one minute.

He picked up his brush and started along the line again, lost in the rhythm of the brush strokes: back, fore; back, fore, making a promise to himself that none of his children – and hopefully, Mary – would ever wear second-hand shoes again. He brushed until all the polish was absorbed by the pliant leather, and every gob of spit fully saturated. Finally, he took a clean, soft cloth and buffed all the shoes in order of size until he could see his face in them. Then he picked up one of his own shoes, and looked hard into the indistinct image in the leather, considering what sort of a man would step into his shoes from now on? He vowed it would be a better one, made a promise to his reflection. He could but try.

Acknowledgements

I would like to thank a host of wonderful people who continue to support me on my writing journey. Firstly, my lovely husband, Philip, who never fails to encourage, especially when the going gets tough; to my strong and clever gang of writerly women friends who prop me up when the words don't come, and say positive things when they do; to writer and academic, Jon Gower, and Film and TV, Director, Euros Lyn, for always being so generous with both time and expertise; to the multi-talented novelist and screenplay writer, and much-respected friend, Fflur Dafydd for motivation and honesty; to my patient literary agent, Gaia Banks of Sheil Land Associates who took a chance on me years ago and has never failed to support me, or stopped believing in my stories. Finally, to Alan Bilton, writer, academic and publisher, who offered me the perfect home for *Weights and Measures* at Watermark Press. Diolch. You all make my 'hard homework' more bearable.

Also published by Watermark Press

Alan Bilton
At Dawn, Two Nightingales

At Dawn, Two Nightingales is rumoured to be the most dangerous poem in the world, its haunted verses said to be invested with mysterious, supernatural powers. The impoverished Count Mitrovsky believes that within the enchanted stanzas lies the key to his beautiful neighbour Mařenka's heart, but other parties are searching for the poem too – sinister censors, dangerous criminals, bandits and brigands of all stripes.

A comic opera in novel form – part quest, part pantomime, part unexpected ghost story – *At Dawn Two Nightingales* is both playful and heartbreaking, an uproarious adventure that upends the conventions of the historical novel at every turn.

'A richly comic and darkly disturbing story of unrequited love, fantastical adventure and the quest for a mysterious poem, masterfully delivered in gloriously luscious prose.'
Carole Hailey

Carolyn Lewis
Time, Again

Time, Again is something Elizabeth feels is her right. From humble beginnings, she has built a successful company, and she sees no reason why, at the age of seventy-three, she should not continue in her role. But what if it is her own children – her beloved daughters – who are seeking to oust her own creation? Sensitively observed and poignantly written, *Time, Again* explores the eternal conflict between youth and age, parents and children, enduring ambition and the passing of time, with both wit and empathy. Has Elizabeth been a good mother? Or did she sacrifice her family in the name of success? Carolyn Lewis' new novel offers no easy answers but thoughtfully examines the choices and challenges faced by all women, at all stages of their life

'How we age and the concerns of who we will become as the years slip by, is a central concern of this novel and touches every one of us. It's a real joy to confront such genuine characters who we get to know rapidly through empathy and realism. A genuinely human story, beautifully written.'
Dr. Peter Nicholls Associate Professor,
Senior Teaching Fellow, Bristol University. Author of *Beginning to See*